She ... **and her c**... **had brushed it.**

"Are you cold?" he breathed.

"No." It wasn't cold—it was much worse. That horrible hot-and-cold tingling ran through her again, but it couldn't be. She needed to marry Robert. She couldn't be attracted to Gabriel. That would lead nowhere and ruin everything. She stood abruptly. "I need to go."

"Go?" He didn't try to hold her. He let her back away, but his expression said it all. He liked her. A lot.

His intensity terrified her. She looked around wildly. The picket fence enclosed the yard, trapping her, stifling her. "I—I need to go," she repeated, even less sure of herself. Stay another moment, and she'd never leave. "I'm sorry."

"Felicity."

She couldn't look at him. The expression on his face would make her stay, and then what? She could have no future with him. She stumbled away, feet as unsure as her heart.

Books by Christine Johnson

Love Inspired Historical

Soaring Home
The Matrimony Plan

CHRISTINE JOHNSON

is a small-town Michigan girl who has lived in every corner of the state's Lower Peninsula. After trying her hand at music and art, she returned to her first love—storytelling. She holds a bachelor's degree in English and a master's degree in library studies from the University of Michigan. She feels blessed to write and to be twice named a finalist for Romance Writers of America's Golden Heart Award. When not at the computer keyboard, she loves to hike and explore God's majestic creation. She participates in her church's healing prayer ministry and has experienced firsthand the power of prayer. These days, she and her husband, a Great Lakes ship pilot, split their time between Northern Michigan and the Florida Keys.

The Matrimony Plan

CHRISTINE JOHNSON

Love Inspired

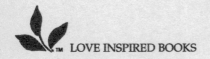

™ LOVE INSPIRED BOOKS

Recycling programs
for this product may
not exist in your area.

ISBN-13: 978-0-373-82880-7

THE MATRIMONY PLAN

For every one that exalteth himself shall be abased;
and he that humbleth himself shall be exalted.
—*Luke* 18:14b

For my parents, who raised me
in the fertile soil of love

Chapter One

❧

Pearlman, Michigan
June 15, 1920

Today, Felicity Kensington was going to meet her future husband. He didn't know this yet, of course, but he had a full two months to come to that conclusion.

She pinched her cheeks for color and took a deep breath for courage. The vanity mirror revealed every imperfection. Her eyes were an odd hue of green, and she was a bit too tall for most men, but Daddy's money could overcome those deficiencies. She pinned her chignon and checked that every pleat of her skirt fell in place. Crisp, conservative, and irresistibly efficient. Mr. Robert Blevins, civil engineer, had to fall in love with her.

A hand bell tinkled downstairs. "Felicity, you're late."

Mother. She was the only hitch in an otherwise flawless plan. She insisted Felicity attend this afternoon's Ladies' Aid Society meeting to greet the new pastor, but that meant she'd miss Mr. Blevins's train. All the other eligible girls would see him before she did. Felicity had to reach the train first.

Hopefully Mother would accept a mere engineer as a son-in-law. He did hail from New York, and Mother always espoused the social superiority of Easterners. If society mattered to Mother, distance was the key for Felicity. Robert Blevins would take her far from Mother's manipulations.

"Felicity." The bell ran with greater urgency. "We're waiting."

Felicity shooed Ms. Priss, the neighbor's sociable cat, out the window with parting advice. "Don't let her see you." The cat wisely scampered across the porch roof and onto the limb of an overhanging elm.

After brushing the bed free of cat hair, which then necessitated cleaning Grandmama's sterling hairbrush, she took a deep breath, cast a quick prayer for courage and descended the sweeping staircase with its polished mahogany rail. Little rainbows danced off the crystals of the hall chandelier and flitted across her arm, but the beauty couldn't calm Felicity's nerves.

"Why did you take so long?" Mother primped in front of the mirror, poking her tight dark curls into place. She looked perfect in her fawn-colored suit. She always looked perfect. "You know we need to leave early so your father can pick up Reverend Meeks."

Reverend Meeks…what a ghastly name. He'd surely be thin and pale with pox scars, a hawkish nose and a receding hairline. He'd never smile or grant the slightest leniency. He would conduct fire and brimstone sermons. Children would cower. Congregants would scurry away, chastened.

Thankfully, she'd be gone soon, married in the wedding of the century—at least for Pearlman. Pearlman, whose cultural center was the drugstore. Pearlman, with its gravel Main Street and single cinema. Pearlman, where everyone knew everything about everyone. She could not wait to arrive in New York City as Mrs. Robert Blevins.

Mother rang the servant's bell, and Smithson, the butler, glided from the kitchen to the front door and opened it without a word. Now was the time to act, before Mother trapped her in the motorcar.

"I'd like to——"

"Don't forget the letter." Mother pressed the ivory vellum envelope from the National Academy of Design into Felicity's hand. "You'll want to show it to everyone."

Felicity wanted to crumple that letter and throw it in the fireplace. The whole idea was Mother's. *She* was the one who wanted to go to art school. *She* was the one with talent. Felicity couldn't draw a straight line. Aside from the humiliation of being the only nonartist at the prestigious art school, Mother would never leave her alone. She'd visit for weeks at a time and fix every one of Felicity's projects. Art school could not happen, and if all went as planned, she'd never set foot in the National Academy.

Mother, of course, never noticed her discomfort. She swooped down the granite steps to the Packard, and Felicity had no choice but to follow—as usual.

Daddy stood by a marble pillar, idly stroking his walrus mustache. He'd gained a little weight around the midsection and had to wear his spectacles all the time now, but he still saw her as his little girl.

"Good luck." He winked at Felicity.

Mother clucked her tongue while she waited for Smithson to open the motorcar's passenger door. "Branford, I thought you were in a hurry. Quit lollygagging."

Daddy rolled his eyes behind his presidential spectacles and sauntered toward the Packard while Smithson opened the rear door for Felicity.

This was her last chance. Though her fingertips tingled and her pulse raced, she mustered the calm smile preached by the Highbury School for Girls, the New York boarding school she'd attended. "I believe I'll walk."

"Walk?" Mother glared through her open window. "In

this heat? Your dress will wilt, and you'll perspire." She said the last word as if it was the most sinful thing in the world. "That's not the image to project when you want to curry favor."

"But I don't want to curry favor."

"Of course you do. It's the only way to get elected chairwoman of the Beautification Committee. You'll ride, and that's that."

Felicity didn't want to chair the Beautification of the Sanctuary Committee, nor did she have the faintest idea how to go about Mother's latest pet project, commissioning a new stained-glass window. The best solution was to avoid the meeting altogether.

"I prefer to walk." She proceeded down the steps and away from the car.

"Now is not the time to show your independence, child." Mother pressed a handkerchief to her forehead. "If only you could have inherited my good sense."

"Eugenia," Daddy warned.

Mother ignored him as always. "Felicity, come here. You are giving me a headache."

Daddy paused at the driver's door, walrus mustache bristling and linen jacket unbuttoned. "A walk'll do her good, Eugenia. Get a little color in her cheeks. Want to make a good impression on the new pastor."

Forget the pastor. Felicity had set her sights on the engineer.

Daddy started the car and put it into gear before Mother gathered wind for the next protest, but as the Packard lurched forward, she found her voice. "Don't be late. Sophie Grattan will hold it over my head forever."

Her plea trailed off as the car rolled down the driveway, leaving Felicity in wondrous calm. The birds chattered. Ms.

Priss crouched beneath a sugar maple, intent on a pair of cardinals who scolded and stayed well out of reach.

She had forty-five minutes until the train arrived, plenty of time to get to the depot before Sally Neidecker and the rest of the girls. The way they'd twittered about Mr. Blevins all week was sickening.

She strolled down the hill through Kensington Estates, passing the Neidecker home with its quaint Victorian gingerbread and the Williams's squat prairie-style house. At the junction of Elm and Main, motorcars mixed with the occasional horse and buggy, and the wood sidewalks were crowded with pedestrians. If Daddy had his way with the city council, the street would be paved by autumn.

Mr. Neidecker's Pierce-Arrow glided past, and she realized Daddy might drive by and catch her before she reached the train station. She quickened her step and passed the drugstore with scarcely a glance in the windows. The early summer heat dampened her brow and made her feel a bit light-headed, but she had to hurry.

She checked the clock on city hall. Three-ten. Daddy would have left Mother at the church by now and headed for the station. If he spotted her, he'd cart her back to the church, but if he didn't see her until after the train arrived, it would be too late, and she would have her Mr. Blevins.

"Good aft'noon." Dennis Allington, the depot manager, crossed the street in front of her.

She nodded slightly and hurried on. She should have taken State Road instead. It was longer and dustier, but Daddy would never have driven the Packard through those potholes.

"Felicity? I'm surprised to see you here." Mrs. Grattan stepped out of Kensington Mercantile and stopped directly in front of her. Ruddy and heavy-jowled, she epitomized the farm wife. Her thick arms could strangle a goose or birth a calf. "Aren't you going to the meeting?"

Felicity stalled. She'd never considered what to say if she met a society member, and Mrs. Grattan always managed to terrify her. Lowering her eyelids, she shrank behind the polite facade preached at Highbury.

"Please inform my mother that I may be a little late."

"Late?" Mrs. Grattan clucked her tongue. "With the new minister coming?"

Felicity gritted her teeth behind an artificial smile. Mrs. Grattan and her husband acted like they held the patent on righteousness, as if owning a dairy farm and a half-dozen delivery trucks made them moral authorities.

"My Eloise can hardly wait to meet him," Mrs. Grattan stated.

Felicity's smile faded. "Eloise is attending?" The eldest Grattan girl never went to society meetings.

"Of course." Mrs. Grattan acted like it was obvious that Eloise, still unwed at twenty-four, would be there.

With a start, Felicity remembered one key fact about the new pastor. Pearlman wasn't welcoming just one bachelor into town today; it was welcoming two. Well, as far as she was concerned, Eloise Grattan could have weaselly, pock-faced Reverend Meeks.

"Wish her luck." She giggled at the thought of the bovine Eloise standing beside a miserly Reverend Meeks.

Mrs. Grattan's eyes narrowed to dots. "No woman can do better than a man of God, Felicity Kensington."

Felicity cringed. "I didn't mean…" she began, but Mrs. Grattan turned away with a harrumph and stalked toward the church.

Discombobulated, Felicity took a few steps in the wrong direction. Then to her horror, she spied Daddy's Packard coming down Main Street. Oh, no. He couldn't see her. Not yet. She looked for an escape and, seeing as she was nearly out of time, slipped into Kensington Mercantile.

The little bell above the door tinkled as she entered, and the clerk, one of the younger Billingsley brothers, nodded at her before returning his attention to Mrs. Evans. Felicity walked just far enough inside so Daddy wouldn't spy her and pretended to examine the contents of the display case.

Since her brother, Blake, had taken over managing Daddy's store, they stocked plain, useful goods that anyone in Pearlman could afford. The few luxuries on hand were displayed in the locked glass display case atop the long oaken counter. A cloisonné jewelry box, scrimshaw ivory pipe, sterling vanity box, pocket watches, assorted pendants and rings and a red leather satchel nestled on royal blue satin. A small sign noted that the satchel was perfect for the university student.

"May I help you decide?" The warm, masculine voice flowed over her like melted chocolate.

Felicity sought the source of that rich baritone and was surprised to find a man perhaps three years older than her, certainly no more than twenty-five. She'd never seen him in town before. Unruly brown curls went unchecked by comb or hat, and his shirtsleeves had been rolled up like a common worker's. His eyes sparkled in a most unnerving way, and his smile suggested mischief.

That smile could disarm the most hardened woman, and Felicity was no exception. She stared at the merchandise as she struggled to regain her composure. "Do you work here?" She didn't recall Blake saying he'd hired anyone new.

"No, but I thought I might help." His reflection in the mirrored back of the case proved just as potent as the real thing, and she prayed he didn't notice the pink hue creeping up her cheeks.

"I don't require any assistance."

He took the hint and stepped away, but she couldn't help watching him in the mirror. First he scanned the nearby bookshelf and then perused the dress goods. A man buying fabric? She couldn't resist a peek. The man strolled back to the books and picked up the volume of Coleridge that had been on the shelf for years. What common worker read poetry?

He looked up, and his eyes met hers. "Are you sure I can't help?"

"No." She jerked her gaze back to the display case. "No, thank you." If she stood in just the right place, she could see him in the mirror. One curl fell across his forehead as he studied the volume. She caught her breath. He *was* handsome.

Oh, dear. He closed the book and headed her way.

"I don't think anything here will do." She darted a panicked glance out the window. Daddy must have driven past by now.

"There are a lot of fine things here." The man stood so close that her skin tingled.

"Are you certain you don't work here?" Her voice squeaked like a schoolgirl asked to her first dance. She swallowed and tried again. "You sound like a salesman."

"I suppose I am, in a manner of speaking." His lips quirked into a semi-smile, and a tremor shook her. What was wrong with her?

"I—I should be going." She stepped into the welcome breeze from an electric fan. The train would be arriving at any moment. "I need to leave."

"But we haven't even met." He extended a hand.

She stared. If she shook his hand, she'd lose all control. Leave, and everyone would know he'd affected her. She chose the lesser of the two evils and dashed for the door. Unfortunately, her hip caught the corner of a table and jostled the display of canned rhubarb.

"Excuse me," she said too loudly as she stilled the wobbling jars.

Mrs. Evans stared. Josh Billingsley snickered. She didn't even want to know what the stranger thought.

Without a glance back, she yanked open the door and rushed out into the heat of the afternoon, glad to hear the soft *shwooft* of the door settling shut behind her. After looking up and down Main Street, she spotted Daddy's Packard parked in front of the bank. She'd never had to go into the mercantile at all. If only she'd walked on. If only she'd kept her composure.

A lady always remembers her station and acts accordingly. Mother had drilled the rules for ladylike behavior into her from childhood. Yet she'd forgotten every single one when she needed them most. She should have politely excused herself. She should never have engaged in such personal conversation, but he flustered her so that she couldn't think straight.

Oh, dear. What had she done? And Robert Blevins was due at any moment. She fanned her face with her handbag. He couldn't see her blushing over another man.

The clock on city hall read nearly three-thirty. The train would arrive at any moment. Felicity hurried toward the depot, perspiration trickling between her shoulder blades and her head buzzing.

Soon the businesses gave way to bungalows with bare yards and unpainted fences. This was the poor part of town where people like the Simmonses lived.

"Ms.?"

She yelped as the stranger from the mercantile planted himself before her. "Why are you following me?" She ducked around him. "I don't want to buy anything." She hurried on, hoping he'd leave her alone.

He didn't. "I'm sorry I startled you. I thought you heard

me." He matched her pace. "I've been calling out for you since you left the store."

"Well, I'm not interested in whatever you have to sell. Good day, sir." She strode as fast as she could, but he easily kept up.

"I'm not selling anything. I wondered if this might be yours." He held up an envelope—an ivory vellum envelope.

She halted. The National Academy letter. She must have dropped it in the store. The man wasn't harassing her; he was trying to return her letter.

"The National Academy has one of the finest art schools in the country," he said. "Congratulations."

Until that moment, she was going to apologize, but not now. He'd read the letter. The man had opened her mail and read it. She snatched the envelope from his hand. "That is private."

"Of course it is."

She hurried on, but he still followed her.

"You don't think…" he said. "Believe me, I would never read a personal letter. I simply assumed, given the time of year and where it was from, that it was an acceptance letter. My apologies if I was wrong."

She silently plodded on, eyes fixed dead ahead.

"What's more, your father—at least I assume he's your father—did happen to mention that his daughter would be attending the academy."

Felicity froze in her tracks. "You know Daddy?"

"We met in New York when he offered me the position."

Felicity gasped as she realized her horrible blunder. This man wasn't a farm laborer; he was Robert Blevins. Of course an engineer would be dressed for the field. Daddy had hired him to construct the new airfield and flight school. Mr. Blevins would want to walk the property and take measurements. That's why he was dressed so casually.

She'd been a fool, a complete fool.

She pressed a gloved hand to her hot cheeks. "Th-then the train already arrived." *Please say no.* Please let her be wrong.

"It was early."

Oh, no. She should have known. Dennis Allington wouldn't be walking through town unless the train had already left.

"I—I," she stammered, backing away, but there wasn't any way to get past the truth. Nothing could erase such an enormous gaffe. The only thing to do was walk away with as much dignity as possible. Less than two hours into the execution of her plan, she'd failed.

"Excuse me," she murmured and took off, not caring where she went as long as it was away from him.

Naturally he followed. "Where are you going? What did I say?"

"Nothing," she cried out, exasperated. Why couldn't he leave her alone?

"Whatever it was, I'm sorry." He drew near.

She walked more briskly.

He reached her side. "Please stop. Let's talk. I'd like to be friends."

"Friends?" She turned from him. "But I've made such a fool of myself. I—I thought you were a farm worker."

"Is that how you normally treat farm workers?"

Shame washed over her as she stilled her steps. She owed him an apology. "No, that is, I'm sorry. It's just that I'm overwrought. The letter…" How could she explain to a mere stranger that her mother had lied and cheated to get her into art school? He wouldn't think any better of her for having such a family. "There's no excuse," she said ruefully.

"Perhaps." He surveyed her for intolerable seconds. "But it takes character to admit fault."

Warmth rose from deep inside, sweeping through her with shocking speed. They'd barely met. She'd insulted him, and yet he forgave her. "Thank you," she whispered.

He laughed and held out an arm. "We all make mistakes. May I escort you to wherever you're going?"

Where was she going? Now that she'd met Mr. Blevins and had even been forgiven by him, she had no destination. *Think of his needs.*

She smiled at him. "You must want to look over the site. Baker's Field is south and east of here. We could walk, but my brother, Blake, should be here with the car soon."

"Your brother? I thought—" His brow furrowed. "I expected your father."

"Daddy? Why?"

Instead of answering, he dropped her hand and took off at a run. What on earth? Felicity spun about and instantly saw what had caught his attention. An envelope—her envelope—bounced along the ground. She must have dropped it in her confusion.

"Oh, no," she cried, running after both the envelope and Mr. Blevins.

Suddenly, a black dog streaked across both their paths, snatched the envelope and took off toward the depot.

"Slinky, no." The town stray would chew the letter. He'd ruin it, and Mother would be furious. Felicity abandoned propriety and hobbled after the dog as fast as she could. "Give it back. Slinky, bring it here."

As if he heard her, the mutt paused, head cocked and one ear flopped over, but as soon as she drew near, he took off again.

"No," she cried in exasperation. Her head spun, and she could barely catch her breath. She'd never get the letter back.

Worse, Mr. Blevins was laughing.

"Stop it," she cried. "It's not funny."

He wiped his eyes and tried his best to keep a straight face. "I'm sorry, Ms. Kensington, but that's no way to get something from a dog. He thinks you're playing a game." He whistled. "Here, boy. What did you call him? Slinky? Here, Slinky." He held out a hand, palm up, and after a little more cajoling, the dog came to him.

He patted Slinky's head and pried the letter from his jaws. He then held it out to her.

The envelope had been chewed, bit through and was soaked in dog saliva. Gingerly, she took hold of one corner. "It's ruined."

"Allow me to wipe it off." He offered his handkerchief.

She sniffled. "That won't help the holes or the dirt."

"The words are still the same. I'm sure we can piece it together."

She shook her head. "It doesn't matter anymore." Indeed it didn't. She'd found her Mr. Blevins, and he was smiling at her. He might be a little less than elegantly attired, but he liked her. Surely he could love her. And she could clean him up. With a little effort, a decent suit and a haircut, he might pass as quite stylish. Yes, she could do this. In two months, maybe less, she'd be Mrs. Robert Blevins.

"Thank you," she breathed, holding his gaze a bit longer than respectable.

His smile curled around her heart. "I'll see you again?"

She nodded, and for a moment she thought he would take her hand, but then a motorcar horn honked. Not just any motorcar. Daddy's Packard. After a backfire and a cloud of blue smoke, the car stopped and Daddy sprang out.

"Sorry I'm late, Pastor Gabriel."

Pastor? Felicity reeled. This man she'd let take her hand, the one she'd promised to see again, was Reverend Meeks? He was supposed to be old and gaunt and ugly, not handsome and charming.

Her head whirled. She gulped the tepid air. Her ears rang. A minister. She'd agreed to see the new minister, *her* new minister, but her plan was to attract Mr. Blevins. Pastor Gabriel wouldn't get her out of Pearlman; he'd tie her to the town—and Mother—forever. Her plan was ruined before it had even begun.

She stifled a sob, and then, as the world around her blurred, she did what any woman in such circumstances would do.

She fainted.

Chapter Two

Gabriel Meeks caught Ms. Kensington a moment after her eyes fluttered shut. She'd paled, and he rushed to her side, knowing she was about to faint.

Time paused the instant he touched her. Such beauty. Delicate veins laced her eyelids. Her ebony hair glistened, its tendrils like spring vines. The artist Alphonse Mucha could not have drawn a more beautiful woman.

The heady scent of roses overwhelmed his ordinarily good sense, leaving him gaping at her as seconds ticked away. From the moment he first saw her in the general store, he longed to know her better. Never did he imagine he'd hold this beauty in his arms. How perfectly she fit the cup of his shoulder and crook of his arm, as if God had made them two halves of the one whole.

"Lay her down," barked her father, head of the Church Council, as he stripped off his jacket. "Get the blood flowing to her head."

Though Gabriel wished he could hold her forever, he did as instructed, placing her head on the folded jacket. Spying the chewed envelope, he snatched it up and began fanning her face.

Still, she showed no sign of coming to.

"Do you have smelling salts?" he inquired.

Mr. Kensington shook his head and squatted beside him. Gabriel fanned harder. Ms. Kensington hadn't moved, and her color hadn't improved.

"What if she doesn't wake?"

"Don't worry, son. She'll come around in a moment. They always do. I've seen my share of ladies dropping off. Why I remember one dance where..."

Mr. Kensington's story brought back a painful memory. Years ago, a girl who Gabriel had escorted to a dance claimed to feel faint. He left her on a sofa and went to fetch water. Upon his return, he spied her escaping to the garden with another man. His older brothers laughingly informed him that he'd just been initiated into high society. According to them, girls used this trick all the time, and he'd fallen for it. The humiliation still stung.

He hoped Ms. Kensington wasn't that type of woman, but her expensive clothing and snobbish attitude put her squarely with the rest of the upper class. He'd been hoodwinked once. Never again.

"Perhaps we should fetch a doctor," he said brusquely.

"Nonsense." Kensington grabbed her handbag. "Let's see if Felicity has some smelling salts with her."

So her name was Felicity, meaning great happiness or bliss. Never had a name flowed so beautifully nor fit so poorly. This Felicity looked anything but happy. The only time she'd shown a glimpse of joy was when she chased the dog. Too bad it had vanished so quickly. Beautiful yet unhappy—how often Gabriel had seen that painful combination. He brushed a strand of silken hair from her eyes.

Kensington cleared his throat. "Pastor?"

He shouldn't have done that. "I, uh, did you find any smelling salts?"

Kensington grinned beneath his mustache. "No, but she's coming to, just like I said she would."

The man was right. Felicity's face had regained some color, and her eyelids opened, revealing splendid green eyes.

She flinched as if alarmed to see him and looked around. "Daddy? Wh-what happened?"

Disappointment knifed through Gabriel.

"You fainted, little one." Kensington knelt beside his daughter, gently helping her to a sitting position.

His love for her was evident. She was cherished, the prize of his life, and completely spoiled. Such women brought nothing but trouble. Gabriel was better off without her.

"Can you stand?" Kensington asked her. "We need to get the pastor to the Ladies' Aid Society meeting."

Gabriel gulped. The Ladies' Aid Society? He'd never been privy to that sacred enclave, but he'd heard tales. If the stories were correct, the ladies would have his entire life laid out for public display before the end of the afternoon. With any luck, that dissection would not include Felicity Kensington.

Felicity convinced Daddy to take her home. She couldn't face Mother and the Ladies' Aid Society, not in front of Gabriel.

Gabriel. Why did he have to be so handsome? She pressed into the dark corner of the Packard's rear seat and watched him talk to Daddy. If he was nervous, he didn't show it. She could grudgingly admire that quality. Most men cowered before her father.

But why had she agreed to see him again? She'd never be able to explain that to Mother, and it would ruin everything with Mr. Blevins.

Daddy stopped the car at the front door, and she scurried into the house before Gabriel could set a date. She slammed the solid oak door shut and leaned against its cool surface, but mere wood couldn't quench the fire inside. Before Smithson or the cook or one of the other servants appeared, she retreated to the sanctity of her room and prepared a cold compress. She pressed it to her blazing cheeks, but even icy water couldn't suppress the wild emotions.

A minister—she had been attracted to a minister. Not to say that there was anything wrong with the ministry but it just wasn't for her. She had to marry wealth and privilege. She had to find a man who lived far from Pearlman if she ever hoped to escape Mother.

She unpinned the useless chignon and let her hair fall free. How could she have been so mistaken? He clearly wasn't socially prominent—the dusty shoes, the rolled-up sleeves. But what pastor walked around so informally dressed? And with a Ladies' Aid Society meeting to attend? Mother would tear him to pieces.

For a minute, she felt sorry for him. The ladies would gasp when he walked in, and Mother...well, no one should have to face that icy stare. Oh, Mother would speak with artificial politeness, but behind every word would be a barb, and at the next Church Council meeting, she'd petition for his removal. Poor Gabriel.

Poor Gabriel? What was she thinking? She'd promised to see him. Mother would have a conniption when she found out.

Felicity gnawed on her nails. Why had the church council hired a minister just out of school? There must have been older, better qualified pastors available, but no, they'd hired someone young and inexperienced and, well, handsome. Those curls, the twinkle in his eye, the hint of mischief... just thinking about him made her cheeks heat.

She dipped the compress in cold water, squeezed and reapplied.

His face had been the first thing she saw when she opened her eyes, and his concern had nearly melted her to the spot. She had to look away.

At first she'd been confused. How had she gotten on the ground? She didn't feel any bruises or bumps, so someone must have caught her when she fainted. She prayed it was Daddy. Just the thought of Gabriel holding her sent hot shivers from her head to her toes.

There'd be no escaping the man or the rumors that would connect them. Practically the whole town had seen them together today including the Billingsley boy who clerked at the mercantile and Mrs. Evans. Felicity sucked in her breath. Mrs. Evans would tell everyone. All of Pearlman would know by tomorrow.

The trail of witnesses didn't stop at the mercantile. Anyone at the businesses between the store and the train depot could have spotted them together, not to mention people on the street. And then there was the depot.

Her stomach flip-flopped. Maybe she was ill. Typhoid, influenza or scarlet fever would be better than facing the ridicule. Even Eloise Grattan, whose parents couldn't buy her a beau, would snicker. And Sally Neidecker would lord it over her.

She groaned and sandwiched her head between two pillows. She could hear her childhood schoolmates now. *Felicity and Gabriel, sweet as can be.* Every childhood rhyme taunted her, each worse than the other. She needed to marry but not someone who would keep her in Pearlman the rest of her life.

What would Mother do when she found out? Felicity tossed the compress in her sink and paced back and forth across the room. Her mother would lecture and impose restrictions: no unsupervised walks, no unsupervised anything. How could Felicity meet the real Robert Blevins with

Mother hounding her every move? It was terrible, horrible, the worst possible thing that could have happened.

She wrung out the compress, plopped on the bed again and pressed the cloth tight to her eyes. She needed a plan. A new plan, a better plan, one that could not fail.

The front door slammed. Mother. When that was followed by the strident ringing of the bell, she popped out of bed and re-pinned her chignon. *A lady never has a hair out of place.*

"Felicity," Mother called out. "We need to talk."

She knew. Daddy must have told her what had happened at the train station. Maybe Gabriel had spilled the whole story at the meeting. They'd doubtless had a jolly laugh over her while they sipped tea and downed Mrs. Simmons's short-bread cookies.

Felicity tucked the last loose strand in place as Mother climbed the stairs. *Thump. Thump.* For such a small woman, Mother had a heavy step.

How could Felicity explain her reaction to Gabriel?

Thump. Thump. Mother's steps matched Felicity's heart-beat.

Heels clattered down the hallway.

Think.

"Felicity?" Mother threw open the door, her expression grim.

Too late. Felicity tried to swallow but her throat was dry. "What?" The word was barely audible.

"I told you not to walk to the meeting. I told you it would make you light-headed, and look what happened. You missed the most important meeting of the year. You left me alone. Why, if I hadn't had Mrs. Williams's support, you wouldn't be chairwoman of the Beautification Committee. There wouldn't even be a Beautification Committee. And the new minister. Felicity Anne Kensington. A lady always keeps her commitments."

Felicity bore the lecture with bated breath, waiting for the worst to fall, but when Mother failed to mention anything about the train station or Daddy finding her with Gabriel Meeks, she relaxed.

"Thank goodness you have me to look out for your best interests," Mother sniffed. "Change out of that filthy gown and try to make yourself presentable. We're having a guest for dinner."

A little knot formed in Felicity's stomach. "A guest?" It had to be the new minister. Oh, how could she endure an evening with Gabriel Meeks? Daddy was bound to make a joke about finding them together. Mother would be horrified when she found out. Somehow she had to stop this dinner party. "Who's coming?"

Mother ignored her question. "I wonder if he has Newport connections."

"Newport?" Felicity gasped. "That's not possible." He was dressed too plainly to come from money, especially that kind of money. If only he didn't have such a welcoming smile and warm brown eyes. The mere thought of him sent that peculiar hot and cold shiver through her again.

"Of course it's possible. A man with his status could easily summer amongst the social elite. Hmm." Mother surveyed her closet. "Nothing too fine in case he isn't from proper society yet expensive enough to impress him if he is. Wear the pale green organdy." She tossed the gown on the bed. "Traditional. You can't go wrong with that."

"Yes Mother." It was always best to agree with Mother, especially when a greater concession was needed. "In fact, let's put off the dinner until we know for certain."

"Put it off?" Eugenia Kensington glared at her. "You can't withdraw an invitation." She pulled a pearl necklace from Felicity's jewelry box and draped it around the neck of the dress. "Pearls will do quite nicely. I expect you downstairs by six o'clock. Try to display some of the social graces we paid for so dearly. Mr. Blevins might prove worth the effort."

"M-Mr. Blevins?" Felicity stammered.

"Of course, Mr. Blevins. Who did you think I was talking about?"

Felicity averted her gaze, not wanting her mother to see that she'd been thinking about Gabriel.

Robert Blevins was coming to dinner. After such a disastrous day, she just might be able to salvage her plan. With any luck, she'd capture his affection before he learned about this afternoon's fiasco.

Nothing about this first day had gone the way Gabriel anticipated. He came to Pearlman expecting a country church filled with salt of the earth, hardworking folk who would appreciate a down-to-earth sermon and a pastor who worked alongside them. The inequities and misery of the city wouldn't exist here—no divide between rich and poor, colored and white, immigrant and citizen, and no stifling poverty or raging crime. The stains of abuse, liquor and hunger wouldn't exist. In Pearlman, he could lead a church that would reach out to the sick and poor, taking them in and nurturing them into strong God-fearing people. It was the mission of his friend Mr. Isaacs's Orphaned Children's Society, and Gabriel planned to make it his own.

Today that idyllic image went right out the window.

The ladies at the meeting had pushed daughter after hapless daughter before him, but the only woman who'd touched his heart was proud and rich.

Then there was the parsonage. Instead of simplicity, he stood in a huge, two-story house large enough for a family of eight. The gleaming cherry Chippendale-style dining set and electric lighting looked to be recent installments, whereas the indoor plumbing had been in place for years judging by the mineral stains on the porcelain. The marble-topped side-board and brocade-upholstered wingback chairs reeked of money. This was not a parsonage; it was a palace.

"Had my man put your trunk upstairs," Branford Kensington said as he opened yet another door. This one led to a handsome library and study. "Encyclopedia, concordance and the Bible in the proper translation." The man blustered around the room like a bull moose. "Of course there's room for your books—" he patted the one empty shelf "—though judging by the size of your trunk, you won't need all this space." He laughed at his own joke.

Gabriel swallowed his irritation. "I guess you're correct there." He'd only brought the necessities, not wanting to put off any of the congregation with his upper-class background.

"I'll give you until six o'clock and then send Smithson down. Come on up to the big house for dinner. Consider it a standing invitation until your housekeeper arrives."

"Housekeeper? I don't—" Gabriel started to correct him, but Kensington had already moved on.

"Fenced yard was installed some years back for Reverend Johanneson. He had four children and thought it would keep them out of mischief." He chuckled at the memory. "Land goes clear to the river."

Gabriel peered through the crystal-clear kitchen window. "It's a fine piece of land."

"Yes, it is." Kensington stuck out his hand. "Well son, I'll leave you to settle in. Smithson'll be here with the car at six sharp."

Gabriel blanched at being driven by a chauffeur. People *would* talk. "No, that won't be necessary. I'd rather spend a quiet night."

"Nonsense. My wife will have my head if you don't come."

Gabriel hesitated. An evening with Branford and Eugenia

Kensington promised to try the patience of a saint. He'd barely made it through the Ladies' Aid Society meeting.

"You'll want to check on Felicity," Kensington noted with a wink, "to see if she's recovered."

Memories of her flooded back: eyes the color of watercress and an elegance seldom seen in small towns. If Gabriel was honest with himself, he did want to see her. "Six o'clock?"

"I'll send the car."

Gabriel shook his head. "I prefer to walk. Just give me the address and point the way."

"Walk, eh?" Kensington eyed him with what seemed to be new respect. "Physical exertion builds a man's character. I recall my trek up Kilimanjaro in 1898—"

"Thank you, sir." Gabriel was too tired for a lengthy story. "The address?"

"Oh, ahem." Kensington cleared his throat. "Naturally you'll want to freshen up first. It's the big Federal on top of the hill. Can't miss it. Twin lions at the head of the drive." He nodded slightly and took his leave.

The house quieted after Kensington left. Gabriel drank in the solitude, spending time in prayer while he unpacked. As he half filled two of the bureau's four large drawers, he wondered if he had made a mistake coming to Pearlman. Mr. Isaacs had asked Gabriel to join him at the Orphaned Children's Society back in New York City.

"We could use a man like you," Isaacs had said. "You've volunteered here for years, and your seminary experience would be a plus. There are other places besides the ministry where you can do God's work. You'd be a splendid agent for the children."

As much as the offer tempted Gabriel, he had to decline. "I need to go to Pearlman. God has called me to pastor there. I don't know why, just that I must go."

Isaacs had understood, as always. "Go then, with my blessing, but if you ever feel your task there is complete, the offer stands."

After today, Gabriel wondered if he misunderstood God's call and should have accepted Mr. Isaacs's offer.

"Why did you bring me here, Lord?" Gabriel asked as he shut the drawer. Today had given him no clue, and the silence of the huge house didn't either. He thought Pearlman might bring him the good, honest wife he'd longed to meet, but instead he'd found Felicity Kensington. For all her beauty, she would never make a good minister's wife. She was too concerned about appearances.

He sighed and walked to the parlor. From the front windows, he could see Main Street and the church's steeple above the rooftops. To the right sat a pretty little park, wooded along its edges and studded with lilac bushes and iris in bloom. He envisioned picnics and revivals, music, laughter and children playing.

Strange to place the parsonage so far from the church. It must be a good two blocks away. From what he'd seen, the parsonage was one of the last homes before farmland. And the property stretched back into the trees. What had Kensington said about a river?

For as long as he could remember, his parents had taken the family to the Catskills in the summer. The cabin emptied onto a lake filled with trout and bass. Gabriel had spent long hours swimming and fishing in that lake. Maybe this river had good fishing. He'd take a look.

The kitchen door opened easily, but the screen door stuck and squeaked. He'd mention it to the church trustees. Two concrete steps led down to the fenced yard. He stretched his back and surveyed the grounds. Other than an overgrown lilac and four-strand clothesline, the yard was bare. The whitewashed picket fence looked solid enough, probably recently painted. Gates pierced both sides and the end.

Beyond the far gate stood the forest, sparse at first but thickening to dense woods. He headed that way, passed through the gate and stepped into the wildness beyond. He clambered over fallen logs and crashed through the undergrowth. When he reached the edge of the river, he dropped to a lichen-covered log to watch the water flow past. He didn't see any fish, but they'd be there in the deep pools.

The river ran dark green over a stony bottom. In the shallows, the color turned to brown, though in a few places it glistened light green over a patch of sand. The same green as Felicity Kensington's eyes.

The thought sent an unwelcome ripple of pleasure through him. He tried to shake some sense into his head. Felicity was precisely the wrong type of woman: rich, controlling parents; a highly cultivated sense of superiority; a society girl. No matter how lovely, Felicity Kensington was one temptation he should avoid. If only he hadn't agreed to dine at the Kensingtons' house tonight.

Lord, lead me not into temptation. But how?

He watched the rustling treetops. They gave no answer. Neither could he hear God's still, small voice. With a sigh, he roused himself. He'd accepted and must attend. Until then, he could take solace in the river. He followed the riverbank away from the park, occasionally peering into the depths to look for fish.

Within minutes, he reached the edge of the wood and the end of the path. A half-fallen barbed-wire fence blocked the way. Since the post had rotted away and the path clearly continued on the other side, Gabriel figured the owner must not have gotten around to removing it.

Two steps into the field, he heard a gun being loaded. Every hair rose on back of his neck.

"Hello?" He slowly lifted his palms to show he was unarmed and looked for the source of the threat. "I'm Reverend Meeks, the new pastor." Never had he been so glad to use the title.

"I dun't care who y'are. This here land's private. Coughlin land, and dun't ye forget it." A narrow-eyed, dungaree-clad man climbed up from the riverbank, shotgun pointed directly at Gabriel.

"Sorry. It looked like the path continued."

"You city folk don't know what a fence is?" He waved Gabriel back with the tip of his gun.

"Uh, I guess not."

"Well, lemme learn you up. This here fence marks my property, Mister Reverend. You stay on your side, and I stay on mine. Understand?"

Gabriel stepped back over the fallen fence, but he didn't dare bring his hands down yet. "I thought the fence was abandoned."

The man's bulbous nose shone red in the sun. "It's them criminals. As soon as I put it up, they take it right back down."

"Criminals? Here?" Though Gabriel had only been in town a few hours, he had a hard time believing it supported a large criminal population.

"City folk." The man spat and aimed his shotgun at Gabriel's head.

"Don't shoot!" Gabriel jumped back, nearly tripping on an exposed root.

The man lifted the gun higher and fired. With a derisive cackle, he said, "I was jess going for a squirrel."

Gabriel's heart pounded so hard that he could barely speak. "Did you get it?" The question barely fit through his constricted throat.

"Naw. Too devilish fast for this old gun." He shook the

discharged shotgun. "R'member. You stay on your side, and I stay on mine." With that declaration, he headed across the field to the distant ramshackle farmhouse.

"Pleased to meet you, Mr. Coughlin," Gabriel called out.

The man either didn't hear or didn't want to. Peculiar man. Peculiar town.

Chapter Three

"You did what?" Mother's screech carried all the way upstairs.

Felicity checked the clock. It was not yet five forty-five.
Mother's conniption fit couldn't be about her. She eased the
emerald-colored taffeta jacket over her shoulders. Conservative would no longer do. She had to dazzle Robert Blevins
tonight, before he heard any malicious gossip connecting her
to Gabriel Meeks.

She pulled a matching ribbon from her vanity drawer and
wove it into her hair. A diamond-headed hairpin secured it
and added the necessary bit of sparkle. Robert had to fall for
her. He just had to.

"How could you?" Mother wailed downstairs.

Felicity inched noiselessly to the stairway landing and
from that perch saw that Mother had pinned Daddy and
Blake at the front door. Blake's wife, Beatrice, a pretty
blonde, hovered near the parlor entrance, anxiously waiting
for Mother to vent the rest of her anger.

"That makes an odd number of guests," Mother cried.

"What's one more?" Daddy waved off her concern. "The
more the merrier, eh, Blake?" He gave a little laugh, meant
to calm her.

Felicity's brother shrugged. "Fine with me. We'll have plenty to discuss."

Apparently Daddy had invited someone else, probably Jack Hunter, since the airfield project most directly involved him. Ever since Jack and Darcy Hunter had attempted the transatlantic crossing last year, Blake and Daddy wanted to bring aviation to Pearlman. Blake had come up with the idea of the airfield and flight school, and Daddy had supplied the funds. Jack Hunter would do the training. Most importantly, Daddy had hired Mr. Robert Blevins to engineer the project, and now Felicity would engineer a marriage.

Mother threw up her hands. "But an odd number means one person won't be paired."

That was strange. If Jack Hunter were coming, wouldn't he bring his wife? Perhaps Daddy hadn't invited Mr. Hunter. A horrible thought raced through Felicity's mind. What if Daddy had invited a lady? And what if that lady was unmarried? Felicity did not need more competition for Mr. Blevins's attention.

Mother pouted. "Fine. Don't consider me. Don't ever consider me. How am I supposed to arrange the table? One gentleman will inevitably be left out."

Thank goodness…another man. It must be Jack Hunter after all. With a smile of satisfaction, Felicity glided down the staircase. "Has our guest arrived?"

"Branford," Mother scolded, "what will people say when they hear we invited an extra guest?"

"They'll think we're generous." Daddy downed his lemonade in one swallow and patted Mother's arm. "It'll be fine, Eugenia." He slipped into the parlor to refill his glass.

Mother's lips had set into a grim line that only grew thinner the moment she saw Felicity. "That jacket doesn't match your gown."

Beatrice shot Felicity a sympathetic look. Everyone in the

family knew how unbearable Mother could be when she was nervous.

"Take it off." Mother waved Felicity upstairs and then glanced at the clock. "Stop. There's not enough time. We'll have to make do. But take that ridiculous ribbon out of your hair. You look like a floozy."

"I think it's lovely," Beatrice said softly, but of course Mother ignored her opinion. She ignored everything about Beatrice except the children.

Before Felicity could remove the offensive ribbon, Daddy returned with his drink and whistled. "Don't you look pretty, little one."

Felicity could always count on him to lift her spirits. "It's just an old gown."

"It looks beautiful to me." He pecked her cheek and escorted her into the parlor with the pomp of a princess to a ball.

"It might be acceptable for a masquerade," Mother sniffed on their heels. "This is merely dinner."

Felicity tried to let the slight bounce off her, but Mother's comments had a way of sticking to her like a burr. No matter how quickly she pulled them away, some of the barbs stuck tight.

"I think I'm past the morning sickness," Beatrice said in an obvious attempt to change the topic. She was expecting her second baby in December.

"I was never sick," said Mother. "Not a single day."

Felicity felt sorry for her sister-in-law, who bravely bore Mother's snubs. Beatrice didn't come from a good enough family to suit Mother. The Foxes ran a dress shop—respectable but not the upper-class connections Mother wanted for her only son.

"How is little Tillie?" Felicity asked. Beatrice had named

her first child Matilda after her grandmother, again irritating Mother.

Beatrice brightened. "She's such a dear, cooing away in her own special language. My mother loves watching her, but I do miss her, even for a few hours."

Blake laughed. "I don't think we'll ever untie Tillie from her mother's apron strings. It was hard enough getting Beattie to turn her over to Grandma so we could come to dinner tonight."

Beatrice blushed. "She's just a baby, dearest."

"Speaking of dinner," Mother said, cutting off the line of conversation, "apparently my wishes are to be ignored. Felicity, set another place at the table."

Despite having a cook, housekeeper, gardener and butler on staff, Mother always expected Felicity to take care of any last-minute changes. Felicity chafed at the directive, but getting upset would not change Mother or charm Robert. She stifled her resentment and obeyed.

Once in the dining room, she discovered the housekeeper had heard Mother's fit and already added a place setting between Felicity and Robert. All Felicity had to do was rearrange the sterling place card holders to put Robert on her right.

Within two minutes, she returned to the foyer to find that Mr. Robert Blevins had arrived. Tall with strawberry blond hair, Mr. Blevins lacked the ideal figure extolled in the ladies' magazines. He was a bit too broad across the midsection and narrow in the shoulders. A little too much brilliantine for her taste, but elegantly coiffed, his wavy hair was parted down the center. He sported a mustache with the tips curled and waxed. The red-and-white-striped silk waistcoat and white linen suit weren't quite appropriate for dinner, which Mother thankfully did not point out.

He tapped his gold-knobbed cane on the slate floor, and

with a flick of the wrist, he caught it midlength before depositing it into the umbrella stand.

Mother batted her eyelashes like a debutante. "Call me Eugenia. Everyone does."

He gave her his full attention. "Very well, Eugenia. And if I may say so, your gown would disgrace every lady at Carnegie Hall."

Mother fairly warbled. "And you are quite handsomely dressed yourself. Blevins, you said? Any relation to the Blevinses of Newport?"

Felicity blushed at her mother's lack of tact, but he didn't seem to notice.

"The very ones," he beamed, chest thrust out.

"You don't say. Felicity!" The screech was a call to battle. "You must meet my daughter."

Felicity glided near. "You called, Mother?"

"Ah, Felicity, there you are. I'd like you to meet the engineer for the airfield project, Mr. Robert Blevins. Do you go by Robert or Bob?"

"Whatever suits you, ma'am." He bent elegantly over Felicity's hand, kissing it lightly. His mustache scratched like Daddy's, and she resisted the urge to giggle. "Or you, Ms. Felicity."

"Ah, such manners," Eugenia crowed. "Few young people today have good manners."

"I can see your daughter does." He gave Felicity a wide smile. "It is a pleasure to make your acquaintance."

Felicity returned his pleasantries, eager to remove Mother from the conversation. "You'll be here long?"

"Some months, I imagine."

Perfect. "Then we'll have a lot of time to get better acquainted."

"Come, Blevins, we're all in the parlor," said Daddy, clapping the man on the back. "You've had a look around the site, I hear. Can the project be done?"

"Of course."

Blake added, "We'll have the airfield completed by August."

"Under budget?" Daddy asked.

Robert nodded. "If Mr. Hunter agrees to the smaller hangar and your figures on the cement are correct, it can be done for two thousand less than projected."

"Two thousand, eh?" In the blink of an eye, Daddy had ripped the man from Felicity's grasp. The three men huddled like schoolboys on a ball diamond plotting the next pitch. How on earth was she to get Robert interested in her with Daddy and Blake monopolizing his attention?

Another knock on the door meant the unwelcome guest had arrived. Felicity edged toward the parlor, looking for a means to recapture Robert's attention. Let Mother greet Jack Hunter. The man was married and of no interest whatsoever.

Smithson opened the front door, and Mother greeted the guest with decided coolness.

"Good evening, Mrs. Kensington. Ms. Kensington." The warm, familiar voice flowed over her like honey. That voice. *His.* Her heart fluttered in a most unwelcome way. It couldn't be. "I'm glad you've recovered."

"Recovered from what?" asked Mother.

Felicity tried without success to fan away the heat that rushed into her cheeks. Everyone was staring at her, expecting an answer, but what could she say? How could she explain away his comment? The only solution was to give a vague answer. She forced a slight smile, the kind used by the elite girls at Highbury. "Yes, I have. Thank you for asking."

He smiled back with such evident pleasure that Felicity half regretted treating him so coldly. He couldn't help his birth. In fact, he'd done well to overcome it. Why tonight

Gabriel looked nothing like he had earlier in the day. His hair had been combed into submission, and he wore a perfectly cut dark gray suit. By all appearances, it had been crafted by an exceptional tailor.

"I'm so glad." His rich baritone embraced her a little too much.

That horrible warm and tingly feeling returned with tidal force. She opened her mouth, but nothing came out. Mother stared at her. Who had invited him, and why had he accepted? Surely he'd known how awkward this would be. Thoughts shot through her head quicker than swallows into a barn.

She must look like a fool, but she couldn't get past the difference in Gabriel. He didn't look like a laborer, a poor man or even a minister.

He looked like a suitor.

Gabriel had never seen such beauty in the parlors and theaters of New York, and he'd been to plenty. Though his parents followed solid Christian values and didn't flaunt their hard-earned income, others of their acquaintance didn't feel the same way. He'd seen more than his share of exquisite gowns and lavish jewels, all of which, his parents pointed out, did nothing to save a person's soul. But on Felicity, the deep green taffeta shone. Her eyes sparkled brighter than the finest jewels. Her hair, drawn exquisitely to the side, gleamed like polished ebony.

He wanted to kiss her hand, a gesture he ordinarily found absurdly elitist, not to mention outdated. Yet such perfection demanded the highest manners. He bowed slightly and held out his hand, expecting to receive her finely tapered fingers.

She didn't move.

He smiled, trying to warm away her fears.

Her mother practically glared at him. "Felicity, have you already met Reverend Meeks?"

Felicity stood as unmoving as a porcelain doll.

"Reverend Meeks?" A foppish redheaded man extended his hand.

Gabriel had seen him on the train. Though they'd shared the last leg of the journey, each man had kept to himself. Gabriel worked on his sermon while this man jotted in a little notebook like those used by reporters. Gabriel had been surprised when he got off the train in Pearlman. Why would a city newsman travel from Detroit to an ordinary small town? Gabriel certainly didn't expect to see him here tonight.

He shook the man's hand. "Pleased to meet you Mr...."

"Blevins. Robert Blevins." The man's idiotic grin betrayed him as a fool, more concerned with appearance than substance.

"He's one of the *Newport* Blevinses," said Mrs. Kensington.

"He's an engineer here to design my new airfield and flight school," Mr. Kensington explained.

An engineer? Gabriel looked again. In his experience, professionals dressed modestly, but perhaps that was only in his circles. It would explain the notepad. He must have been making notes on the project.

Kensington then quickly introduced his son, Blake, and daughter-in-law, Beatrice, a blue-eyed blonde that most men would find attractive but who paled beside Felicity. Both greeted him warmly, and he hoped they could become friends.

Mrs. Kensington maintained an artificially bright smile throughout the introductions but did not echo the warmth of Beatrice's greeting. "We will be a bit crowded at the table tonight," she sniffed, darting a glance at him, as if he was somehow the cause.

Kensington laughed, a deep guttural chortle meant to put everyone at ease while simultaneously exerting control. "The better to get to know each other, eh? I told Eugenia that you're an easygoing fellow, Pastor, and won't mind sharing a full table."

That wasn't all Gabriel had to share, judging by the glances Felicity cast at Blevins. The engineer rewarded her with an extended arm. "May I escort you to the parlor, Ms. Kensington?"

She eagerly accepted, and Blevins cast a look of triumph at Gabriel. "After you, Reverend."

"No, no." Mrs. Kensington brought the procession to a halt. "Dinner is ready." She took her husband's arm and headed in the opposite direction, drawing her daughter and Blevins with her. "Mr. Blevins, you will sit in the place of honor."

The change in direction put all the couples in front of Gabriel. Eugenia and Branford Kensington led the way, followed by Felicity and Blevins and then Blake and Beatrice. Gabriel trailed behind, the only one without a partner.

At the entrance to the dining salon, ostentatiously outfitted with Irish linen, gold table service and English porcelain warmed by gold chargers, Eugenia Kensington turned to Gabriel, almost as an afterthought. "You may say grace, Reverend."

At that moment, Gabriel saw the future stretching before him in one long, straight road through a barren desert. Gone were the camaraderie and familiar joking he'd enjoyed at dinners in the past. Gone were friendships and openness. Now he was Reverend Meeks, the pitiable wallflower, never truly welcome except in crisis. These people didn't want a leader. They wanted to put him in a cupboard and take him out for Sunday worship and weddings, none of which would be his. Mrs. Kensington's excessive attention to Blevins made it perfectly clear that Felicity was off-limits.

His place setting was the only one without a hand-scripted place card perched on the back of a sterling swan. He was the unanticipated guest, the outsider. Mr. Kensington's invitation must have been made on the spur of the moment, a gaffe that his wife could not forgive. Everything was meant to demean Gabriel, yet as he stepped to the table, he couldn't help but be pleased.

Eugenia Kensington's stained red lips pursed so tightly that they looked like the tied-off end of a balloon. Felicity blushed madly. Gabriel folded his hands and closed his eyes in grateful prayer.

He was seated beside Felicity.

If Felicity had known Gabriel Meeks was the extra guest, she would have placed him as far away as possible, certainly not in the chair beside her. Every step toward the table was torture. Robert was on her right, and Gabriel was on her left. How could she bear it?

Robert pulled out her chair, and though she glued her attention on him, she felt Gabriel's presence. His clean cotton scent rivaled Robert's perfumed hair treatment. She sensed when Gabriel lifted the water glass to his lips, when he put the napkin on his lap, when he picked up his fork. She felt it all with the combined excitement and dread of waiting for her first dance. Would he try to talk to her? Did he feel anything for her? Would he tell Mother that she'd swooned? Worst of all, was he here to press his suit?

The cook placed steaming Chesapeake clams on the table, and Felicity's stomach turned.

"Let me serve you, Ms. Felicity." Robert proceeded to fill her plate with shells.

She stared at the clams, not daring to touch them lest she lose the contents of her stomach.

"Had them shipped fresh from the Bay," Daddy bragged.

"I prefer Littlenecks myself." Robert grinned round at the whole table. "We dig 'em up on the Island every summer." He smiled directly at her, the wrinkles at the corners of his eyes betraying his age. He had to be at least thirty-five. "You'd like it there."

The hint should have made her heart dance, but Gabriel ruined that opportunity with a volley from her left. "I thought you summered in Newport, Mr. Blevins."

Felicity picked at the clams. Gabriel was trying to trip up Robert. She could guess why, but it didn't make her any more comfortable.

Robert laughed. "True, true, but we visit friends on Long Island from time to time. Need to keep in touch and all."

Daddy seconded that, defusing the crisis. Felicity took a deep breath, but she still couldn't stomach the clams. She pushed her plate away.

"Not hungry?" Robert asked.

She nodded, and he scooped her clams onto his plate.

"Clams don't settle well for me either," Beatrice said.

Felicity could have blessed her for that but not the next comment that came out of her mouth.

"Do you have a beau, Pastor?"

Felicity choked and coughed into her napkin.

Gabriel handed her a glass of water. "Are you all right?"

She was definitely not, but she nodded and sipped the water to calm her throat.

Then to her dismay, he proceeded to answer Beatrice. "No, Mrs. Kensington. Not yet, that is."

Beatrice smiled. "If I can do anything to help."

Help? Felicity glared at her sister-in-law.

"No, thank you," Gabriel said hastily. "If you don't mind, this is something I'd rather do on my own."

"Ah," murmured Beatrice, prolonging the conversation unnecessarily. "Then you have someone in mind?"

Felicity intensified her glare, and Beatrice smiled. Gabriel had paused, but Felicity didn't dare look at him. She held her breath and waited excruciating seconds until he answered.

"Not yet."

She breathed out with a whoosh. Thank goodness. He didn't feel the same way she did. Her peculiar attraction was nothing more than a physical reaction based on the chance occurrence of thinking he was someone else. Once she got to know Robert, this unnatural feeling for Gabriel would vanish.

"But I do have an idea what I want in a wife," Gabriel added, sending Felicity back to her napkin.

Mother's eyebrows rose, and Daddy roared. "That's the way to do it, son. Know what you want and go after it."

"This is hardly a hunt, Branford," Mother chided. "We're talking about marriage."

"And romance." Beatrice smiled at Felicity. "Every woman longs for romance."

Perhaps, but Felicity couldn't afford it. She had to marry this summer before that horrid art school begins. "I've always believed a match is best made between two social equals with like minds." She glanced at Robert to make her point perfectly clear. "Love can grow from there."

"I suppose you're right," Beatrice conceded. "I didn't always love Blake the way I do now. When we were young, I found him a bit of a rascal."

"I was." Blake laughed.

"Most boys are," Gabriel said. "From what my sister says, I was, too. You ladies are right that love can grow over time.

It's gentle and kind, two things we men are not too good at in our youth."

"Gentle?" Robert snickered. "Very pastorly of you, Reverend, but in my experience, love is passionate and wild." He gazed at Felicity. "It throws caution to the wind."

Her pulse raced but not in an entirely pleasant way. His words should have thrilled, but a shiver of unease made her look away. She shook it off. He was merely telling her that he was interested—exactly what she wanted.

"Speaking of the wind," Daddy said, "Blake tells me Hunter has some ideas on runway direction that contradict what you have on the blueprints."

As the beef Wellington was served, Daddy, Blake and Mr. Blevins descended into talk about the airfield project. Felicity swallowed her disappointment. If only Daddy hadn't changed the subject, Robert would have asked to see her again. She pulled the pastry off the beef and absently swirled it in gravy.

"I hear you've been accepted at a prestigious art college," Beatrice suddenly said.

Felicity started. Why was Beatrice stirring up trouble tonight? On most occasions, she barely said a word.

Gabriel set down his fork. Was he going to tell everyone about their encounter this afternoon? She felt that awful heat wash over her again.

"Yes," she said hastily, "an art academy."

"The National Academy of Design to be precise," Mother said haughtily. She leaned ever so slightly toward Gabriel. "That's the finest art school in New York."

Felicity blushed wildly. Gabriel knew that. "Mother," she hissed.

"Well, it is."

"And one of the finest in the country," Gabriel said.

Once Mother got over the initial shock that he knew about

art academies, she looked pleased. "See, Felicity. I told you that *everyone* has heard of the National Academy."

Felicity squirmed. How could Mother slight Gabriel like that? He might be poor, but he wasn't ignorant.

To his credit, Gabriel fielded the derogatory comment with grace. "You're probably right, Mrs. Kensington." Then he ruined everything. "Ms. Kensington, your sketches are very well done. That still life of the rose is particularly good."

Felicity didn't have to follow his gaze to know he meant Mother's sketch hanging on the opposite wall. "It's not mine," she said stiffly.

"It might as well be," Mother said with a wave of the hand. "Felicity's work is charming."

She would lie to a minister? That was practically like lying to God. "No it's not," Felicity said in a moment of contrariness. "I can't draw a thing."

"Felicity," Mother hissed.

"I'm sure that's not true," Beatrice graciously said. "You did a lovely sketch of a horse when we were in school."

Mother did it. Mother always did Felicity's sketches. Either the teachers didn't know or they looked the other way.

"That's why my Felicity is the perfect chairwoman of the Beautification Committee," Mother stated, deftly turning the conversation in a new direction.

"Beautification Committee?" Gabriel asked.

Beatrice raised guileless blue eyes. "The Beautification of the Sanctuary Committee."

Mother explained, "We've decided to replace the plate glass window inside the entry with stained glass."

"We?" Gabriel looked around the table. "Why haven't I heard about this?"

Felicity wanted to hide. Mother should have told him at the Ladies' Aid Society meeting. She should have laid out all her plans to the new minister. It was just like her to settle the matter before he arrived to avoid any opposition.

Mother waved off the question. "Don't fret. You'll hear all about it at our next meeting."

Gabriel gulped. "Are you telling me this is a Ladies' Aid Society project?"

"Of course, and my Felicity is chairing the committee."

Gabriel's expression hardened. "I thought the Ladies' Aid Society raised funds to help the poor."

Mother's artificial smile tightened in preparation for a fight. "That is one of our missions. Helping our church is another."

"But the poor—"

"Pardon me, Reverend, but you've been in Pearlman less than a day. I believe we know a bit more about our town than you do." Though Mother spoke in a singsong tone, her words cut with the efficiency of a scalpel.

Gabriel's jaw dropped, and for a moment Felicity wanted to encourage him, but then she heard Robert snicker and realized what a fool Gabriel was making of himself. Mortified for him, she tried to think of another topic of conversation, but her mind had gone blank.

Looking stricken, Beatrice took the lead. "Felicity, when is the first meeting? We can discuss this all then, not at dinner."

How could she answer? She didn't know a thing about the project or the committee, not even who was on it, but she couldn't admit ignorance. She lifted her jaw and squared her shoulders. "I will contact you when a date is set."

"But shouldn't we begin soon?" Beatrice asked. "I understand it can take some time for a window to be constructed. Bad weather will be here before we realize it."

A lady always maintains her composure. Felicity kept her head high. "Everything is under control." It clearly was not.

Gabriel was upset with Mother's project, and Robert had resumed talking about the airfield. If she didn't do something quickly, she'd lose her chance to claim his attention.

"I'm terribly hot," she exclaimed, setting her napkin on the table. "May I be excused, Daddy? I'd like to take some air." She didn't wait for his approval to push her chair back.

"May I escort you, Ms. Kensington?" Robert asked, setting aside his napkin. He held out a hand.

Perfect. She beamed as she placed her hand on his. At last, her plan was underway.

Gabriel itched to follow Felicity, but she could never care for a man who chased after her. So he waited anxiously for the meal to end.

The Wellington lost its flavor, and he couldn't ignore the empty places beside him. What would they say to each other? What would they do? No small part of him wanted to run out and protect her, for what kind of man spoke so carelessly of passion, equating it with lasting love? He knew the answer: a man who wanted to use a woman for his own pleasure.

"It *is* hot in here," Kensington said, interrupting Gabriel's thoughts. "Let's all take our dessert in the garden."

Though Gabriel eagerly assented, judging by the grim set of Eugenia Kensington's lips, she supported her daughter's withdrawal with Blevins. Thankfully her father had better sense.

They caught up with the pair on the porch. A waning moon couldn't compete with the bright gas lanterns lining the driveway. Moths fluttered against the globes, hopelessly attracted to what would kill them.

Felicity still hung on Blevins's arm, gazing into his ridiculous face with adoration.

Peeved, Gabriel asked if she felt cooler now.

Felicity ignored his question. "Founder's Day," she whispered to Blevins. "Remember, green satin ribbon."

Judging by Blevins's grin, he understood what she meant, but instead of answering, he kissed her hand and broke away just as Kensington approached.

"Mr. Blevins, join Blake and me in the study," the patriarch said. "I have a question about your blueprints."

Blevins of course obeyed. He had little choice, since Kensington employed him, but that left Gabriel to reap the rewards of being alone with the ladies. He snared a crystal bowl of strawberries with cream and offered it to Felicity.

"Would you care for dessert?"

She hugged her arms and shivered. "No, thank you. I'm still a bit fatigued." Without asking his pardon, she departed, leaving a faint scent of roses lingering in the air.

Gabriel knew a brush-off when he saw one. Felicity Kensington not only preferred Blevins but she disliked *him* intensely. The feelings he had for her were not mutual.

He gathered the remnants of his battered pride and faced the remaining women. Eugenia and Beatrice Kensington had watched the entire exchange. Felicity's mother smirked, while Beatrice looked dismayed. Gabriel forced a smile. "Nice evening."

They exchanged small talk, but he could barely keep his mind on the conversation. He wondered what Felicity meant by those furtive instructions to Blevins. Clearly they'd planned to do something on Founder's Day, whenever that was, but what did the green satin ribbon mean? Was it to indicate where they could meet in secret? Surely there was no need. Eugenia Kensington clearly supported a match between her daughter and Blevins. Clandestine meetings always led to no good. Gabriel had seen his share of unwed mothers, abandoned by their lovers as soon as they were with child. He shuddered to think that might happen to

Felicity, but he didn't trust Blevins. Something wasn't right about the man.

"Pastor, glad to see you're still here." The hearty greeting came from Branford Kensington, flanked by his son and Blevins. He shook Blevins's hand. "Shall we call it a night? You'll want to start first thing in the morning."

Blevins apparently understood a dismissal when he heard one, for he gathered his hat and cane and thanked Mrs. Kensington for a fine dinner. As the man passed, Gabriel smelled whiskey. That shouldn't be—not with prohibition. Yet somehow he'd gotten liquor.

Kensington's intense gaze honed in on Gabriel. "You and I have a little unfinished business, Pastor. Let's go to my study."

That was not a suggestion; it was a command. Gabriel swallowed a nut of worry. What had he done to upset Kensington? Had he been too forward with Felicity? Did Kensington suspect his interest in her? Every step down the long hall intensified his dread.

The study was paneled in mahogany and filled with heavy furniture. A gun rack with nine hunting rifles spanned the wall behind him. A Cape buffalo head stared blankly with dark, glassy eyes while gazelle, moose and antelope mounts graced the other walls.

Rather than sit in the low chair across the massive desk from Kensington, Gabriel remained standing. He'd been forced low enough for one night.

"Care for a drink?" Kensington pulled the stopper off a crystal decanter filled with a dark liquid.

Whiskey. Fingers of dread danced along Gabriel's spine. That's where Blevins got it. Kensington might have stockpiled a legal supply before the law took effect. Even if he hadn't, like most rich men he would think he was above the law.

"I don't drink," he said with quiet condemnation.

Kensington held the stopper in midair and laughed. "It's sarsaparilla, son, not alcohol."

But Gabriel had smelled whiskey on Blevins. Perhaps Blevins carried a flask, or maybe Kensington put the liquor away for the minister.

"I'm not thirsty."

"Suit yourself." The man rapped his knuckles on the desktop before taking his seat. "I'm a man who likes to get straight to business." He leaned back in his chair, at ease with the world and whatever he had to tell Gabriel. "You've seen the town, inspected the church, met a good portion of our congregation. You're a man of education, correct?"

Gabriel nodded, though the question was rhetorical.

"Then you see how things add up around here."

Gabriel saw nothing of the sort. "What adds up?"

Kensington smiled paternally. "You're a bright young man and can see how things run in this town." He steepled his fingers. "There's one thing I'd like you to keep in mind."

Gabriel's mind raced through the hundred things Kensington could demand: silence about illicit alcohol, blinders for every indiscretion. He could even dictate the sermon topics.

Kensington leaned forward, gaze intent. "Remember who's in charge."

"What?" Gabriel backed up, not believing what he'd just heard. The man was threatening him, telling him that he had to get approval for every idea.

"I think you know what I mean."

The initial shock settled in Gabriel's belly with a dull fire that grew with each successive thought. He had ignored every slight and innuendo tonight. He'd endured Eugenia Kensington's derogatory comments and turned a cheek to Blevins's superior attitude, but he could not accept bullying.

Nor could he remain silent when the evil of drink was seeping into this town. Gabriel Meeks did not bow to any man.

"Yes, I do, sir." He trembled beneath shackled ire, ready to fight. "I know exactly who's in charge. God is."

Gabriel spun away but not before glimpsing a peculiar grin on Kensington's face. The man thought he had Gabriel exactly where he wanted him. Well, he was wrong.

Without a word, Gabriel left the room, the house and very likely his first pastorate.

Chapter Four

Day two, and Felicity's plan was progressing on schedule. Even though Robert hadn't asked to see her again, he would have if the rest of the dinner party hadn't shown up at the most inopportune time. Still, she'd won his assurance that he would bid on her Founder's Day picnic basket. A little trinket inside would assure him of her interest.

That's why she deliberated over the small collection of luxury goods in the mercantile's display case. The morning sun streamed through the store window, sending a thousand sparkles off the paste jewelry. She drew her attention to those items suitable for a man of recent acquaintance. Sterling hat brush, watch or pocketknife. None of them struck her as perfect. She wondered if Blake had any stock not yet on the shelves.

"No, Ms. Kensington," Josh Billingsley said in answer to her query.

"Any due in over the next week?"

"I wouldn't know."

He didn't even look at the order book. Honestly, her brother should hire better help. She examined her options again. Perhaps a book. The slender volume of Wordsworth had a calfskin cover and ribbon place marker, but would

Robert read poetry? Gabriel yes, but Robert? She imagined Robert reclining at the picnic, reading love poems to her. Though she could picture his strawberry-blond hair and outrageous mustache, the voice was always Gabriel's rich baritone.

Definitely not Wordsworth. Perhaps the hat brush? Too impersonal. The pocketknife? Too masculine. Besides, he'd already have one.

She bit her lip, trying to decide, and overheard a pair of giggling voices—Sally Neidecker and Eloise Grattan, if she wasn't mistaken. The two stood directly behind her, hidden by the tall candy display. They'd been inseparable since the first day of primary school. Whiplike Sally, whose parents' wealth was second only to Felicity's, stuck her nose into everyone else's business while Eloise blundered along blindly with everything Sally suggested.

"He looked at me," Eloise giggled. "Did you see it?"

"Who didn't?" Sally whispered. "He likes you. I can tell."

Felicity could guess whom they were talking about. Gabriel. Good. She needed to wipe him from her mind. The image of Gabriel kissing Eloise Grattan was just the thing. She picked up the book of Wordsworth and leafed through it.

"Do you really think so? I'm not too young?" Eloise's voice fluttered with nervous worry.

Too young? He couldn't be more than a year or two older than her. She stifled a laugh, and the book accidentally knocked the glass of the display case.

"Shh," Sally said. "Someone's listening."

"Who?" asked a panicked Eloise.

Felicity buried her head in the book and pressed into the corner, out of their line of sight.

"It's only Felicity Kensington," Sally said after a moment,

"and she's busy reading, but just to be safe, pretend you're looking at the candy."

"But I am looking at the candy."

"To buy some, silly."

"I was going to get some horehound drops," Eloise said, and for a moment Felicity felt sorry for her. Sally was sure to ridicule the choice.

"Horehound? That's for sore throats."

"Pa likes them," Eloise said weakly.

After that, the conversation stopped for so long that Felicity thought they'd left. She edged out of the corner and spied the two girls still at the candy counter.

"You don't think I'm too young?" Eloise asked again.

"Not at all," Sally said flippantly. "Some men like younger women."

Felicity rolled her eyes.

"But my size—"

"My brother says men like a woman with some meat."

Joe Neidecker might like substantial women, but Felicity doubted Gabriel did.

"Do you think I have a chance?" Eloise whispered.

Sally's voice lowered, but Felicity could just make out the last bit. "...the barn after lunch."

They were going to the barn? Felicity nearly dropped the book. Eloise wasn't infatuated with Gabriel. She wanted Robert. Impossible. He would never fall in love with someone like Eloise. She had no breeding or wealth. She brought nothing to a marriage.

"Don't worry. I'll be with you every step of the way," Sally said.

Felicity's pulse beat faster. Sally didn't offer her assistance unless she expected to gain something, even from her sidekick. Eloise might think Sally was joining her to help, but in the end, Sally, not Eloise, would have Robert—unless Felicity got there first.

She snapped the book shut. She couldn't wait for the Founder's Day picnic. If she wanted to secure Robert, she had to act now. But how? She couldn't pester him like Eloise. That was sure to drive the man away. No, she needed a good, logical reason to interrupt his business or he'd only be annoyed. Business. That was it. She set the book back on the shelf.

"Oh, Felicity," said Sally, sliding past her, "I didn't see you. When is the committee meeting?"

"I'll contact you," Felicity said sweetly, as if she hadn't overheard a thing. "I'm glad you're helping."

"Oh, not me. Eloise is on the committee. I'm far too busy to be on some silly old committee."

"It's hardly silly." Felicity couldn't believe she was defending Mother's pet project. "The new window is important to the church."

Sally shrugged. "Everyone knows the only person who really wants it is your mother. That's why she named you chairwoman."

Felicity clenched her fists. "No one supports this community more. Why, if it weren't for the Kensingtons—"

"Kensington," Sally snorted and rolled her eyes at Eloise, who giggled. "I wouldn't throw that name around so much if I were you."

"What do you mean?" Felicity demanded.

Again, Sally laughed. "Not a thing." She took Eloise by the arm, and the two girls walked off, whispering to each other.

Felicity stood dumbfounded before the candy display. People disparaged the Kensington name on occasion, but no one had ever done so to her face.

"Kin I help you, Ms. Kensington?" Josh Billingsley asked.

She shook her head. Sally and Eloise's snide comments didn't matter. They were just trying to distract her from Robert. Well, they would not succeed. Felicity had one option they didn't. As committee chairwoman, she could request Robert Blevins's assistance with the new stained glass window. A man liked nothing better than to demonstrate his skill, and it would give her all the time with him that she needed.

Gabriel awoke the next morning with a sense of purpose and a stomachache. The former would propel his new sermon for Sunday, assuming he wasn't fired before then. The latter undoubtedly sprang from that meeting last night.

After stewing about Kensington's threat for almost an hour, he'd paid the exorbitant cost to place a long distance telephone call home. Dad could tell him what to do. Unfortunately, Mom and Dad were at the opera, and he could only talk with his sister, Mariah.

Though she usually made sense of the worst muddles, last night she'd offered no solution.

"Do what you must, Gabe," she'd said over the crackling line. "And pray first."

Prayer hadn't brought sleep or a calm stomach, so first thing in the morning he headed to the drugstore for medicine. Before he'd walked a block, the one Ladies' Aid Society member who hadn't asked for a favor stopped him. Short and plump, Mrs. Simmons epitomized the loving mother. Her round cheeks glowed, and her blue eyes twinkled merrily.

"Pastor Meeks. How good to see you."

Gabriel greeted her and smiled at her gawky teenage

daughter, who hung back holding a basket covered in cheap gingham. He wished he could remember the girl's name.

"Anna and I were just on our way to the parsonage with some cinnamon rolls."

Anna. That was it. The delicious aroma of fresh bread and cinnamon revived his downtrodden spirit. "For me?"

Mrs. Simmons smiled broadly, her rosy cheeks round as apples. "You're looking mighty thin." She clucked her tongue softly. "No housekeeper or wife to keep meat on those bones. If you're hiring, my Anna's a hard worker."

The girl kept her face averted, but Gabriel saw her blush.

"I'll keep that in mind," he said, "after my sister visits."

If he wasn't fired first.

"Oh my, you have a sister. Is she younger than you?"

Mrs. Simmons had such a kindly manner that Gabriel easily confided in her. After a few minutes talking about his older sister, Gabriel saw Blake Kensington drive by. Though the son had proven companionable, any Kensington reminded him that his fate still hung in the balance. The bile rose in his throat.

"Please excuse me." He hated cutting off a parishioner, but he couldn't concentrate on what she was saying when his gut hurt. "Can you tell me where I might buy something for a stomachache?"

"Mercy me, here I am prattling away when you need medicine. The drugstore's across the street at the end of this block. You hurry on now, and I'll leave the rolls on your porch."

Though Gabriel insisted he could carry them, she would have none of it. "I'll send Anna." And before he could protest further, the girl sped off.

Mrs. Simmons then motioned him close and whispered, "Be sure to use the front entrance."

"Why wouldn't I?" he asked, puzzled, but she only bid him goodbye and headed for the post office.

What an odd thing to say. Customers never used the back door of a business. That was for deliveries and employees. He stopped outside the drugstore and examined the storefront. It looked like any drugstore with advertisements for tonic and perfume and lotions in the front windows. The interior was lined to the ceiling with narrow shelves and bottles. A long wooden counter, manned by an attractive, dark-haired woman of perhaps forty, kept customers from the strongest drugs.

He stepped to the counter. "I'd like something for stomach upset."

The woman smiled pleasantly between the curled ends of her bobbed hair. "You're the new minister in town, aren't you?"

"Yes, I am. Reverend Meeks."

"I'm Mrs. Lawrence. Would you prefer dyspepsia tablets or bicarbonate of soda?"

"The tablets, please, a half dozen." If he didn't butt heads with Kensington too often, he wouldn't need more.

She slid the tablets into a tiny paper envelope. "That will be twenty cents."

As he handed over the dimes, he heard two young ladies whisper behind gloved hands. He recognized them from the Ladies' Aid Society meeting. One had been pushed by her mother to meet him, if he recalled correctly. Unfortunately, he couldn't remember their names, a poor start for their pastor.

"May I help you, Eloise?" Mrs. Lawrence asked pointedly.

Eloise Grattan. That was it. And the one with the pointed nose must be Sally something-or-other.

"No, not today," Ms. Grattan giggled, darting a glance his way.

Her mother had brazenly offered her daughter as a potential wife. Though Gabriel had come to town hoping to find a bride, he didn't want one thrust on him.

"Ladies." He nodded, eliciting yet another round of giggles.

The bell above the door tinkled when he left, replacing his irritation with a warm homey feeling. This was small-town America, the rural ideal he'd envisioned—girls giggled, boys played, clean air, bright storefronts and friendly townspeople—well, at least for the most part.

He waited at the corner for a motorcar to pass. The Packard approached quickly, and the driver blew the horn to warn everyone to scatter. For a second, the significance didn't hit Gabriel. Then he remembered. This was Kensington's car. Gabriel watched it turn into the alley behind the drugstore. What had Mrs. Simmons said? To be certain to use the front door?

Curious, he hurried down the street and reached the alley just as the motorcar was driving away. The heel of a man's shoe vanished into the drugstore's back door—Kensington, no doubt. Gabriel strode down the alley and tried the door. Locked. Whatever was going on, it wasn't good.

Evil hides from the light.

What this town needed was someone to shine a bright light into the dark corners. They needed their eyes opened to the corruption around them. The people of this town needed a leader who would stand up to Kensington, not another puppet giving bland sermons and lukewarm advice. This town needed its spiritual and social fire relit. God had called him, Gabriel Meeks, to Pearlman for a reason. He now knew what that reason was.

Reinvigorated, Gabriel strode past the church to the park.

This whole business began in the woods behind the parsonage. Criminals, Coughlin had said. Gabriel now knew what the man meant. Something was going on near that broken-down fence, and he intended to find out what.

The route to Baker's Field took Felicity past the park and the parsonage with its hedge of furiously blooming bridal's veil. If she could get to the barn first, she could ask for Robert's assistance before Sally and Eloise claimed his time.

She hurried past the cramped fields of Einer Coughlin, the last farmhouse before Baker's Field. Though she couldn't spot Robert in the field, a motorcar was parked near the barn. It looked like Blake's, meaning Robert had to be there.

If she cut across Coughlin's hayfield, she'd save precious minutes, but the man was the meanest farmer in town. Everyone blamed it on his wife's untimely death and son's running away, but Felicity sympathized with the wife and son. He'd likely driven them to their rash actions. Shiftless and stingy, Mr. Coughlin grew hay on the richest farmland in the township.

She hated walking by Coughlin's land. Sometimes he'd yell at passersby. Occasionally he'd threaten them. She hurried past the ramshackle house surrounded by garbage and broken equipment. It was an eyesore and a disgrace and so close to the parsonage, too. Poor Gabriel.

Poor Gabriel? What was she thinking? She had set her cap on Robert Blevins, not Gabriel Meeks.

With a shudder, she scurried by the Coughlin place, head down. Just a few yards more, she thought. Then a pitiful whining made her stop. That came from a dog, and judging by its plaintive cry, it was hurt. Was the animal caught in one of the rusting buggies or plows near the house? If so, Coughlin would shoot it out of spite.

A horrible yelp set her in motion. She had to save the poor

thing before it was too late, but where was it? At first, the cries seemed to come from near the house, but as she went farther into the newly reaped field, she realized the animal was behind the house, toward the river.

When she rounded the decaying wagon, she saw. Mr. Coughlin, rifle slung over his shoulder, dragging poor Slinky toward the river on a rope.

"Stop," she cried, racing toward them.

The dog struggled against the rope with all his might, but Mr. Coughlin didn't let go. With a jerk, the knot tightened around Slinky's neck.

"Stop. You'll strangle him."

Coughlin kept walking.

The wet earth sucked the ivory satin pumps off her feet. She yanked the shoes out of the mud and tried again, but two steps later, the shoes came off again. It was no use. She grabbed the shoes and ran in her stocking feet. The hay stubble stabbed her soles, but she had to save Slinky.

"Stop. Stop." She waved the shoes, but Coughlin didn't hear her.

He steamed onward, slowed only by Slinky's desperate resistance. The black-and-white dog snapped and nipped at the rope, but Coughlin yanked harder.

"Stop that," she cried. "You're hurting him." She threw a shoe past the man's head.

That stopped him. He squinted in her direction while Slinky tried desperately to rub the rope off his neck.

"Mr. Coughlin," she panted, "don't do it."

Coughlin raised the rifle. "Yer on my land."

"P-please." She could barely get the word out. He wouldn't shoot her, would he? "You have no right."

"I have every right. This mutt has et his last chicken. Now get off my land."

Slinky jumped joyfully against her pale yellow gown,

planting muddy paw prints on the delicate chiffon. Coughlin yanked the dog back with a harsh jerk.

"No," Felicity cried with frustration. How could she stop Coughlin? How could she prevent this murder? She looked around for help and spotted the broken fence ten feet back. "In case you haven't noticed, we're standing on parsonage property."

His eyes narrowed as he followed her line of sight and then he dragged Slinky back over the fence line. "Now I'm on my land. Git."

Not without Slinky. But Coughlin would never let the dog go. He operated on the eye-for-an-eye system. Somehow she had to convince him to turn the dog over to her.

Heart hammering in her ears, she said, "I can stand here if I want. My father gave this land to the church."

"Yer choice." Coughlin pointed his rifle at Slinky.

"No," she cried. "Don't. I'll pay you for the chicken."

"You got money?"

"No, but my father does."

"And what about the next 'un and the next?" He aimed.

"You can't kill him," she cried. "Everyone would hear. There'd be an outcry."

"Don't care what no one thinks." He cocked the gun.

Felicity wildly searched for a way to stop him. "Even your son Benjamin?"

The rifle barrel dipped.

"I knew Ben," she said in a hurry, "and he'd never want you to kill an innocent animal."

"Ain't innocent." His aim steadied. "Besides, what do I care what Ben thinks when he done run oft?"

Felicity scrambled for a better reason. "What if someone owns the dog? They could insist you pay them for their loss."

"This here's a stray. You know it an' I know it."

"B-but he deserves to live. He only needs to be trained.

Why, it's no different than a child. Without proper training, a child goes wild. Slinky can be trained. I know it."

Coughlin stared her in the eye. "You planning to take him on?"

Felicity swallowed. Mother would never allow it. She claimed the smell of them made her sick, and that was one point even Daddy couldn't fight. No pets. Yet Slinky looked at her with such desperation, the little white eyebrows lifted, one ear cocked and one flopped over. She couldn't bear to see him get shot.

"Didn't think so." He raised the gun again. Slinky cowered, whining.

"No! I—I—I'll take him."

"Where? Your daddy don't keep no pets. He sure ain't gonna want this chicken-stealing varmint." Coughlin aimed.

Felicity squeezed her eyes shut against the tears and gave one last plea. "Any dog can be saved with a little love."

"She's right," said a calm, clear and very familiar voice.

Felicity opened her eyes to see Gabriel standing between herself and Coughlin. He was dressed as plainly as yesterday afternoon, his shirtsleeves rolled to the elbow, revealing strong, capable forearms.

"Gabriel," she breathed, and then realizing that was disrespectful said, "Pastor."

Coughlin waved him away. "This is none of your business, Rev'rend."

But Gabriel didn't back down. "Ms. Kensington is correct. Love will cure many faults. It might even save a chicken-stealing varmint."

Felicity almost laughed at those rough words coming from his educated tongue. Yes, educated. His diction was as fine as any orator. In that moment, she saw him anew. He might dress a little too informally, but he had a generous heart. Even if he wasn't husband material, he was a good and decent man.

"You feel that way," spat Coughlin, "then you take 'im." He put the rope in Gabriel's hand. "If that dog ever sets foot on my property again, this bullet is goin' straight through his head, pastor or no pastor."

Coughlin returned the way he came, and Gabriel led Slinky onto the parsonage's side of the fence.

Now that the danger had passed, Felicity began to shake. Coughlin had aimed his gun at her. What if he'd shot? She hugged her arms and wished she were home in her room. Instead, she stood awkwardly with Gabriel, who stared at Slinky.

Finally, he raised his eyes and held out the rope. "It looks like you've got yourself a dog, Ms. Kensington."

"What do you mean?" She backed away and rubbed the muddy grains off her hands. "My parents won't let me have a pet. And I'll be leaving by September."

"Well, I can't have a dog. You did say you'd take him. I believe those were your exact words."

"I didn't want Mr. Coughlin to kill Slinky, so I promised."

"Do you generally promise what you don't intend to fulfill?" His eyes glittered with gold flecks in the sunlight.

"I, uh." No one had ever questioned her before. She was Felicity Kensington. She squared her shoulders. "No innocent creature deserves to die, no matter what he's done. Slinky can be rehabilitated by the right owner, someone who understands dogs, someone who knows how to call them, for instance." She gazed right into those deep brown eyes and knew he understood. "I don't suppose…?" She left the sentence hanging.

"No."

"Just for a while," she implored. "Until Mr. Coughlin simmers down. Please?"

"What happens then? You'll turn him loose again?"

"No," she said hastily. Slinky could never run loose again, or Coughlin would kill him. "I'll find him a home."

He hesitated. "The Church Council might not want a dog in the parsonage."

"The Johannesons had a cat."

Gabriel rubbed his forehead as Slinky cocked his head and looked at him with big, hopeful eyes. Good boy, Slinky. She felt Gabriel's resistance break.

"Two months," he said. "You need to find him a new home within two months."

"All right." Perhaps she could convince Robert to bring Slinky with them or find a farmer willing to take him on.

"And you will help train him," he added.

She swallowed hard. That meant hours working with Gabriel, hours by his side. "Me?"

"You. That point is not negotiable." He put the rope in her hand. "You can start by bringing him to the parsonage."

"Now?" Her legs turned to jelly.

"Of course now."

He took off, leaving her no choice but to follow.

Chapter Five

Gabriel guided her through the woods. "We'll begin with a bath."

"A bath?" For one humiliating moment, Felicity thought he meant her.

"I'm not letting that dog into the parsonage without a bath."

Of course he was talking about Slinky, who, come to mention it, did stink. Gabriel led the way, and the dog trotted along beside her, eager to go wherever they led.

"But I have things to do." She couldn't exactly tell Gabriel that she had to see Robert before Sally and Eloise got to him.

"Duty first." Gabriel opened the gate to the parsonage's backyard and held it for her. He sounded just like a parent, though he couldn't be more than her twenty-one years.

"I shouldn't be here alone," she pointed out.

"You're not alone." He motioned for her to enter the yard.

Felicity tentatively stepped through the gate. Though she'd been to the parsonage numerous times, she had never set foot in the expansive backyard, partially shaded by a huge oak nestled just outside the whitewashed picket fence.

A solitary lilac and a clothesline broke the expanse of mowed grass.

After closing the gate behind her, Gabriel strode quickly across the yard, a man at ease with his surroundings. At the stoop, he turned to check her progress.

"I thought you were in a hurry," he called out as she inched closer.

"How long is this going to take?" She had to get to the barn before Robert left.

Gabriel's mouth curved into a soft smile. "We'll find out, won't we?" He turned the screen door's handle.

"You don't expect me to go inside, do you?" She glanced to her left and right. There was no one there now, but anyone could walk through the park or down Elm Street.

"Of course not." But still he grinned at her in the most alarming manner. "I'll fetch the water. You hang on to the dog."

"Slinky. His name is Slinky."

Gabriel's eyebrow lifted. "We're going to have to do something about that name. Somehow Slinky doesn't seem quite right for a minister's dog."

She laughed. She couldn't help it. Gabriel had made a joke on himself, something she didn't expect. Ministers were somber and judging, not funny and warmhearted like Gabriel.

"I'll be right back," he said, opening the screen door. "You just keep hold of Slinky."

He vanished inside, and she once again felt vulnerable. Even here, close to the house, she was exposed, but if she stood behind the lilac, no one would see her.

"Follow me." She patted Slinky's head and headed toward the bush.

He didn't budge.

She tugged gently on the rope. "Come, Slinky."

He tilted his head in bemusement.

She held out her hand the way Gabriel had at the train depot, and at last the dog bounded toward her. By backing up and repeating the process, she led him bit by bit to the lilac.

Then she waited…and waited. The noon hour must have come and gone. Sally and Eloise would be at the barn by now. What could be taking so long? She fumed and crossed her arms. If not for Slinky, she'd leave.

At last, Gabriel pushed open the door with his shoulder. He carried a bright tin washtub brimming with water. Towels hung over his shoulder—the new towels.

"You can't use those," she cried. "My mother had them monogrammed in New York City."

Gabriel searched left and right until he spotted her. "What are you doing way over there?"

"It's shady here."

"We don't want to be in the shade." He set the tub down in the middle of the yard and stretched his back. "Phew, that's heavy."

"The towels," she said at the exact moment he tossed them on the ground. Too late. They were ruined now.

She edged closer to the tub. Only the less fortunate used a tin tub to bathe anymore. Felicity had never set foot in one herself, though the mercantile still sold them to local farmers and tradesmen. Slinky sniffed the water and began slurping it up.

Felicity tried to pull him back. "Stop it. Don't drink that."

"Why not? He's probably thirsty, and it's not soapy yet." Gabriel produced a cake of castile soap from his pocket. "Shall we?"

Felicity had no idea what to do next, but she hardly wanted to admit it. He'd laughed at her inability to get the letter from Slinky yesterday. How much harder he'd laugh if he knew she had no idea how to wash a dog. If she'd been allowed to have a pet, she would have known what to do, but Mother insisted animals did not belong in the house, and Daddy only brought them inside after they'd been stuffed.

She held out the rope, indicating Gabriel should take the lead.

He didn't make a move. "He's your dog."

But she didn't know how to bathe a dog.

Gabriel held out the soap.

She folded her arms. "It's your soap."

"You don't know how, do you?"

Felicity jutted out her jaw. "Our home is too nice for pets."

"Too nice?"

He was flustering her. "Mother doesn't want the furniture ruined."

Instead of criticizing her upbringing, his expression softened. "Do you mean you never had a pet?"

Felicity bit back a wave of emotion and shook her head. Ms. Priss didn't count since she belonged to the neighbors. "Blake had a hunting dog once, a long time ago, but he let Blackie in the house one day, and Mother found out. Daddy took poor Blackie away, and we never saw him again."

"I'm sorry."

He looked at her so kindly that her throat tightened. "It doesn't matter. Proper young ladies don't get attached to smelly old dogs."

"You don't really believe that, do you?"

Mother did. Animals belonged on farms, not in nice houses. To her they were objects, like a vase or a doorstop, not creatures with souls, but Felicity had worried and prayed for that dog for weeks. Mother had told her to grow up and stop fussing.

"It was a long time ago," she said with a shrug, hoping he didn't notice how painful the memory was.

"I always had a lot of dogs and cats." He smiled softly. "Too many, Dad would say, but Mom put up with it."

Felicity wondered what it would be like to have parents who accepted their children's interests. "My mother would never allow them. You must understand. You've met her."

"Yes, I have." He laughed, easing her discomfort. "Do you have a big family?"

"Just Blake. He's four years older than me."

"That means we're both the babies of our families. I have four older brothers and one older sister, Mariah."

"Six? There are six of you in all? How did you all find a place to sleep?" She'd heard many of the poor had large families, but six children? How had they all fit into a tiny tenement apartment? And with dogs and cats, too?

"We took shifts," he said solemnly.

"You did? Then you had to sleep in the daytime—" She halted when Gabriel roared. He'd been teasing her, and she fell for it. "You made that up."

He nodded, still laughing. "I'm sorry, I shouldn't have done that, but the thought of my brothers and I sharing a bed was too funny. Charlie, the oldest, doesn't like anyone talking to him, least of all snoring next to him."

She knew he was trying to soothe her hurt feelings, but it still stung that she'd been so gullible. At least she wasn't poor. "Well, I never had to share anything."

He sobered, looking at her with clear eyes. "I imagine that's true."

Slinky barked, reminding them of the business at hand.

"Do you want to hold or scrub?" Gabriel asked.

"Excuse me?"

He nodded at the dog. "One of us has to hold, uh, Slinky, while the other scrubs."

One holding and one scrubbing, all around a little wash-tub. There'd be soap and water, and they'd be far too close.

"Well," he asked again. "Which will it be?"

What if water splashed onto her dress? What if Gabriel accidentally touched her? Which was most ladylike? Which was proper?

"I—I—I'll hold him," she finally said.

"Fine. Bring him here."

"Here, boy. Have a nice bath." She tugged on the leash, but Slinky had other ideas. He barked and danced away, nearly pulling the rope from her hands.

With a laugh, Gabriel scooped up the dog and plopped him into the tub. The water splashed out, soaking Felicity's skirt.

"Oh," she cried, pulling the wet chiffon from her legs. "Be careful."

Slinky stood in shock for an instant before leaping from the water and tearing away. The rope ripped through Felicity's hands, burning her palm. The wet dog ran around the yard barking. At least he didn't hurdle the fence. After making the circuit, he stopped by Felicity and shook.

"Stop, stop!" she cried, turning from the spray of doggy-smelling drops.

Gabriel, to his credit, stifled any laughter. He merely walked over to Slinky, picked up the rope and handed it to Felicity. "You might want to hold him around the neck."

That meant practically hugging the wet dog. Gingerly she stepped close, bent over and held the collar part of the rope between her index finger and thumb.

"That's never going to keep him still," Gabriel remarked as he lathered up the soap. "Get a good hold of him."

"But he's wet," she cried. "My dress."

She wanted to walk away, to leave Slinky to the fate he deserved, but then he looked up at her with those big brown eyes. His little white eyebrows pressed together as if he was worried she'd leave him, too.

"All right," she sighed, kneeling on the grass and ruining her dress entirely. "For your sake." She wrapped her arms around his wet, smelly body.

"Hold him tight," Gabriel said. "He's probably not going to like this."

That was an understatement. The moment the soap hit Slinky's fur, he yanked out of Felicity's grasp, sending her tumbling to the ground.

"Don't let go," Gabriel cried, but it was too late.

This time Slinky was making a break for it.

Gabriel chased him around the yard, hollering the dog's name and alternately calling him bad or good. Neither worked. Slinky stayed just beyond reach, like that day at the depot. Felicity couldn't help but laugh. By the time the dog, with Gabriel in pursuit, had made a second circuit, she was doubled over.

"You could help," he panted, making a flying leap for Slinky's rope.

He crashed to the ground but missed the rope, which Slinky pulled just out of reach. The mutt ran ten feet away and barked, but Gabriel lay facedown, unmoving.

"That's no way to call a dog," she said, echoing his words at the depot. She leaned over and held out her hand. "Here, Slinky. Here, boy."

The dog came straight to her, and she grabbed the rope, pleased that she'd turned the tables on Reverend Gabriel Meeks. She glanced at him, expecting a sheepish grin, but he hadn't budged. He was still facedown. A jolt of fear shot through her. What if he was injured? And she'd been making fun of him—a minister of God.

Horrified, she went to him. "Are you all right?"

He didn't move. What if he'd hit his head on a rock? What if he was...dead? Felicity couldn't breathe. She let go of Slinky, who sniffed Gabriel's mop of curls.

"Gabriel?" She still couldn't bring herself to call him pastor. "Please wake up. Lord, don't let him be hurt."

He groaned.

"Thank God," she sighed. "Are you all right?" She still didn't want to touch him.

He groaned again and rolled over. "Rotten dog. Fits his name." He winked at her.

She could have slapped him. "You're not injured."

He sat up and dusted the bits of grass from his shirt. "Just winded. You had a good chuckle at my expense though."

"You have to admit it was humorous."

Slinky barked his agreement, and Gabriel grinned. "And I no doubt deserved it. This dog does have the better of us, I'd say." His voice softened with every word, and Felicity became aware of how close they were, within inches.

"Can you stand?" she whispered.

He wasn't smiling anymore. Instead he gazed deep into her eyes, clear to her soul. "Your eyes are the most unusual color, not quite emerald but darker than jade."

Ordinarily she disliked being reminded of her eyes, which didn't match anyone else's in the family, but Gabriel made their uniqueness sound special. "Some say it's the green of water."

"Like a deep spot in the river." He pulled a damp lock of hair from her cheek.

She involuntarily trembled, and her cheek burned where his finger had brushed it.

"Are you cold?" he breathed.

"No." It wasn't cold; it was much worse. That horrible hot and cold tingling ran through her again, but it couldn't be. She needed to marry Robert. She couldn't be attracted to Gabriel. That would lead nowhere and ruin everything. She stood abruptly. "I need to go."

"Go?" He didn't try to hold her. He let her back away, but his expression said it all. He liked her—a lot.

His intensity terrified her. She looked around wildly. The picket fence enclosed the yard, trapping her, stifling her. "I—I need to go," she repeated, even less sure of herself. If she stayed another moment, she'd never leave. "I'm sorry."

"Felicity."

She couldn't look at him. The expression on his face would make her stay, and then what? She could have no future with him. She stumbled away, feet as unsure as her heart.

"Felicity?" He was coming after her. "What did I do?"

"Nothing." She pushed at the air, trying to keep him back. "I'm sorry," she mumbled, unable to explain. She stumbled backward, just out of reach. She had to leave. She had to go now.

Spotting the gate, she fled.

Felicity kept to the park and out of the public eye as long as she could, but inevitably she had to walk past houses. The only way to avoid the streets was to follow the riverbank upstream, a route she hadn't used since childhood, when she'd hide from her parents in a little cave near the river's edge. But so many years had passed that the route no longer looked familiar. Neither could she navigate the treacherous ground in pumps. No, she had to walk through Kensington Estates, where everyone would see her damp and muddy dress.

She hurried her step, hoping Mrs. Neidecker was at the Women's Club and Mrs. Vanderloo had left to play tennis. Though it wasn't much consolation, Sally and Eloise would be long gone. By now, they'd have captured Robert's attention.

"I hope they annoy him to death," she muttered and promptly tripped over a tree root. Why didn't this town install real sidewalks? Why didn't they pave their roads? Pearlman was so backward.

She kept to the shadowed side of Elm Street, somewhat hidden beneath the stately trees that had given the street its name. Tall hedges lined many of the yards, affording cover from prying eyes inside the estates. If no motorcars passed, she'd get home unscathed. She hurried along. There were only two more blocks to go. She'd slip in the servants' entrance and run upstairs. She'd wash, change and hurry to the barn. With luck, she'd find Robert eager for intelligent conversation after a trying afternoon with Sally and Eloise.

"Hey, sis, what happened to you?" Blake had driven his car up to her so quietly that she jumped at the sound of his voice.

"Blake, what are you doing here? It's not polite to sneak up on people."

He slowed the car to a crawl, keeping pace with her walking. "Want a ride? You look like you fell in the river."

She kept her focus dead ahead as she plodded up the hill. "I did not fall in the river, and I don't need your help."

He laughed. "You and the reverend go swimming?"

He'd seen her? Her cheeks heated. "Certainly not."

He laughed. "Loosen up, sis. You could use a good swim."

"I do not swim, especially not with the new minister."

Blake was grinning like an idiot, taking far too much pleasure in her discomfort. "Then why'd you run out of the parsonage's backyard?"

Oh, no. He had seen her, and if he'd seen her, others might have, too. By supper, it would be all over town. "Don't tell anyone. Please?"

His grin grew wider. "You and the reverend have a little romance going? Beattie says—"

"I don't care two pins what Beatrice says. She's wrong. There's absolutely nothing between us. Understand?

Nothing." She could not say that strongly enough. "Never ever in a hundred lifetimes."

He chuckled. "That bad, eh?"

All those years of teasing rushed back: too skinny, too tall, didn't look like a Kensington, must have been switched at birth. Every stupid taunt Blake had thrown at her during childhood returned. "Stop it. Just stop it." She wasn't going to cry. She bit her lip and stiffened her spine. *A lady always maintains her composure.* But a sniffle escaped.

"I'm sorry, sis. Let me give you a ride home." He stopped the car, leaned over and opened the passenger door.

Felicity relented. She really didn't want to walk past the Neidecker house looking like this. Besides, she could pester Blake about Robert. She slipped into the car and closed the door.

"So what did happen?" Blake put the car in gear.

Felicity should have known he wouldn't give up. "A dog. Slinky, to be precise."

"Slinky got you all wet? That had better not be dog urine soaking into my seats."

"It's not dog urine," she snapped. "It's wash water, if you must know."

Blake snorted, tried to stifle it when she glared at him, and then roared the minute she looked away. "You tried to bathe Slinky?"

"Gabriel, uh, the pastor, is taking him in."

"Gabriel?" Blake's tone intimated something more than dog washing had gone on.

Well, she'd put an end to that kind of thinking. "Slinky needs a new home. Yours would do."

"That mutt?" Blake cast her a disparaging look. "If I get a dog, it's going to be a hunting dog, purebred."

Figures. He was just like Daddy. She crossed her arms. "Can't you go any faster?"

"What's the hurry? Anxious to have Mother yell at you?"

"No." She tossed her head and stared out the passenger window. Blake could be such a brother sometimes. He also couldn't be trusted to keep a secret. If she told him she wanted to talk to Robert, he'd blab it to Beatrice and Jack Hunter and even Robert. Still, she needed to know where to find the man.

"What's going on this afternoon at the airfield?" she asked casually.

He shrugged. "We called it a day, what with the dinner party tonight."

"Robert, too?"

If Blake thought it odd she used Robert's given name, he didn't remark on it. "Of course. We're all invited to the Hunters'."

That meant the talk would center on the airfield and flight school. At least Darcy and Jack Hunter wouldn't try to match some girl with Robert...she hoped.

"Did Sally and Eloise stop by?" she ventured, exposing her hand.

Blake thankfully didn't put two and two together. "Couldn't say. We were out in the field."

Thank goodness. Felicity sighed with satisfaction. She'd have another chance tomorrow.

"We're here." Blake pulled into the circular drive, stopping at the front door where Mother was sure to see her.

"Couldn't you have dropped me in back?" she huffed as she got out.

Blake just grinned. "No way to sneak past old eagle eye."

She heaved a sigh and slammed the door shut. "I suppose you're right."

With a tip of the finger to his cap, Blake said, "Pick you up tonight at seven."

"Tonight? Do you mean I'm invited, too?" she stammered, but he was already driving away.

Oh, dear. If she was attending dinner at the Hunters', she had a lot to do. She only had a few hours to wash off the doggy smell, dry her hair and put together the perfect outfit to attract a Newport man.

And she had to pray that Robert hadn't yet heard what had happened at the parsonage that afternoon.

That evening, Gabriel couldn't concentrate. The day had passed without a word from Kensington or any of the Church Council. He'd like to assume his position was secure, but there were still three days before Sunday. He could receive notice at any moment.

He sat at the rolltop desk in the study and leafed through the Bible looking for the proper verse, but the words swam before his eyes. The meaning muddled in his mind. His sermon, full of fire that morning, stagnated.

He couldn't get Felicity out of his mind: her green eyes, her ebony hair, her tall and slender shape. He scrawled poetic lines in the margins of his sermon like an infatuated school-boy.

How ludicrous. She'd run away the moment he drew close. Her father had practically threatened him. Gabriel didn't relish seeing what the man did with those nine guns. He pitied the poor buffalo, king of the African plain, taken down by a small bullet. Gabriel had witnessed his share of the cruel unfairness in this world. That was one reason he came to the ministry, and one reason he chose to pastor in a small town. Justice should prevail.

But what justice is there in denying a child the companionship of a pet? He'd glimpsed Felicity's painful longing when she talked about her brother's dog. She must have had a lonely childhood. The age gap would have kept brother and sister from playing together. Add to that an emotionally distant mother, and it was natural she'd both yearn for affection and fear it wouldn't last.

He rubbed his face. "Gabe, you're getting soft."

That's what Dad would say. Mom would reach over and pat his father on the sleeve with a "now Edmund." The scold would inevitably accompany a peck of affection. How Gabriel longed for such a partnership, so in step with each other that one look or word communicated everything. But he'd fallen for a woman who hid her feelings behind snobbery.

Dad would know what to do. Though Edmund Meeks was nearly forty years older, Gabriel missed him. Those years had given him a wealth of wisdom not found in younger fathers. Dad had never been one to fuss about money or social standing or what people thought. He'd have found the Kensingtons absurd and shared a good laugh. He'd know exactly how to crack the shell around Felicity's heart.

Gabriel sighed. His entrance into the ministry was the only thing that had puzzled his father.

"It's a hard life, son," Dad had said. "Lots of heartache and strife and disillusionment. Don't think you can escape it. Every human flaw in greater society can be found in a church. In my opinion, you'd get more satisfaction working with Mr. Isaacs and the orphans."

At the time, that seemed hard to believe. Gabriel had chafed with frustration over increasing regulation of orphan placement. The older children were hard to place, and many ran away to a life on the streets. More than once Mr. Isaacs had pulled a girl from prostitution or a boy from thieving only to lose them again to the same vices.

If only Gabriel could find a place with hearts big enough to take in those children, a place like his parents' home. At first he'd agreed with Dad that his place was with the orphans, but then he'd heard the call to minister in Pearlman.

He couldn't explain it; he just knew he had to go. He imagined the apostles James and John had faced similar disbelief when they told their father they were abandoning fishing to follow an itinerant preacher. Dad let him go, but Gabriel knew he worried for him.

"I'll be all right, Dad," he whispered aloud.

The quiet parsonage didn't answer. Even Slinky yawned.

Gabriel glanced down at the dog, which had settled patiently at his feet. "I don't suppose you can help with my sermon?"

Slinky lifted his head, pricked his ear and gave Gabriel an eager look.

"All right. I suppose a walk will do us both good."

He shut the Bible, turned off the lamp and went to the kitchen, where he'd left the rope. He'd have to get a proper leash tomorrow. After getting Slinky ready, he headed out into the still though not silent night. Frogs trilled their mating calls in an escalating chorus. The river raced and splashed over rapids.

Gabriel walked through the park, shadowy at late dusk. Someone giggled in the pavilion, so he skirted around it, hoping the female voice didn't belong to Felicity. Horrible images of Blevins kissing her came to mind. He shook it off and headed downtown. Better to be amongst those going to the cinema or strolling the sidewalks, but Main Street didn't prove any easier to take.

A young couple held hands before a store window. Their attention was so devoted to each other that they didn't notice him. With meaningful glances, they pointed out which furniture they'd buy after they married. How he wished he had someone to love, someone who looked to him with adoring eyes, someone who would discuss the mundane details of everyday life.

"It'll be difficult to find a wife," his mom had said when

he announced that he was entering the ministry. "It takes a special woman to bear the burden of a minister's wife."

Felicity Kensington certainly didn't fit that mold. She'd never be able to summon the sympathy and compassion necessary for the position—or the patience. Chances were she'd end up like her mother. He shuddered and walked past the young couple.

At the corner, Slinky barked and tugged him toward the alley.

"What is it, boy?"

Gabriel gave him the lead. At the head of the dark lane, the dog halted, hair bristling as a deep growl rolled from within. Fear ran its cold finger down Gabriel's spine.

He couldn't see a thing now that dusk had turned to moonless night, but he could tell that something was wrong.

He let his eyes grow accustomed to the dark. As he dropped to his haunches to pet Slinky, he kept his eyes open and ears alert.

He heard the noises before he saw anything—a creak, creak, creak of a heavily laden cart or wagon and then a jingle, like glass tipping against glass.

"Who's there?" he whispered.

The sound stopped.

He stared into the inky black. Was that a cart ahead of him or a pile of garbage? But the creaking didn't resume, and with no moon, he couldn't see.

Then he remembered Kensington's guns and the trophies hanging from his walls. Gabriel was alone and unarmed. That sound might have been nothing, a delivery cart or a cat rattling the garbage. Or it might have been a man who'd gladly put a bullet through his head, someone like Branford Kensington. Whichever it was, he could do nothing on his own.

"Come on, Slinky," Gabriel whispered, urging the dog backward. "It's nothing," he said more loudly.

His legs shook, and his heart raced. He'd get the sheriff to investigate. Even if the thieves or smugglers were gone by the time the law arrived, Gabriel would have served notice. Kensington might convince the Church Council to fire him, but Gabriel would go down swinging.

He backed out of the alley more certain than ever that he was needed here. God had sent him to Pearlman for a reason. On Sunday morning, his congregation would hear why.

Chapter Six

To Felicity's relief, just three couples attended the Hunters' dinner, and none were her parents. Daddy would have monopolized conversation, and Mother would have invariably chased away prospective suitors. Tonight, Felicity had Robert all to herself. Still, talk of the airfield dominated conversation during the meal.

Afterward, everyone gathered for charades in the small living room. Jack and Darcy claimed the ragged loveseat, while Blake and Beatrice took most of the faded sofa. Robert offered Felicity the chair, the newest of all the furnishings, but she perched instead beside Beatrice. That isolated Robert to her left, where no one could steal his attention.

After Jack Hunter pantomimed an airplane, which his wife guessed in seconds, Blake stymied everyone with *Knute Rockne.*

"No one would ever guess that," Darcy protested.

"Why not? It's a person, place or thing. Anyone could see this meant *newt.*" He pantomimed short legs by extending his hands from his armpits. "Add to that *rock* plus *knee,* and you have Knute Rockne. Easy."

"For football players," Felicity challenged. She loved charades, but Blake always came up with the most impossible phrases, usually having to do with football, which he had played in college.

Her brother pouted.

"Now that's a charade anyone could guess," Felicity jabbed.

Everyone chuckled, and Blake mockingly bowed.

Next Robert leaped to his feet. "My turn." He twirled one end of his mustache as if deep in thought.

"Dandy," said Beatrice.

Darcy laughed.

Felicity scowled at both of them. Robert might be a bit overdressed but better that than the chronically underdressed Jack Hunter. "He hasn't begun yet, have you, Robert?"

"That's right," Robert said brightly, unfazed by the barb. "Ready?"

When everyone nodded, he held up one hand, curved into an arc. Felicity wrinkled her nose, trying to guess what he could mean. No doubt it would be something to do with engineering, considering Jack Hunter had chosen aviation and Blake football.

"Oh, oh," she called out before anyone else. "What's that instrument called that draws circles?"

"A pencil?" said Blake.

Everyone laughed, but Robert shook his head and indicated he'd start over. He then laid his head on his folded hands and closed his eyes.

"Sleep," said Beatrice.

"Slumber," Felicity guessed.

Robert shook his head and held up two fingers for the second word and proceeded to mimic a shoeshine. Within moments, the group had narrowed it to *shine*.

"Something shine," said Beatrice.

Dozens of guesses followed, but in the end no one could fathom what phrase Robert was acting out.

"It's *moonshine*," he finally said in exasperation. "My hand was supposed to be the moon. When you didn't understand that, I tried to indicate it was at night. See? Moon plus shine."

"You said two words," Darcy cried out. "Moonshine is only one."

Beatrice had turned rose pink. "I'm not sure it's proper."

"I don't see why not," Robert said. "It's a thing. No one put any restrictions on which words we could use."

He looked around the room for support, but Blake couldn't go against his wife, Darcy supported her best friend and Jack Hunter had to agree with his wife. That left Felicity.

"Robert's right," she said quickly. "No one said we had to use certain words."

But the convivial atmosphere had been destroyed. Beatrice examined her skirt. Darcy whispered something to her husband, and Blake looked oddly lost.

Robert, however, didn't seem to notice their discomfort. "Guess one of you ladies is next."

"I—I'm not feeling too well," Beatrice said, touching her slightly swollen belly.

Darcy hopped up. "You're not sick, are you? Jack, I told you roast beef was too heavy."

"No, no." Beatrice shook her head. "It's the baby."

Darcy gasped. "Are you having pains?"

"Oh, no. It's just normal queasy stomach."

"That's my cue." Blake rose and helped Beattie to her feet. "I think we'll call it a night."

Jack Hunter stretched. "Just as well. We have a long day ahead of us tomorrow."

Felicity watched with growing alarm. She still needed to ask Robert for help with the stained glass window. "Already? It's not even dark yet."

"I can come back for you, sis," Blake offered as Beatrice

gathered her bag and took her leave. "It'll give you a few more minutes." He grinned and winked.

She scowled at him. "I can't imagine what you mean."

"Don't trouble yourself, Blake," said Robert as he helped Felicity from the sofa. "It's a lovely evening. I'll escort your sister home."

Felicity smiled in triumph. A long walk offered ample opportunity to gain both Robert's assistance and his interest.

The goodbyes took so long that by the time they reached the street, the sun had dipped below the trees and dusk spread its filtered light over the town. Crickets and frogs hummed their night chorus, and cool calm settled in, a perfect night for romance.

Robert extended an arm. "Shall we?"

She should have felt a thrill, but his somewhat nasal tenor grated on her ears. Gabriel's warm baritone was much more pleasant. Robert reeked of perfumed hair treatment whereas Gabriel smelled of soap and fresh air. Gabriel was always proper and polite, whereas Robert...

Stop this. She wanted to marry Robert, not Gabriel.

"Penny for your thoughts," he said, patting her gloved hand.

"Nothing important." She smiled up at him. Up. Of course. Robert was taller than Gabriel, a decided virtue. "Were you born in New York?"

"Philadelphia."

She wrinkled her nose. "But I thought your family was from New York City."

"True, true, but technically speaking, I was born in Philadelphia. My mother was visiting family at the time."

"Ah."

After that, conversation lagged. Felicity couldn't figure out how to transition to her question, and Robert peered down every side street and alley. When he stopped to survey the lane beside the cinema, she had to ask what he was doing.

"Just getting the lay of the land." Again he patted her hand. "I'm sorry. I should have been paying more attention to you."

"That's quite all right." She smiled, but again conversation languished.

They ambled down Oak Street, together yet miles apart. Dusk quickly darkened into night, and the first stars appeared, bright pinpoints in the velvet sky.

"Lovely night, isn't it?" she mused.

He nodded. "I'll be able to get a good day's work in tomorrow if it doesn't rain."

Just like a man to think of work instead of romance. A rebuke rose to her lips, but criticism would not win his heart. She held her tongue as they approached Elm Street and the parsonage. The parsonage. She couldn't walk past Gabriel's house with Robert. She slowed her steps, and he stopped, dropping her hand to withdraw a cigarette case from his jacket pocket.

"Do you mind?"

Though she shook her head, she minded very much. The body was a temple that shouldn't be defiled by vices like drinking and smoking. If he truly cared for her, he'd see her displeasure and put it away.

He lit the cigarette.

She looked away to hide her disappointment. The rooftops faded in the waning light, and the church steeple was barely visible.

Do it now.

"I was wondering," she began as he blew out a cloud of smoke, "if you might help me with a project."

"What sort of project?" He peered into the gloom.

She shook off a chill. "I'm heading the committee to

replace a plate glass window in the church with stained glass, and it occurred to me that I should get your advice."

"I'm no artist."

"That's not what I meant. I have an engineering question." At least she thought it was an engineering question.

"Ask away."

She took a deep breath. "Do I need to worry about the size of the window?"

He flicked an ash to the ground. "Do you mean because of the added weight? Well, I'd need to see the structure. Stained glass is considerably heavier. It's thicker, you see, and then there's the lead. I'd need to take some measurements and run the calculations."

"You could come to worship this Sunday."

He ground out the butt with his heel, leaving the ugly remnants in the street. "That'll work."

Relief flooded through her. He was a Christian. "The service begins at ten o'clock."

"Ten o'clock." His gaze drifted back to her, and the tips of his mustache twitched in the faint light.

"Ten o'clock," she breathed.

Darkness improved his appearance. The years melted away, and the painfully bright clothing was muted. She could learn to love him in such light.

He held out his arm again. "Mind if we walk on the far side of Elm?"

That would take them past the parsonage and the park. She swallowed. Gabriel might be home. He might see her with Robert.

"I—I," she stammered, but she didn't have a good excuse. "All right."

"Wonderful." He led her across the street. "The park is so lovely."

The park? Her heart pounded a little harder. Lovers met in

the park. If he suggested the park, he must already love her. She glanced at the parsonage, which thankfully was dark. Gabriel must be out for the evening. Nothing could stop her plan.

She squeezed Robert's arm, and he inclined his head toward her.

"Ready?" he asked.

She smiled up at him. "There's a pavilion a little farther into the park." She could just make out its shape.

"Sounds perfect." He led her into the darkness.

The pudgy young deputy refused to budge from the chair behind his spotless desk. "I'm sorry, Reverend. Sheriff Ilsley isn't here." He took a form from a file. "You can make a report."

Gabriel was losing patience with the procedurally minded deputy. "Don't you understand? The crime is in progress now. If we wait until the sheriff returns, it'll be too late."

"Your name?" The deputy poised his pen over the form.

"Gabriel Meeks, but there's no time to waste. There are bootleggers bringing liquor into this town."

"What makes you think that?" the deputy said lazily. "Do you have evidence?"

Gabriel swallowed his exasperation. Precious minutes were ticking away. "Only what I heard. The sound of bottles being unloaded in the alley behind the drugstore."

The deputy looked disgusted. "Most drugs come in bottles. Maybe that's what you heard."

After five minutes of such nonsense, Gabriel realized he was getting nowhere. Either the deputy had no intention of getting up from his desk, or he was colluding with the bootleggers.

"Never mind. I'll speak with Sheriff Ilsley tomorrow."

The deputy looked up in surprise. "Then you don't want to file a report?"

"It can wait."

Gabriel let the door slam shut behind him but felt little satisfaction in the noise. Slinky got up and cocked his head expectantly. Sighing, Gabriel untied his rope leash and headed back to the parsonage.

What would convince the law to act? The sheriff might be more willing than his deputy, but then again he could be pressed from the same mold. To ensure action, Gabriel needed evidence. To get evidence, he needed to find the bootleggers' route into town. He had a good idea where that might be.

Gabriel cut through the parsonage backyard. He'd make his way to the river, then downriver to the fence at Coughlin's land. The man said out-of-town criminals broke it down. That's where the bootleggers were bringing in the whiskey. They took it downriver by boat and then supplied the back alley speakeasy, which locals called a blind pig, at night. If he was fast enough, he might catch them.

After closing the far gate, he and Slinky made their way through the woods. The dog happily tugged at the rope while Gabriel tried his best to hold him back. The moonless night made navigation hazardous, and more than once on his way to the river he stumbled over a root or rock.

This whole thing sickened him. Prohibition was supposed to put an end to the scourge of drink. Instead, it lived on under cover of darkness. He expected it in big cities, but not here. Why didn't God-fearing citizens rise against it? Why did they let it happen under their noses? Well, they wouldn't anymore, not after he unveiled the crime and its instigators.

He picked his way to the river path, Slinky pulling steadily on the rope. Thank goodness the mutt kept quiet. Barking might alert the rumrunners and send them scampering. On the other hand, a good bark or two could interrupt the operation and keep liquor out of the hands of people like Robert Blevins.

Gabriel recalled the smell of whiskey on the man's breath. His gut twisted at the thought of that pompous engineer holding Felicity close—maybe even kissing her.

He shook away the image. She deserved better. She deserved someone who would treat her with respect, someone who would honor her the way God intended a man to honor a woman.

Suddenly Slinky froze, bristling, and a low growl came from deep inside, just like it had at the alley. Gabriel halted, the hair on his arms and neck standing on end.

A light breeze rustled the leaves around him. The river chattered below, not twenty feet away. An owl hooted. And then, quieter than even those sounds, Gabriel heard the clink of glass or metal, the grunt of men and a murmur of low voices.

He'd caught them. It must be exactly like he thought. The liquor came down the river by boat, was unloaded on Coughlin's land and then shipped to the blind pig under cover of darkness.

He crawled forward to get a better view, taking care not to snap any twigs. The woods were even darker than the park, where light from town allowed a man to see the dim outlines of trees and the pavilion. Here, he saw nothing.

Realizing any further progress was bound to alert the bootleggers to his presence, he halted and tried to calm his hammering pulse. *Lord, help me expose the truth.*

He waited but saw and heard nothing for a long time. His eyes gradually began to pick out dim shapes, and his ears heard yet more rustling.

Then a man's voice said, "Last of 'em."

That came from the river, if he was any judge of direction.

A grunted reply told him two or more men were there. Then he heard steps coming toward him.

He backed up, and a twig snapped.

Slinky barked.

The voices stopped, and a gun cocked. Footsteps shuffled closer and then ran.

Slinky trembled at his feet, the low growl beginning again. Don't bark. Gabriel reached to stroke Slinky's head, but then he realized that was just the thing he needed to distract the bootleggers. He let go of Slinky's rope and prayed God would protect them both.

The dog ran upriver along the path, barking. Gabriel heard the men crash after him and followed. With any luck, Slinky would flush the bootleggers out into the open of the park or even to Main Street, where they could be stopped and held until their boat was found. The sheriff couldn't dismiss evidence like that. Gabriel would put a stop to this bootlegging business tonight.

He plunged through the woods, heedless of noise. They were getting close to the park. Soon he'd have his quarry. Then his foot hit something solid and he tripped, falling right into a patch of bushes.

Raspberry bushes.

Felicity grew more excited with every step. Soon Robert would kiss her. Soon he'd be hers.

The grass was soft underfoot, already damp with dew. He began to whistle last year's popular song, "I'll Say She Does."

The tune grated on her nerves. "Could you please stop?"

He halted, staring into the blackness of the park, as if he'd seen something.

"I meant the whistling."

"You don't care for whistling?"

She pressed her temple. "I'm getting a headache."

"No problem, chickadee." However, he started up again when they resumed walking.

It's all right, she told herself. She could correct that flaw later. Tonight she would secure his affection, and then soon afterward she would be Mrs. Robert Blevins of Newport with an engagement ring so large even Mother would gasp. She'd walk down the aisle of a large cathedral. Nothing in Pearlman would do. They'd wed in New York City. Her gown would be encrusted with pearls, the train a mile long. Every girl at Highbury and in Pearlman would weep with envy.

They reached the pavilion, and Robert stepped aside to let her ascend first. Heart pounding at what was to come, she climbed one then two then three steps. Then she heard voices and scampered back down. "Someone's already here."

Robert took her hand. "Then follow me." He pointed toward the inky black forest.

She ignored the quiet voice that told her not to go and followed. Robert would never hurt her.

"Let's walk by the river," she suggested.

"My thoughts exactly." This time he didn't whistle.

"Amazing how we think alike," she laughed, trying to settle her nerves.

"Indeed." But his words didn't calm her like Gabriel's did.

The moonless night had extinguished the warm light from people's windows. She couldn't even see where she was walking. She'd never find her way back to Elm Street. Each step twisted her stomach one turn tighter.

"Here we are." Robert guided her a few steps to the left, and she soon felt the gravel of the path underfoot.

A few more steps forward, and the black of the forest swallowed them.

He stopped. "Ah, my little chickadee." He lifted her hand to his lips and twirled her about so she came to rest in his arms. "You are a lady after my heart." His rough finger scratched along her jaw, not at all the pleasurable sensation she'd experienced with Gabriel.

This was wrong. Panic struggled to surface, but she reasoned that Robert wouldn't dare hurt her. She was a Kensington. He worked for Daddy. She was just being foolish.

"You're so tense," he murmured, far too close to her ear.

His heat overwhelmed her, like standing alongside a blazing fire, but she fought the urge to break away. "We can't be long. Daddy's waiting for me." It wouldn't hurt to reinforce that point.

"Forget your father." He tipped her chin up. "Tonight there's only us."

"Yes, us." She tried to ignore the growing knot in her stomach. They shouldn't be alone together. They shouldn't be in the park alone, and they absolutely shouldn't be there in the dark.

He bent close. He was going to kiss her.

"I didn't know how we'd ever get together," she blurted.

"Lovers always find opportunity." His voice had gotten husky and syrupy at the same time, and his lips brushed her ear.

"Lovers?" she gasped. "Is that what we are?" Her heart was battering its way through her rib cage.

"Hush, my little chickadee."

He pinned her so close that his waistcoat buttons bit into her abdomen. His breath reeked of ashes. His mustache scratched her face. Every instinct told her to flee.

"Felicity." His voice seduced. "How beautiful you are." He cupped the back of her head and drew her face toward his.

She felt a tremor, small at first but escalating rapidly as he bent toward her. Was this love, this terrible nerve-racking fear? Before she could say a word, he pressed his lips to hers. The scratch of his mustache was quickly replaced by the tawdry taste of tobacco.

She shoved at his chest. "L-let go."

"What's wrong, darling?" He relaxed slightly but didn't let her go. "We've just begun."

No, no, no. Every part of her revolted. "I—I can't breathe."

"That's normal." He crushed his lips to hers again.

Panic welled. This was wrong, and she no longer cared if she ruined everything. She couldn't talk with his lips smothering hers. She was too weak to break free. She was too far from help. No one knew she was here. No one would hear her scream. Dear God, what had she done?

"Felicity," he murmured, breaking the kiss.

A cry burbled in her throat but refused to come out. What if he took advantage of her? What if he…?

No. She opened her mouth, but nothing came out.

He kissed her neck. She twisted aside. His lips followed, so she dug her fingernails into his fleshy wrist.

"Hey." He jerked away, shaking his hand. "What was that for?"

She staggered backward, free at last, but where could she go? Blackness surrounded her in every direction. She'd get lost and maybe twist an ankle, but that was better than another minute in Robert's clutches. She stumbled to her right and quickly got entangled in the brush.

Woof. At that moment, a dog leaped onto her.

"Help, stop," she cried, even though it would bring Robert.

Rather than back off, the animal ran around her barking. Though she couldn't see more than a shape in the darkness, she recognized that bark. Slinky. She grabbed his rope collar and hugged him close. She didn't care why or how he'd gotten here, only that he had.

Seconds later, the glow of a lantern bounced through the trees. Gabriel. It had to be. He'd come for her.

The light swept the woods, revealing everything. Robert stood not five feet from her, smirking. She looked a sight.

"It's not what you think," she cried.

"Then what is it?" The lantern lowered to reveal the holder's face.

She gasped, "Daddy."

Chapter Seven

"Young lady, you have some mighty big explaining to do."

Felicity searched for words to answer her father. How much had he seen? The kiss? The way Robert held her? Thank heavens it was dark. Her father couldn't have seen everything, but clearly he'd seen enough.

His spectacles reflected the lantern light. "I'm waiting."

"I—I," she stammered, mind blank.

She looked to Robert for help, but he avoided her gaze. Shouldn't he stand up for her? A real gentleman would explain everything. A lover would take the blame. Robert stood silent.

"Felicity." A disheveled Gabriel burst into the clearing. "Thank goodness you caught up to Slinky."

Daddy's brow furrowed as he glanced from Gabriel to Felicity and back again. "Are you saying you two were together?"

Felicity held her breath. What would Gabriel say? A minister couldn't lie, nor could he respect her if she lied for him.

His gaze met hers, and she knew he would do it. She couldn't let him.

"I was walking home." That much *was* true. She scratched Slinky's neck, praying Daddy didn't ask more questions.

Robert finally found his voice. "Everyone's safe now. Guess it's time to head back." He made a show of checking his pocket watch in the lantern light.

Robert's nonchalance left Felicity speechless. How could he stand before Daddy pretending nothing had happened?

"Indeed it is," Daddy growled, holding out his hand to her. "Come along, Felicity."

She stared, dumbfounded. Daddy had found her alone in the dark with Robert, yet he didn't ask one single question of the man.

Gabriel stepped into the light. "I assure you, sir, that I have only the deepest respect for Felicity and would never harm her reputation." He glared at Robert.

Gabriel knew what had happened. He knew she'd stumbled badly. Yet he spoke up for her when Robert stood silent. She blinked back tears. No one had ever done that for her before.

"Of course, you wouldn't." Daddy clapped Gabriel on the back. "You're a man of God. All I ask is that you let me know the next time you want to walk with my daughter."

Gabriel fidgeted, eyes downcast. "Yes, sir."

How that must have cost him. Felicity wished she could tell him how much his sacrifice meant to her, but that would expose the truth.

He lifted his eyes, and she could see the hope flickering inside. "I'll walk you home."

Daddy cut that idea short. "There's been quite enough walking around in the dark for one night. I will escort my daughter home, Pastor. Good night, Mr. Blevins."

Both men nodded their understanding and then went their separate ways, leaving her alone with Daddy. With the lantern to guide them, he led her through the park. She waited for the lecture, but he said nothing until they passed the pavilion.

"Be certain what you want, little one." The words dripped with disappointment, and her heart lurched. How could she have been so foolish?

"I'm sorry, Daddy."

He patted her hand, but it didn't make her feel any better. At the end of day two, her plan lay in ruins.

Two days and much soul-searching later, Felicity stood on the parsonage's front porch with a package wrapped in brown paper. The wide-brimmed hat hid her swollen eyes but did nothing to bolster her courage.

She lifted a fisted hand to knock, then let it drop for the twentieth time. A hasty glance backward showed she was still alone, but someone she knew could go down Elm Street at any moment. If she was going to do this, she had to do it now.

She rapped on the oak door. The hard wood stung the knuckles. She pressed an ear close, listening for movement inside but heard nothing. He probably wasn't home. She should leave.

Then she heard a bark.

"Hush," said Gabriel.

Oh dear, he was there. She dipped the brim of her hat to hide her eyes. What should she say?

The door opened.

"Good morn..." The rest of his greeting evaporated, and her heart sank.

He hated her.

She sneaked a peek. He looked the same as always, with that intoxicating smell of fresh-pressed cotton, his sleeves rolled up. She couldn't read his expression. He neither looked pleased nor frowned.

She offered a hesitant smile. "You're here."

"I am." He cleared the roughness from his throat.

She stared at her feet. How could she look at him when he knew what had happened? The embarrassment was killing her, but she had to make amends. She needed to thank him for stepping forward on her behalf.

She thrust out the package. "For you."

He didn't budge. "I can't accept a gift."

She dropped her hands, deflated. How could she persuade him? "Ministers accept gifts of thanksgiving all the time." She held it out again.

Again he shook his head. "It's not necessary."

Tears of frustration threatened. "I know it's not necessary. It's a gift."

"Felicity," he sighed, "you must see that accepting a gift from an unmarried woman in my congregation would not be proper."

She averted her gaze at the gaffe. Still, if she couldn't make amends, he would never speak to her again, at least not as a friend. "It's a thank-you. That's all."

"Then I accept your thanks as more than adequate. A gift is not needed."

How could she get him to accept the gift, her unspoken apology? Slinky nuzzled against her leg, begging to be petted. That was it.

She held out the gift again. "It's not for you. It's for Slinky."

"For Slinky?" His eyebrows rose.

"I thought perhaps you'd like a proper collar and leash— that is, that Slinky would like them. H-he saved me, in a manner of speaking."

Still, he didn't take the package.

"Please?" she pleaded. "He is my responsibility. You said so yourself. It's the least I can do."

At last Gabriel took the package. "I guess it's all right if it's for Slinky." The paper crackled under his fingertips.

"Go ahead. Open it. I had Mr. Jones at the harness shop make it."

Gabriel tugged open the string and unfolded the paper to reveal the beautifully crafted leather collar and leash, embossed SLINKY in block letters.

His lips slowly curved upward. "I guess I can't change his name now."

She laughed, though it came out bubbly and half-teary. "I'm sorry. I forgot you wanted to change his name. I'll have Mr. Jones make a new one."

"No, no, this is perfect." He turned it over in his hands, but he was no longer looking at the collar. "You're so thoughtful." His gaze softened.

She sucked in her breath, startled by the depth of feeling. That crazy hot and cold tingling started again, and she reached for the porch rail to steady herself. She had to leave—now—before she lost all control.

"That's all I wanted," she said, edging down the steps. "I should be going."

"But don't you want to see the collar on Slinky?"

"No, no." She couldn't stay another moment. What had she been thinking? Gabriel Meeks was her minister. He'd witnessed her disaster in the park. Deep down, he must condemn her. Oh why had she thought a gift would right things between them? She should never have come.

"I—I'm sorry." She backed down the last step. "I have to go."

She flew down the walkway and almost crashed into Mrs. Grattan, who gave her a stern look. Felicity murmured an apology without breaking stride. She had to get away. She had to get home.

For the first time that she could recall, Felicity anticipated Sunday worship with a flutter of nerves. It would be Gabriel's first sermon. She prayed it would soar, that he'd stand proudly before the congregation, inspiring them with profound stories and fiery rhetoric like the popular evangelist Billy Sunday. Even though she couldn't contemplate falling in love with him, she could cheer his success.

While Mother politicked for her stained glass window, Felicity settled into the family pew and waited for the service to begin. Before long, she heard whispers behind her that could only belong to Sally Neidecker, Eloise Grattan and Anna Simmons.

"Did you hear the news?" Sally whispered none too quietly. "It's all over town."

Felicity stared ahead, back straight. That night in the park had been bad enough, but Sally Neidecker crowing over it was intolerable. Still, *a lady always maintains her composure*. Felicity would show them she possessed poise under duress.

"What news?" asked Eloise.

As if she didn't know.

"I don't think we should talk in church," Anna said, and the conversation ceased.

Dear gawky Anna, forever trying to be one of the popular girls but never succeeding. Perhaps Felicity had misjudged her.

The quiet lasted less than a minute.

"It *will* be interesting to see them together," Sally giggled. "I can't wait."

Felicity felt the old heat rush to her cheeks. How she wanted to slap that Sally Neidecker.

"Me, too," gushed Eloise. "I wonder what he'll look like in robes."

Robes? Robert didn't wear robes. Her eyes widened. They were talking about Gabriel. But then with whom did they want to see him? Was he courting someone? Is that why he'd been so cold to her?

"Please, be quiet," Anna whispered.

Eloise prattled on unhindered. "I hope you-know-who will pick my basket at the picnic next Saturday. I'm putting a blue ribbon on the handle. I practically told him which one would be mine and that I'm making my strawberry pie. Everyone knows I make the best strawberry pie."

A week ago Felicity would have fretted about Eloise pursuing Robert, but what if her real quarry was Gabriel? He was the better catch.

Her heart caught as she realized what she'd just thought. Gabriel was the better catch. Mother would die if she knew Felicity was even thinking such a thing. Of course it was impossible, but Gabriel marry Eloise? That was worse yet.

"Who do you hope picks your basket?" Eloise asked.

After a brief pause, Anna said quietly, "I don't care."

"Yes, you do. You're in love with someone," Sally pestered. "Tell me. I promise not to tell a soul." Her voice lowered, purring confidence, but Anna Simmons refused to divulge a thing.

Thankfully Mother and Daddy arrived to put an end to the chatter. The congregation hushed as Gabriel entered and the opening hymn began. Felicity followed along, singing the words by rote. She couldn't take her eyes off Gabriel and how distinguished he looked in the black robes. He'd combed his hair and looked quite solemn and proper—very much the minister.

He handled the service beautifully, speaking clearly and with authority. The congregation listened, if not with enthusiasm then at least with respect. They liked him. They accepted him. She didn't know why she should care so much, but she hung on his every word and movement, smiling encouragement.

Strangely, he chose temperance as his sermon topic. Considering Prohibition was in force across the nation and had been the law in Michigan since 1917, it didn't carry the force another sermon might have. Mother stifled a yawn behind her gloved hand, and Daddy's head bobbed more than once. Felicity shot a quick look at the congregation. He had lost them.

"And most of all," he finished, looking directly at her. "Love each other."

Felicity sat stunned. Love. He'd spoken the word while looking at her. Was it possible that Gabriel meant her? Was the way she felt around him love?

Everyone stood for the closing hymn. Though Felicity sang, the words of the hymn didn't register. She could only think about what had just happened. Gabriel had declared love before the congregation. She hazarded a glance at Mother, who mouthed the words to the hymn. She hadn't noticed. Maybe no one else had either. That statement had been for her alone. Her spirits soared with the last stanzas of the hymn.

Then she heard the whispers.

"Did you see him look at me?" Eloise crowed. "He was talking about love and looked right at me."

No, he wasn't.

Felicity turned to refute Eloise and discovered the girl was indeed seated behind her. From the pulpit, they sat directly in line. What if Gabriel was looking at Eloise, not Felicity? Embarrassed, she turned back around.

The words of the benediction floated past unheard. Gabriel couldn't love Eloise—impossible. No, that look had been for her, Felicity Kensington. But he didn't glance her way again, not even when exiting down the center aisle.

The congregation filed out, and Felicity followed mindlessly. Progress proved slow since everyone was greeting

Gabriel. Felicity watched him—how perfectly at ease he was, welcoming every member of the church as if they were part of his family.

As Mrs. Grattan stepped forward to greet him, Felicity gasped. There, leaning against the wall, stood Robert Blevins. She'd forgotten she asked him to come to church this Sunday.

He nodded at her, the tips of his mustache bobbing.

She looked away. Clearly he expected her to join him, but if she did, any and all rumors would be confirmed. She balled her fists, praying Mother wouldn't spot him.

Mrs. Grattan finished greeting Gabriel, and Felicity stepped forward.

"Good morning, Pastor." The title sounded strange. "Very nice sermon." For some reason, she couldn't think of anything intelligent to say.

"Thank you. I was nervous."

"I wouldn't have known. You looked so secure."

He smiled politely. "I wasn't."

Their exchange dwindled. The most important things couldn't be said in front of her parents or anyone else. What's more, Robert was walking toward them. Mother nudged her with an elbow. Felicity fixed her attention on Gabriel.

"I particularly liked the part about loving each other." Just mentioning the word *love* made her cheeks burn.

"Thank you," Gabriel said softly. "And thank you for the collar. It fits perfectly."

"What collar?" Mother demanded, simultaneously pinching Felicity's arm to warn that she was not to proceed further.

"Reverend." Robert pushed past Felicity. "Good to see you again. Interesting sermon, but a bit too political for my taste."

Gabriel dutifully shook Robert's hand. "I think that's a compliment."

"Mr. Blevins is quite right," said Mother, nose in the air. "Politics and religion don't mix. You'd do well to remember that, Reverend."

Felicity blushed and silently apologized.

"Dear Ms. Kensington." Robert took her hand and placed it on his arm. "Before we address business, I understand the Founder's Day celebration includes a dance."

Felicity recoiled, taking back her hand. Robert was headed in a direction she did not want to go. That night in the park had shown her where her heart lay, and it was not with Robert Blevins.

"I don't recall," she said vaguely.

"Yes, it does," Daddy said, wrecking any chance she had of sliding out of this. "The Founder's Day dance."

"Then I'd like to ask your daughter to join me at those festivities." Robert glanced at Gabriel. "If someone hasn't asked already."

Felicity prayed Gabriel would save her again.

Instead, he dashed her hopes. "My sister, Mariah, is coming to visit. I'll be busy."

Felicity could barely hide her disappointment.

"Excellent," Robert said, "then Ms. Kensington can join me."

No. That's what she wanted to say, but for some reason she couldn't get the word out. All she could remember was the rough kiss. Every fiber of her body said to refuse, so why couldn't she say it? She opened her mouth.

"Of course, she will," Mother gushed. "She'd be delighted."

Robert grinned broadly. "Now then, Ms. Felicity, let's talk about that stained glass window."

He led her toward the window, but she couldn't keep her

mind on trivial business. She was committed to attend the dance with Robert, but she so wanted to be there with Gabriel. He must sense how she felt. Why hadn't he seized the chance to escort her to the dance? Instead he'd offered the flimsy excuse of a sister. No sister could stand in the way of a romance, unless...

She caught her breath.

Unless he loved someone else.

Chapter Eight

The window project forced Felicity to spend far too many hours in Robert's company over the following days. He assessed the structural support. He measured and calculated and measured again, and through it all, he expected her to fetch and carry. She wished she'd never asked for his help.

Each day she looked for Gabriel. Surely he would come to the church, but each day she was disappointed.

"He's making home visits," Florabelle Williams sniffed while typing at breakneck speed, "and they're not even sick." Florabelle had been the church secretary—and Mother's intimate insider—for as long as Felicity could remember.

Felicity's stomach knotted as she searched for an explanation that didn't involve a budding romance. "Perhaps he's getting to know members of the congregation."

Florabelle tossed her graying head. "He hasn't come to *my* house yet."

Wise man. Florabelle and her daughter Cora, the postmistress and telephone operator, spread most of the gossip in Pearlman. Felicity would have saved that visit for last, too.

"Who is he visiting today?"

Ding. Without breaking rhythm, Florabelle whipped the

typewriter carriage back. "How should I know? Now if you don't mind, I have work to do."

Her tone intimated Felicity did not have work, and considering most of her time was spent retrieving Robert's instruments, Felicity had to agree. She returned to the window no wiser.

"Where's that eighteen-inch ruler?" Robert asked.

For an engineer, he was remarkably disorganized. Each day he'd bring some of his measuring tapes and tools but forget others.

"Why don't you keep everything in a case?" she snapped as she handed him the ruler.

Instead of taking it, he whistled. "That's it."

"That's what?"

"The new window must weigh less than three hundred eighteen pounds."

"And what size would that be?"

He looked at her as if she'd asked the stupidest question on earth. "That depends on the thickness of the glass and the quantity of leading, of course."

She hadn't thought of that. "Well, about how big would it be with average thickness?"

He snapped his notepad shut and patted her hand, a condescending gesture he used far too often. "Just specify the maximum weight when you place the order."

She bristled. "It's not an order. It's a commission."

She might as well have spoken to a brick. No matter how many times she corrected Robert, he never remembered. It was amazing that a Newport man would have no sense of the arts.

She mentioned that to her mother when she relayed Robert's conclusion.

"Well, of course he doesn't," Mother said, pushing aside the slip of paper with the window specifications. It fluttered off the hall table, and Felicity snatched it midair. "A man's head is filled with numbers and business, as it should be. It's the wife's role to bring art and culture into the home. And so you shall with your academy education."

Felicity didn't know why Mother continued to insist on art school when her idea of the perfect suitor was at hand. "Suppose I receive a proposal this summer?"

"Robert proposed?" Eugenia Kensington stopped fussing in the mirror.

The idea nauseated Felicity, yet she had little choice. No other suitable man could be found. Gabriel didn't have enough wealth and social standing to pass muster with her parents, and considering the way he was avoiding her, he didn't even like her.

"Well?" Mother glared at her. "Did Mr. Blevins propose or not?"

Felicity jerked out of her wishful thinking. "Not yet, but it might happen."

Mother returned to her primping. "Goodness, child, you nearly stopped my heart. Now listen, if such a proposal should come, you must simply tell him to wait until you finish school. A man of quality will understand." She blotted her lip color. "Oh, and this came for you while you were gone." Mother pointed to a small envelope before donning her hat and gloves. "It's from the minister."

"Gabri—uh, Reverend Meeks?" A jolt of pleasure shot through Felicity. "What would he want?"

"He's having some sort of dinner for his sister tonight and asked you and Blake and Beatrice to attend."

"Oh right, his sister." Felicity had not forgotten that was why he couldn't escort her to the Founder's Day dance. "Her name is Mariah, right?"

Mother shrugged. "Whatever it is, she's come to visit. Mrs. Evans tells me she's very mannish and without the slightest social grace. A spinster. Why she's nearly thirty and without a prospect in sight."

Apparently thirty defined spinsterhood, a fate that held increasing appeal of late. Felicity lifted the envelope and noticed the seal was broken. "You read my invitation?"

"I needed to send your regrets."

"My regrets? But suppose I want to attend?"

Mother opened the door. "Don't be silly. Why would you attend the pastor's dinner when Robert isn't invited? Tell the cook I'll be back at six and expect dinner promptly at seven. Oh, and get a bouquet of flowers for the table. The current ones are getting rather sad." Without so much as a goodbye, she whisked out the door to the motorcar, where Smithson waited.

Felicity seethed. Mother had no right to interfere. The sooner she could get away from here, the better. Alas, that meant marrying Robert and all his faults, but she didn't have to submit to her ultimate fate this instant. Tonight she could enjoy Gabriel's friendship. Blake and Beatrice would be there and so would his sister. That was reason enough to attend.

She checked the invitation. The dinner began at six o'clock. If she hurried, she could retract her mother's refusal.

After changing into a cool, yet conservative ivory linen suit, she walked down the hill. The parsonage looked quiet. Slinky wasn't in the backyard, and the front porch, easily the coolest place on a hot day, sat vacant. They were either indoors or gone.

As she approached the porch, she caught a glimpse of a motorcar on the far side of the house and altered her path to get a closer look.

Yes, it was a dusty touring sedan with a canvas roof and rather large tires caked in mud. Perhaps everyone was wrong, and Mariah did have a husband, or a brother drove her here.

"Do you like it?"

Felicity started.

A plain, simply dressed woman with a strong resemblance to Gabriel approached from the backyard. "I'm sorry. I didn't mean to frighten you. I'm Mariah Meeks, Gabriel's sister."

Felicity saw the family resemblance. Mariah had the same square shoulders and curling dark hair, bobbed in the latest fashion. She carried herself with the same confidence. Felicity immediately liked her.

"Felicity Kensington. I'm a friend of your brother's." That awkward blush flashed over her cheeks. "Is this your car?"

"She's an Overland Model 90, self-starting." Mariah opened the hood. "Four cylinders, very reliable, which is a good thing on a long trip."

"You drive?"

"Of course." She closed the hood. "How else would I get here?"

Felicity stared first at the motorcar and then at Mariah. "You drove all the way here by yourself?"

"Absolutely. The machine ran beautifully, and I only had to change two tires."

"You changed a tire?" Felicity could hardly believe a woman would do such a thing. Well, maybe Darcy Hunter. She was forever fussing over engines but not a minister's sister.

"Someone had to." Mariah laughed. "Seeing as I was the only one around, it fell to me."

Felicity marveled at her frank manner. "But wasn't it difficult? And dirty?"

"It's not my favorite thing to do, and yes, it's dirty, but a little soap and water takes care of that." She ran a loving hand down the front fender. "Gabriel had a fit when I drove up. He went on and on about how dangerous it was and how I could have been hurt and every other foolish excuse a brother can throw at you. I don't suppose you have brothers."

"I'm afraid I do. One."

Mariah laughed. "Then you understand how overprotective they can be. Even though Gabriel is four years younger, he thinks it's his responsibility to look after me. I expect it from my four older brothers, but not from him."

"Four?" The moment Felicity said it, she recalled Gabriel's assertion he had five siblings. "I can't imagine having that many brothers."

"Mom had her hands full." Mariah threaded her arm around Felicity's. "Would you care for a glass of iced tea? I discovered the icehouse still has a good supply of ice despite the heat." Within moments, Mariah drew Felicity into the kitchen, where they were greeted by Slinky, sporting his new collar.

The dog barked eagerly, and Felicity had to stoop for kisses.

Mariah wiped her hands and poured two cups of tea from the pitcher on the table. "He really likes you. What a name, though. I can't believe Gabe would call him that."

"Oh, Slinky was already his name. He's the town stray, and everyone calls him Slinky because, well, because he tends to get into places he shouldn't."

Mariah's laughter warmed Felicity. So this is what it was like to have a sister.

"Perfect for Gabe. He was always getting into places he shouldn't."

"Really?" Felicity sipped her cool tea. "He seems so formal and, well, righteous."

"Righteous?" Mariah's laughter pealed through the house, making Slinky bark.

Felicity looked around in alarm. "Shh, he'll hear you."

"Don't worry. Gabe's not here. Not that his presence would stop me. He gets too serious sometimes and needs a little boot in the behind to remind him he wasn't always so perfect. Let me give you an example. When he was little, he took Mom's favorite dress and cut it to pieces to make bandages for our dogs and cats. He told Mom he was curing their injuries."

Felicity had difficulty imagining this side of Gabriel. "What did your mother do?" Her mother would have had her sent to her room without supper.

"Oh, she was angry at first, but when she saw the dogs and cats running around with their colorful little bandages, she just couldn't yell at Gabe." She paused, growing serious. "The day before, he'd seen a neighbor's dog get hit by a motor truck."

A pang of sympathy tore through Felicity's heart—the poor dog, poor little Gabriel. A flash of memory brought sudden tears. Years ago, she'd stumbled upon a possum, shot for sport. It struggled for life, its legs pawing at the air for long, horrible minutes. She'd prayed for God to take away the creature's pain. She'd wept over its still body. And she hoped God made a place in heaven for the innocent whose lives had been stolen away too soon.

"It's all right." Mariah wrapped an arm around Felicity's shoulder and handed her a handkerchief. "Making bandages was Gabe's way of coping. He takes things too much to heart sometimes. That's why Mom and Dad worry about him choosing the ministry. There's so much heartache a pastor must bear, and they don't know if he'll be able to hold up." She gave Felicity a final squeeze. "Forgive me. I'm babbling on and on about my family without giving you a chance to tell me about yours."

"Mine?" Felicity searched for what to say as she folded

and refolded Mariah's handkerchief. Everyone in Pearlman knew the Kensingtons. The girls at Highbury cared only that her family came from the country. They didn't want to hear about her lavish home and expensive gowns. She was not sophisticated enough to be one of them. But all of that seemed foolish next to Mariah's honest and caring family.

She handed the handkerchief back to Mariah. "There's nothing much to say."

"You mentioned a brother," Mariah urged. "Older or younger?"

"Older. Blake manages the mercantile and helps with a couple other family businesses. Oh, and he's involved in the new airfield project. We funded Jack Hunter's transatlantic flight attempt last year." At last she found something worth mentioning.

"Hunter? I don't recall reading his name in the newspapers."

"They crashed."

Mariah gasped. "Did they…?"

"Everyone was all right," Felicity said, "but it was a big event around here."

"I imagine so. I'm glad to hear your brother wasn't injured."

"Oh, he doesn't fly. He's just interested in aviation. You'll meet Blake and his wife tonight at dinner. In fact, that's why I'm here. Contrary to what my mother told you, I would like to attend."

"We'd be glad to have you." Mariah didn't miss a beat in the conversation. "Is Blake your only sibling?"

"Yes." Once again, she felt deficient. Mariah had so many brothers, a house filled with laughter and activity, not the cold mansion Felicity had grown up in. "I always wondered what it would be like to have a sister."

Mariah squeezed her hand. "Me, too."

Time flew past as Felicity and Mariah shared stories about their families. Felicity sucked in every tale about Gabriel and reluctantly shared her own unexciting childhood. With Mariah, Felicity didn't need to worry about making a good impression or upholding the family name. Felicity wished they could talk forever, but at last Mariah noted the time.

"Goodness, it's nearly four-thirty. I need to start cooking."

Felicity blinked in surprise. "You're cooking?" For the first time in her life, she felt ashamed to have a cook and servants to wait on her. How much happier Mariah seemed than anyone in her family—how much more content and able to cope with life's troubles.

"It won't be fancy, but it'll taste good. Would you like to help?"

Felicity had never so much as lifted a spoon, but she wasn't about to admit her ignorance. "I'm sorry. I need to go to the florist. Mother will be furious if I don't have a fresh bouquet sent."

"Go." Mariah waved her away. "I'm sorry I kept you."

"Don't be." Felicity smiled at her new friend. "I enjoyed talking."

If only she and Gabriel could converse with the same ease.

Try as he might, Gabriel couldn't take his eyes off Felicity during dinner. He cooed over Beatrice's baby before she fell asleep and tried to concentrate on what Blake had to say, but a mere turning of Felicity's head sent his thoughts spinning. In addition to beauty and grace, Gabriel saw much more of her true nature. She and Mariah chattered away like old friends, and Gabriel soaked in her unguarded enthusiasm. Beatrice had been right to suggest the dinner at the parsonage.

"Weren't you afraid?" Felicity asked when Mariah related her driving adventures.

Mariah gave one of her low, throaty laughs. "Only that I'd run out of fuel."

"Did you?" Felicity set down her fork, attention riveted on his sister.

"Only once, and then a very nice gentleman gave me a ride to the nearest filling station."

"Aha," said Beatrice. "A very nice and handsome gentleman?"

His sister knew a matchmaker when she saw one. "I didn't notice. I was too busy correcting his poor driving."

Gabriel stifled a snicker. Mariah had probably tormented the poor man by criticizing his every move.

"But…" Felicity said, "weren't you concerned that he might take advantage?"

Mariah shrugged. "The Lord is always with me. What have I to fear?"

Felicity stared, as if that concept was as useless as Confederate money. Gabriel had sensed Felicity's faith wasn't as solid as it could be. Maybe under Mariah's tutelage it would grow.

After the guests left, he and Mariah cleaned up. She washed the dishes while he dried and put them in the cupboards.

"She's a lovely woman, Gabe," Mariah said, breaking their silent work.

"I understand Beatrice Kensington is considered the prettiest girl in Pearlman."

Mariah clucked her tongue. "I'm not talking about Beatrice, and you know it."

Gabriel ducked into a cupboard, pretending to straighten

the plates. "It sure does get hot in this room. I wonder why they didn't build a summer kitchen."

"You can't avoid the subject, Gabriel John, and I can't see why you'd want to. Felicity Kensington has a natural grace and compassion that makes her quite likable."

"Compassion?" Gabriel would never apply that word to Felicity. "I've found her a bit proud."

Mariah set a soapy kettle on the soaked towel. "Pride is just a defense."

"Against what?" Gabriel dunked the kettle in rinse water.

"Fear, I guess. Fear of being hurt." Mariah looked off into the black night, hands finally still. "Sometimes a person just feels too much."

"What do you mean?"

"Some rare people are born that way, with exceptionally tender souls. Every little hurt becomes magnified a hundredfold. The pain is so intense that they can't bear it. To preserve themselves, they hide behind something else, like pride."

"And you think Felicity is prideful because she has a tender soul?" Gabriel snorted. "Well, you're wrong. She's been pampered and coddled and lets everyone know it. She went to Highbury School for Girls and has been accepted into the National Academy of Design. I don't see a tender soul there."

Mariah's lips curved into a slight, private smile. "Diamonds are formed from coal."

"What are you talking about?"

Rather than answer, she began humming "Nearer My God to Thee." Sometimes his sister could be exasperating, but he loved her dearly, and soon he joined her in the hymn, singing out the verses, off-key but from the heart.

"All done," she said as she lifted the last of the dishes

onto the towel. "Whew, that's a lot. I don't know how Mom managed six children."

"We helped," Gabriel pointed out. "Remember the rotation? Each day we either set the table, cleared the table, washed the dishes, dried the dishes, took out the garbage, swept the floors or scrubbed the sink and stove."

"Ah, yes," she laughed. "I remember that well. Thankfully with just me at home, there's a lot less to do, or I'd be up all night."

"Speaking of still being at home, have you met anyone special?" Gabriel loved provoking his sister.

As usual, she didn't bite. "If you mean men, no, I haven't met the right one yet, but I know that if God has someone in mind for me, He will bring him around at the right time. Just like He'll bring the right woman for you."

Gabriel wasn't so sure. He was attracted to someone, but she wasn't the right woman for a minister. Besides, she liked the pompous Robert Blevins.

"I do have something important to discuss with you," Mariah said. "Shall we take our tea to the parlor?"

After they were settled in the comfortable wingback chairs, Mariah ran a fingertip around the rim of her teacup. "Your friend Mr. Isaacs stopped by the house before I left."

"Why would he do that when he knew I was here?"

She set her teacup on the cherry end table. "He had a proposal and wanted me to bring it to you. It's important work, Gabriel, a mission dear to your heart."

Gabriel felt his throat squeeze shut. Isaacs wanted him to work at the orphanage. "I've just begun here."

Mariah studied him. "Even so, you've gained enough contacts to form an appropriate board. Why, just your guests tonight would make a fine selection committee."

"Board? Committee? What are you talking about?"

"I'm talking about orphans, Gabriel. Mr. Isaacs said they

need to place five children in foster homes. They're older and
difficult to place. Everyone wants toddlers now. He asked me
to look over Pearlman to see if it would be an appropriate,
God-fearing community. If it was, then I was to ask you to
assemble a committee of three or four and contact him for
guidance. They'd send an advance agent and arrange everything. You know the procedure."

He did, but Pearlman? Illegal liquor flowed into its homes
and businesses.

"I'm not sure it's the best place. Isn't there any town closer
to New York City?"

"Actually, the orphans are at the Detroit mission. That's
why he's looking for a Michigan community. Pearlman
would be perfect. The people are good and caring. The town
blossoms with generosity. Tell me about the congregation,
Gabe. Do they love the Lord?"

He wasn't sure. Some surely did, but others? Eugenia
Kensington promoted her ill-conceived idea to use Ladies'
Aid Society funds for self-aggrandizement. On the other
hand, Mrs. Shea and Mrs. Grattan staunchly fought with
him to abandon the window project in favor of giving to the
poor. Perhaps if they brought in the orphans, he could convince the Ladies' Aid Society to divert the funds to the children's care. Just seeing the orphans usually struck a chord
deep in people's hearts. Yes, this might be just the thing to
turn Pearlman around.

"Let's do it."

Mariah smiled softly. "I suggest you put Felicity Kensington on the selection committee. You can ask her at Saturday's picnic."

His momentary certainty crumbled. He couldn't work side
by side with Felicity. "I'm not sure she's the best choice."

"Of course, she is." Mariah exuded confidence. "She's
precisely the person who needs to be on that committee.

God has brought this opportunity to Pearlman for a reason, and Felicity could very well be that reason."

Gabriel rubbed his head, which was beginning to ache. "The committee is supposed to be composed of town leaders and people with experience, not young women without children."

Mariah leveled her calm gaze at him. "Mr. Isaacs will respect your selections. Make one of them Felicity."

He shook his head. "I can't." On this point, he would stand firm. No matter what his sister thought, Felicity Kensington lacked the compassion for the selection committee. He rose to go to bed. "And that's my final decision."

Chapter Nine

Founder's Day dawned a bit crisp for late June but with no sign of rain. Felicity stood alone at the kitchen worktable putting the finishing touches on her picnic basket.

The cook had prepared the food yesterday. Felicity added the creative accents. The table overflowed with ribbons and paper and flowers fresh from the garden. She rolled the silverware in white linen napkins and tied them with green ribbon. A sprig of fresh-cut pinks completed each set. She wrapped the cold fried chicken in butcher paper and then prettied it with green checked gingham. Ribbons encircled the jars of pickled asparagus and lemonade. Crystal, linen and silver were included as well—nothing but the best. Strawberry tarts, still in their tins, crowned the feast.

Any man would enjoy such a lunch. She hoped that man would be Gabriel. If Mariah kept her end of the bargain, it would. Felicity couldn't bear an entire day with Robert, and he'd already claimed supper and the dance. The afternoon had to belong to Gabriel.

She tucked the red satchel from the mercantile between the jars. It would be perfect for Gabriel's books. He could take them to the river, and she would join him there, whiling away lazy summer days. They'd talk and share a jar of lemonade. Perhaps their fingertips would brush.

Just thinking of it made her skin tingle. His kiss wouldn't be rough like Robert's. He would never take what she hadn't offered to give.

"Are you ready yet?" Mother's question yanked her from the dream. "Stop fussing over that silly basket. I don't know why you bother with the auction. Considering how much your father contributes to the event, there's no reason for you to raise money. After all, Mr. Blevins is the only respectable bidder." She repositioned the bow on the basket handle.

Felicity lifted her basket off the table before Mother ruined it. "Someone else might outbid him."

"Who? Your father has been given strict instructions not to bid."

Felicity walked to the hall with Mother on her heels. "I didn't mean Daddy."

"Another man? Don't worry, dearest, I've ensured Robert will make the highest bid."

"You have? How?"

"Don't fret. It'll ruin your complexion. Just be thankful that someone is looking out for your best interests." Mother snared her gloves from the hall table and thrust the front door open. "Hurry now. Your father is waiting."

Felicity clutched the basket handle tightly. Mother had struck again.

She could not escape this town fast enough.

"Are you going to bid on Felicity's basket?" Mariah stretched out on the heavy wool blanket as the flies danced and buzzed in the warming noon air.

"No." Though the little park bustled with joyous Founder's Day festivities, Gabriel fought a tumult of negative emotions. Just seeing Felicity agitated him, seeing her with Blevins made him angry. The man didn't deserve her.

"Why not?" His sister plucked a fresh strawberry from their lunch basket, a rather plain affair compared to the large decorated ones that lined the long table before the pavilion. Though the display was meant to attract men, only the women hovered near, eagerly waiting to see who displayed interest in which basket.

He watched Hendrick Simmons approach the table. The ladies whispered to each other, watching to see which basket he'd examine, but the man shied away. Gabriel didn't blame him. The scene reminded him of those awkward dances where the girls congregated on one side and the boys on the other, each too afraid to approach the other.

"I don't need to bid on a basket," he said, "when we already have lunch."

"What makes you think I'm going to share it with you? Maybe I've invited someone else to join me."

"Who?" His sister had only been in town a few days. Granted she met people easily, but to have a beau already? Impossible. She must mean a female friend.

Mariah laughed. "None of your business, nosy brother." She straightened her skirts, an odd gesture for Mariah, who didn't care a bit about appearances. Gabriel glanced around but saw only the usual crowd.

"If I'm going to lose my housekeeper, it is my business."

"You'd just have to get another. I believe Ms. Kensington is available. She likes you, you know."

"No, she doesn't." He'd watched Felicity walk beside Blevins since she arrived. "She likes Robert Blevins."

"Hmm. Maybe that's because he's the only man to approach her." Mariah tipped her hat a bit forward, putting her hazel eyes in shadow. "If you outbid him, you'll be able to eat lunch with her."

"I know how the auction works," he snapped, feeling heat shinny up his neck.

Mariah leaned closer. "I happen to know which basket is hers."

So did he. She'd told Blevins to look for the green satin ribbon. Only one basket matched that description.

"The one on the far right," Mariah said, pointing, "with the green bow."

"I'm not interested." He waved at Jack and Darcy Hunter as they passed. "I'm not going to make a spectacle of myself in front of the community."

Mariah burst into laughter. "Foolish pride."

"It is not pride. I'm a minister and need to uphold a high standard. People expect proper behavior from clergy. Besides," he fished for a reasonable excuse, "she clearly likes Robert Blevins. I overheard her tell him which basket to bid on."

"Snooping again, little brother?"

"I wouldn't do that." He picked at a bit of straw stuck in the wool blanket. "I just don't think I should interfere."

"It's not interference to let her know you're interested."

"Did I say I was interested?" Gabriel squirmed under her relentless pressure. "Even if I was, which I'm not, she's a member of my congregation."

"So?"

"So, having a romantic relationship with someone under my pastoral care is ethically wrong."

She laughed. "It happens all the time. Where do you think Reverend Mills found his wife?"

Gabriel felt his face heat up. "This is hardly appropriate conversation." He turned away. "Besides, Reverend Mills handled the courtship quite properly and discreetly."

"Ah, so that's it. Well, if discretion is what's worrying you, I have the perfect solution. Ask her to be on the Selection Committee."

He groaned. Not that again. "I told you I don't want Felicity on the Selection Committee."

She clucked her tongue. "Maybe she needs to be."

He scowled. "You must be ready to marry, sis, because you nag like a wife."

Mariah laughed, deep and hearty. "That's what sisters are for. After a few weeks living with me, a wife will be easy."

Gabriel doubted that. Other than Mariah's constant matchmaking attempts, she went very easy on him. Sure, she insisted he put his dirty clothes in a hamper and wash dishes on occasion, but all in all they got along famously.

"The advance agent will be here in two days," Mariah said. "Have you asked anyone yet?"

"I'm considering Dermott Shea, the bank manager. He's an upstanding member of the community. I'll ask him tomorrow after the service."

"So why not ask Felicity today? The basket auction provides the perfect opportunity."

Gabriel rolled his eyes. Why couldn't she let this go? "Even if I did want Felicity on the committee, I don't need to buy her picnic basket to ask her. I can just call on her."

"Then why haven't you done so?"

"Because she's not the best candidate." Aside from her pretentiousness, he didn't want any Kensington near the committee. Her mother would turn the event to her own agenda, and her father had his fingers in bootlegging. The rack of guns, Kensington's visit to the blind pig, and his nearness to the delivery added up.

Mariah shook her head in disgust. "I think you're wrong."

Gabriel did not want to argue the point and was glad when Dermott Shea mounted the pavilion steps and raised his hands to quiet the chatter.

"Gather around, men, for the picnic basket auction," Shea called out. "All proceeds go toward the community improvement fund, so be generous. This year, we hope to build a new roof for the pavilion."

The first basket was held up, a frilly blue-checked gingham. Only one man bid on it, but the amount was high, and the pleased girl popped up to present it to the winning bidder. Judging by their shy smiles, she'd told him which basket was hers, just like Felicity had told Blevins. The next two baskets offered little competition, though each ended up less costly than the gingham one.

Next came Felicity's green-ribboned basket. Judging by the whispers, a great deal of anticipation coursed through the crowd. Blevins opened the bidding at once, though his two-dollar bid was low.

"Do I hear two-fifty?" said Mr. Shea, glancing at Kensington. The man remained mute. "Two-fifty anyone?"

It was a pitifully small amount.

Mariah jabbed an elbow into Gabriel's side. "Bid."

Gabriel raised his hand, and Shea looked relieved.

"Two-fifty from the minister."

Felicity's head whipped around, and their eyes met. Gabriel felt the spark, but whether she was delighted or angry, he couldn't tell.

Mr. Shea continued the bidding. "Do I hear three dollars?"

Blevins nodded and lifted his hand.

"Five dollars," Gabriel called out.

The crowd murmured, glancing from Felicity and Robert to Gabriel.

"Five-fifty," countered Robert.

"Seven dollars." Gabriel rose to his feet. He couldn't let Blevins get the basket. He couldn't let that pompous fool get Felicity.

"Seven-fifty." Blevins glared, his ridiculous mustache quivering.

Gabriel edged closer to the baskets, reeled in by the hopeful expression on Felicity's face. She wanted him to outbid Blevins. She wanted him to claim the basket. Gabriel fingered the ten-dollar bill in his pocket. "Eight dollars."

Blevins's face turned firecracker-red. "Fifteen."

Fifteen? Gabriel didn't have fifteen dollars. He looked apologetically at Felicity, trying to let her know he couldn't afford more, but her face slowly turned to stone.

Mr. Shea hurried the count, probably so Blevins couldn't reconsider. "Fifteen once, fifteen twice, sold to Mr. Robert Blevins for fifteen dollars."

Gabriel stood defeated in front of the entire town. He heard a snicker and several whispers. Felicity stared at the ground until Blevins, bearing the basket triumphantly, seized her arm and jerked her away from the grandstand. Gabriel had made his play and lost.

"Next we have a lovely basket that smells so good I could eat its contents right now," said Mr. Shea, holding up a modest basket covered in red gingham.

Judging by the blush on Anna Simmons's cheeks, the basket belonged to her.

"Do I have an opening bid?"

Shea's question was met by silence.

"One dollar?" he prompted.

Again, there was silence until Hendrick Simmons raised his hand. Anna blinked her eyes rapidly, and Gabriel felt her humiliation—to have only your brother bid on your basket and offer just one dollar. Poor girl. The Simmons's didn't have much money, but they worked hard and loved God and their neighbors. They deserved better.

"Ten dollars," Gabriel said, raising his hand.

A collective gasp rippled through the crowd as Mr. Shea

hurriedly closed the bidding. Again, every eye focused on Gabriel, but he only cared what Felicity thought. Her lips had pressed into a tight line, and the moment he looked her way, she turned her face and took Blevins's arm.

Gabriel's elation plummeted. He'd hurt her, but he didn't have time to repair the damage. Anna Simmons raced toward him, basket bouncing so much the contents nearly spilled out. The awkward colt of a girl beamed like Cinderella at the ball. He'd done the right thing.

Felicity watched Gabriel take Anna Simmons to meet his sister. That should have been her. Mariah must have encouraged Gabriel to bid on her basket, but then he stopped bidding. Worse, he'd paid more for Anna's basket than he bid on hers. Felicity blinked back tears. Now Robert would get the satchel. Now Anna Simmons got to eat with Gabriel.

"Let's dine by the river," suggested Robert.

"The river?" Felicity followed his outstretched hand. "It's damp there." She didn't want to go anywhere secluded with Robert. She also had to see what happened between Gabriel and Anna. "Over by the parsonage is drier."

"The parsonage? That's hardly romantic."

This time she would not allow Robert to lead her into seclusion. She marched to the spot and waited for the reluctant man to drag the basket there. Sally Neidecker watched Felicity with an envious glare. Her basket had fetched a pretty price but clearly not from the right suitor. Likewise, Eloise Grattan looked glum. Felicity held her head a bit higher. At least in their eyes, she'd won the big prize.

"The sun is warmer here," she said when Robert finally arrived.

She pointed to a flat, grassy area, and he lifted the pressed linen tablecloth from the top of the basket. It snapped and fluttered in the breeze, threatening to blow away until she sat down. The ground was hard and lumpy and would stain the tablecloth, but from here she could watch Gabriel.

Robert pulled one item after another from the basket, commenting on each. "Lemonade. And little crystal glasses. How charming. Silverware tied with ribbons with a little flower tucked in. How dainty."

Felicity detested each word. Gabriel and Anna chattered away like best friends while Anna's brother, Hendrick, captured Mariah's attention. Why oh why hadn't Gabriel outbid Robert?

"What on earth is this?" Robert held up the gift she'd meant for Gabriel and shook the satchel as if he expected a snake to tumble out.

Felicity thought fast. "It's for your instruments. You can use it when you work in the field."

"Hmm." He examined the interior. "Looks like a plain old knapsack to me."

How rude. Gabriel wouldn't have disparaged her gift, even if he already had a satchel. He would have thanked her profusely and used it every day.

"It's just a trifle." She waved her hand the way Mother did to indicate her lack of concern, but Robert's words stung. The gift, once blessed with hopeful dreams, turned cheap in his hands. Gabriel, Gabriel, why didn't you bid more?

Robert tossed the satchel onto the corner of the blanket. "You were awfully sure I'd win your basket, weren't you? What if that minister fellow outbid me?"

She looked away lest he realize that's exactly what she'd wanted.

"I suppose your mother told you she gave me more than enough to outbid a poor minister." He laughed, stark and harsh, not like Gabriel's warm inviting laughter. Then he shoved a whole tart into his mouth. His cheeks bulged like a chipmunk's.

"Those were meant for dessert."

He shrugged. "Why not grab the best part first?" he mumbled with his mouth half full, crumbs clinging to his whiskers.

Her rebuke didn't slow him. He downed another and another until she couldn't stand it. "There is such a thing as manners."

He guzzled half the lemonade and wiped his mouth with the back of his hand. "You sound like the reverend, all proper and reserved. Let your feelings out a little."

"Certainly not."

"Forget the sermons and what you learned in Sunday school." Robert leaned close. "A woman like you needs to be free to express herself. You don't belong with the religious types."

His heavy cologne made her nose itch. She tried to ignore it. She tried not to fixate on the absurd waxed mustache. She tried to find something to admire about the man but couldn't. He'd just denigrated the sacred.

"I attend church," she stated flatly. "I believe in God."

Robert found that immensely amusing, and the wave of cold fear that had rolled over her that night in the park returned. Something about Robert felt wrong, hidden, as if he wasn't who he said he was.

She instinctively sought Gabriel, who was talking with Anna and Mariah. How she longed to be with them. How she wished Gabriel had won her basket.

She nervously glanced at Robert. He was consuming the chicken, never having offered her a bite. Robert Blevins only took. If she gave herself, he'd take that too and throw her aside like the chicken bones. Why hadn't she realized that earlier? Why had she let him think she cared? She knew why—that foolish plan of hers.

That's what got her into trouble in the park that night.

That's what led her here. That's what would force her to spend the evening with Robert. And after the dance... She shivered. What was she to do?

"I say." Robert sat bolt upright, dropping his half-eaten drumstick.

Felicity looked around to see what had startled him. It didn't take long to spot the cause. Slinky had snatched the red satchel and was running full speed toward the woods.

"Rotten dog," Robert said, throwing a table knife at him. "That's mine." He picked up the fork.

"Stop it." Afraid Robert would hurt Slinky, Felicity grabbed the fork from his hand and scrambled to her feet. "Let him go."

Robert twisted the fork from her hand. "That dog has my knapsack."

"Don't worry," said a calm baritone voice from behind her. "I'll get your bag from Slinky."

Felicity whirled around to see Gabriel's wonderful brown eyes and welcoming smile. He tipped his hat and took off after Slinky. She instinctively stumbled a few steps after him.

"Come back, chickadee," said Robert, patting the table-cloth.

Without a look in his direction, Felicity ran after Gabriel. She couldn't match his pace, and by the time she reached the parsonage fence, he'd disappeared from view. He could be all the way to the river or on Mr. Coughlin's land. She stopped to catch her breath and was relieved to see that Robert hadn't followed.

The broken-down fence stood twenty feet away on her right. The trees were thicker here except for the occasional glade, rippling with bright green grass and ferns. Out of view and to the left the river raced south before turning west.

"Gabriel?" she said hesitantly.

"Down here." His voice sounded oddly far away, as if he was in a cave, but she'd explored these woods in childhood, and there weren't any caves here, only upriver where the springtime rapids had carved a hole into the bank.

"Where? I don't see you."

His head popped out of the ground not twelve feet ahead, face ashen, like he'd seen something terrible. "Stay there."

"Why?"

He scrambled up. "Go to the parsonage and get the rope, the one Mr. Coughlin used to tie up Slinky. It's just inside the back door."

"Why?" Something was wrong, and he didn't want her to see it. "Is Slinky hurt?"

"I think so. Just get the rope. Please?" He touched her arm, gently directing her toward the house.

She nodded and obeyed. The old Felicity would have questioned or refused, but this one knew Gabriel was deadly serious. Slinky was hurt, and Gabriel needed her. No one had ever needed her before.

She ran as fast as she could to the parsonage.

Chapter Ten

Sending Felicity to get a rope had been a diversion. Gabriel wasn't sure how much she knew about her father's involvement in the bootlegging ring, and he didn't want to be the one to enlighten her.

He climbed back into the root cellar and stepped between the toppled cases of liquor, avoiding the broken bottles. Slinky whimpered and quaked, definitely hurt.

"It's all right, boy." Gabriel hooked his arms under the big dog. "I've got you."

He struggled to carry Slinky from the cellar. Why would the bootleggers leave the doors open on Founder's Day? Someone was bound to happen upon it. This reeked of stupidity or laziness, neither of which he'd attribute to Kensington.

The dog panted and whined but didn't bite. Once out of the cellar, Gabriel set him down.

"Stay," he commanded, probably unnecessarily considering the way the dog favored his right front paw.

He returned to the cellar to fetch the red satchel, but halfway in, he heard thrashing. Someone was coming. He did not need Blevins showing up right now. He quickly exited, closed the cellar doors and carried Slinky a short distance away.

"Gabriel?" That voice could only belong to Felicity.

He exhaled. "Thank goodness it's you."

"Who else would it be?" She pushed through the underbrush, snagging her fine navy suit. "I found it." She held up the rope.

"Good. Bring it here."

Instead she headed toward the root cellar. Gabriel panicked. He'd forgotten to kick leaves over the doors. She'd find it and know where Slinky had been.

"We're over here." He waved.

"I know. I'm just going around a rotten log." Her cheeks were pleasantly flushed, making her infinitely lovelier than the studied sophistication she assumed at dinner parties. "Are we in time?" She halted when she saw Slinky. "I thought you needed to lift him from a hole."

"I got him out, but he seems to be favoring his right leg."

"Poor dear." Felicity knelt and gently lifted Slinky's paw. "I won't hurt you, big boy." Her soft tones calmed the dog. "Let's look at your paw." She spotted the problem in seconds. "See?" She motioned for Gabriel to look at the shard of glass embedded in one of his pads. "This must hurt terribly. We'll need to clean out the wound with hydrogen peroxide."

Gabriel had no idea if he had any, but Felicity didn't pause long enough for him to tell her that.

"It's not far to the parsonage, but we shouldn't make Slinky walk on the injury."

"I'll carry him." Gabriel liked this new Felicity. In an emergency, she took charge. Even better, her concern and gentleness with Slinky showed a surprising depth of character.

"I wonder how it happened," Felicity mused. "You said you found him in a hole? And with glass, too. How odd."

Gabriel held his tongue.

"The foundation of the old Warren homestead is around here somewhere. Maybe he fell into it."

Gabriel wondered again how much she knew about her father's smuggling operation. She hadn't mentioned the root cellar, but she did know about the homestead.

Felicity led the way to the parsonage, all business. By the time they reached the fence, his arms burned and he was panting as much as Slinky. Felicity opened the gate and closed it behind him. She also held the screen door for him and followed him into the kitchen without one word about propriety. She whipped the precious monogrammed towels out of the linen closet and laid them on the floor. Then she barged into the pantry.

"If I remember right, the hydrogen peroxide is in here."

"You've been in the pantry before?"

"Mother and I helped stock it before you arrived," she said, emerging with bottle in hand. "I'll need some tweezers."

"I don't think we have tweezers," he said helplessly.

She knelt beside Slinky, gently caressing the dog's head. "Very well, we'll make do."

Her tender touch calmed Slinky to the point that he nuzzled into her arms like a lap dog. Maybe Mariah was right. Maybe her pretentious veneer did hide a tender nature.

"Peroxide." She held out a hand.

Gabriel uncapped the bottle, and she poured some on a cloth and dabbed at the injured paw.

"It's tough to see with all the mud."

That mud had come from the bottom of the root cellar, a fact best kept to himself. "Do you want some water?"

She shook her head. "This will do."

Felicity carefully cleaned the footpads and then, bending

close, pulled the sliver of glass from Slinky's paw. The dog whined but didn't nip her.

"Got it." She sat back with a sigh of relief.

"Is that the only one?"

"As near as I can tell." She applied more hydrogen peroxide to the wound.

This time Slinky pulled away, fed up with the entire procedure, and retreated to his bed.

"He looks better already," Felicity said hopefully as she recapped the peroxide. Her hands were flecked with blood, but she didn't seem to care.

He liked her this way, without the self-consciousness and pretension. Helping animals changed her. "You'd make a good veterinarian."

She looked up in surprise. "Me?"

"You're good with animals."

She shook her head. "There's no such thing as a woman veterinarian."

"Why not? Why shouldn't women be veterinarians?"

She shrugged. "They just aren't. Besides, even if a veterinary college accepted me, Mother would never allow it."

Not allow her to help animals? Not allow her to use her God-given gifts? Even though her mother forbade pets in the house, that prohibition shouldn't extend to her daughter choosing a career. "Why not?"

Her far-off gaze looked so sad that Gabriel ached for her. Mariah had often talked of the fewer opportunities granted to women, but his sister didn't let that stop her. Felicity did, and that was a tragedy.

"I shouldn't have spoken so openly," he said. "You might find it difficult to believe, but I think women should have the same opportunity to pursue their dreams that men have."

She averted her gaze. "Maybe I don't have dreams."

"I don't believe that for a minute." He touched her blood-stained hand. "You deserve every opportunity."

She shook her head but didn't pull away. "It doesn't work that way."

"It should."

Her mouth twisted into a wry smile. "It doesn't."

Gabriel couldn't get her into veterinary college, but he could change her life in another way, by entrusting her with solemn responsibility.

He took a deep breath. "Will you promise to consider something for me?"

She looked up, wary. "What is it?"

"A friend from New York, Mr. Isaacs, arranges foster homes for orphaned and abandoned children. His Detroit mission needs to place five children in good Christian homes. He thought Pearlman might be a good place for them. You know the community and everyone in it. Would you serve on the Selection Committee?"

She didn't answer at first, the disbelief evident on her face. "Me? Are you sure?"

He recognized the seeds of self-doubt. No wonder she flaunted her social status. She didn't believe she had anything else of value. "Yes, I'm sure. With your compassion for the less fortunate, you'd be perfect."

For a moment her confidence lifted, but then she lowered her eyes. "I'm not certain—"

"Don't answer now. Think about it." He needed to find a reason she couldn't resist. "Just remember, these children are no different than Slinky. They need love and a place to call home. They need someone who cares enough to help them."

She squared her shoulders and looked him in the eye. "I don't need to think it over. I'll do it. I'll be on your committee."

"Thank you. You won't regret it." He smiled, and when she smiled back, he had to envelop her in a hug. "Thank you," he whispered, closing his eyes and breathing in the rosewater scent that belonged only to her.

He wanted to stay with her forever, but the kitchen door creaked open.

"Gabriel?"

He jerked away from Felicity. It was Mariah, and beside her stood Anna Simmons and Blevins.

Felicity leaped to her feet and smoothed her skirt, embarrassed to be caught in an embrace. "We were just taking care of Slinky." She waved at the dog, who watched the uncomfortable scene from his bed.

Mariah looked surprised. "Is that where you went? You were gone so long that Anna and I searched the park while Mr. Blevins checked the woods."

Poor Anna looked like she was going to cry, but Robert leaned confidently against the doorway, arms crossed. He was going to hold this against her.

"Slinky was hurt," Felicity hurriedly explained, "so Gabriel carried him here." She smiled at the memory of him lugging the big dog through the woods. He'd had to lean backward to balance the weight, but he'd never once set Slinky down.

Robert smirked. "And you went along with the good pastor because?"

Felicity swallowed. She shouldn't have come into the parsonage with Gabriel. As soon as the gossips heard, they'd whisper scandalous things about the minister and Ms. Kensington. All Anna Simmons had to do was tell Eloise Grattan or Sally Neidecker, and the tongues would wag. People seized any chance to disparage the Kensington name.

"I, uh..." She couldn't think of a single excuse.

Gabriel stepped in. "Ms. Kensington removed some glass from Slinky's paw."

"Glass? What glass?" Mariah looked around, confused.

"He fell into a hole," Gabriel explained. "In the woods."

"A hole in the woods. I thought you were chasing him because he took my knapsack." Robert crossed his arms. "Just where is this hole?"

How Felicity wished she'd never come up with that foolish plan to marry Robert. Every minute that passed made her despise the man more.

Gabriel's jaw tensed. "It's part of an old foundation, near the parsonage land. Perhaps you know the spot?"

Robert laughed unkindly. "How could I when I'm new to town, Reverend?" He took great delight in stressing Gabriel's title.

"So am I, Mr. Blevins, but I can't help wondering why we didn't see you. If you were searching the woods like my sister said, you should have found us."

"I must have been searching in another part of the woods."

Felicity had had enough. "Stop it, both of you. No one cares where Slinky got hurt. The fact is he did, we found him and he's safe now."

"Amen," murmured Mariah.

Gabriel picked up the bloody towels. "Ms. Kensington is as skilled as any veterinarian."

Warmth spread all the way to her toes. He believed in her, Felicity Kensington, a woman without a single talent or skill. She shot him a smile of gratitude, which he reflected back.

Mariah cleared her throat. "Thank God all ended well."

As if on cue, Slinky raised his head and barked.

"We need to keep his paw clean until the wound heals," Felicity mumbled, still watching Gabriel. "I don't suppose he'll tolerate a bandage, though."

"I'll keep him inside as much as possible," Gabriel promised.

Gabriel didn't mock or question her advice. He treated her like a trained professional.

"That's good," she breathed.

"Sorry to break up this little medical conference," Robert said, moving into her line of sight, "but it's getting late and we still have to attend supper with your parents and go to the dance."

The room came abruptly into focus. The dance. She wanted to avoid it, but how could she when her parents expected her?

Robert opened the door. "Shall we, chickadee?"

The pet name grated on her nerves. "I—I'm not sure I'm done." She looked around for an excuse to stay.

Anna Simmons, clutching her lunch basket, lifted her eyes to Gabriel. "We didn't eat dessert yet." Her quavering voice drew him to her side.

"Thank you, Felicity," Mariah said dismissively.

"Yes, thank you," Gabriel echoed with the briefest of glances.

Why didn't he look at her? Moments before, he'd gathered her in his arms. His gentle embrace spoke of compassion and maybe even a little more. His smile promised the feelings ran deeper, but now he only had eyes for Anna Simmons. Had she been wrong? Had the hug been nothing more than a minister encouraging a member of his congregation? Jealousy fevered her thoughts. What a fool Felicity had been to think he cared for her.

"Come along, darling," said Robert, holding out his hand, "your parents are waiting."

Felicity stared at Robert's outstretched hand. Never had a man so repulsed her. Gabriel opened Anna's basket and took out the cake while Anna placed napkins on the thick oak table. *That was supposed to be her.* It should have been her.

But it wasn't.

With a sigh of resignation, she left with Robert.

Gabriel skipped the dance. He couldn't bear to see Felicity in Blevins's arms. Chickadee. The man had nerve calling her that, but then he had taken liberties before. At least this time they'd be under her parents' supervision.

"You should go," Mariah urged from the doorway of the study. "The Grange Hall is a short walk from here or you can ride with me."

"I need to review my sermon," he said blackly as he buried his nose in his notes. But he couldn't concentrate on the words.

Why had he asked Felicity to be on the Selection Committee? Compassion alone wouldn't give her the strength to make life-changing decisions. If today was any indication, she'd do whatever her parents or even Robert Blevins wanted.

He scrubbed his face, irritated with himself. With only three people on the Selection Committee, every voice counted. To balance her inexperience and his relative lack of knowledge about Pearlman, he needed a strong Christian community leader like Dermott Shea as the third member. Gabriel had seen enough of the man to trust his opinion. Yes, Mr. Shea would provide good balance. He would ask him after the service on Sunday.

Unfortunately, Branford Kensington had other ideas. While Gabriel greeted the members of his congregation and waited for Mr. Shea to leave the sanctuary, Kensington pulled him aside.

"Fine sermon, Reverend, though you might want to make

it a little lighter for the ladies." Kensington elbowed him in the ribs with a wink. "Speaking of ladies, my Felicity is a bit inexperienced for your orphan committee. Don't get me wrong. She's a fine young lady, but she's never spent a single hour with a baby."

Gabriel watched Dermott Shea leave the church with growing irritation. If he hurried, he might catch the man outside. "These aren't infants, sir. They're older children. Excuse me, please. I should greet the rest of the congregation."

Kensington blocked his retreat. "My point exactly. She hasn't got a bit of experience with children. Besides, she's a woman. You know how emotional they are. Let a woman near an orphan and she'll get all weepy on you."

Any thought of replacing Felicity vanished. This committee would give her a chance to stand on her own, to make decisions and act on behalf of others.

"Felicity is an intelligent young lady who will do a splendid job," Gabriel insisted as he watched her chat with the Hunters and the Simmonses, two families with whom she didn't generally converse.

"Exactly, but aren't these committees usually comprised of the finest and most upstanding members of the community?"

Gabriel flinched. "I consider Ms. Kensington to be a fine, upstanding member of the community."

Kensington did not relent. "I mean professionals, son. Doctors and businessmen. Those are the usual members of one of those orphan committees, aren't they?"

Gabriel gritted his teeth. Kensington was right, but that didn't mean past practice was always the best choice. "I'd like a woman on the committee."

Eugenia Kensington had spotted them and was steaming their way, fire in her stride.

Kensington noted his wife's approach and dropped the jovial attitude. "Let me put this plainly, son. I want to be on that committee. No one is better qualified—certainly not my daughter."

Before Gabriel could think of a polite yet firm way to refuse, Eugenia interrupted.

"Reverend Meeks. The Ladies' Aid Society would like your opinion on the new window. The artist sent five sketches. Do you have a moment?"

Gabriel's sympathy for Felicity increased tenfold. "I thought your daughter was chairing that committee."

Eugenia waved her smartly gloved hand. "She's too busy, so I'm helping her out."

"Too busy? Doing what?"

Eugenia stiffened, and Gabriel realized he would get nowhere protesting her plan. It was better to soften her heart and lead her gently to the right conclusion. "Very well, I'll look at your drawings, but first I could use the Ladies' Aid Society's help on a new project."

"What new project? I haven't heard anything."

Gabriel plunged in. "Mr. Isaacs of the Orphaned Children's Society would like to place five children with foster families in Pearlman."

Her face went stark white and her stained red lips trembled slightly. For a moment, he thought she was going to faint and held out an arm to brace her, but she regained her composure. "What, pray tell, does that have to do with us?"

"I hoped the Ladies' Aid Society would consider helping the children and save the window project for later."

"Help them? How? Don't the foster families take on that expense?" Her jaw had tightened so much that a crowbar couldn't open it.

"Yes, but the initial expense can be overwhelming for

some families. The children arrive with only one change of clothing."

"Well, if they can't afford to take on a child, they shouldn't be given one."

Gabriel's stomach rolled. Had this woman no heart? He was amazed Felicity possessed any tenderness at all, given her parents. He tried again. "I feel the society's mission would be better served helping these children than putting in a window we don't need."

Her face turned an ugly shade of red. "May I remind you, Pastor, the Ladies' Aid Society decides how to spend its funds, not you."

Felicity, who must have overheard the exchange, hurried near. "As chairwoman of the committee, I agree with Reverend Meeks."

Eugenia Kensington looked like she would explode, but Gabriel saw only Felicity. She'd supported him over her mother. That took fortitude, the kind needed on the Selection Committee.

"Felicity," Eugenia hissed, "this is already decided." She grabbed her daughter's hand, and Felicity's confidence began to crumble.

Gabriel had to save her. "Your daughter is on the Selection Committee."

Eugenia Kensington went dead white.

"No," she gasped. "Branford." Her knees wobbled, and her husband rushed to support her.

"Don't worry, dear," Kensington blustered as he held his wife. "The pastor here has named me to the committee, too."

"That's not—" Gabriel began, but Kensington was already leading this wife away.

"How could you?" Felicity cried, fists balled. "Put Daddy on the committee? I thought you had better sense."

"But I didn't put him on it," he said to no one, for

Felicity had stormed out of the church before he could get the words out.

In five short minutes, the Kensingtons had steamrolled him yet again.

Chapter Eleven

By the time June faded into July, Felicity's plan had acquired so many holes that she needed to rethink the situation. Art school was Mother's dream, not hers. Felicity would never break free of her there. Marriage wasn't the answer, but Robert appeared beyond reform, and she did not want to wait until marriage to discover he would not change. Eliminating him as a suitor left her with no prospects.

Gabriel had turned out to be just as fickle. How could he ask Daddy to be on the Selection Committee? He must know that would destroy any chance of spending time with her. Then again, perhaps that was his plan. Perhaps he was seeing someone, someone like Anna Simmons. At seventeen, Anna was awfully young, but Gabriel might like younger women. He had leaped to buy her picnic basket.

Felicity worried about it when she went to bed and resumed fretting when she awoke. Could it be? She considered every possible candidate in town and was able to dismiss most but not all. She listened to the gossips at the post office and in the mercantile, but no one said a word about Gabriel. Finally, she couldn't stand it anymore and went directly to the source.

"Is your brother seeing anyone?" she asked Mariah one afternoon while helping her make strawberry jam.

Mariah laughed. "Gabe? He doesn't know a good prospect when it bites him on the nose." She handed the filled lightning jar to Felicity, who cleaned the rim and clamped down the glass lid.

The kitchen was steamy hot, and Felicity had to constantly wipe her face on her apron to keep the perspiration from running into her eyes.

"What about Anna Simmons?" she whispered.

Mariah moved the bubbling preserves off the hottest part of the stove. "What about her?"

"They seemed to get along on Founder's Day."

"She's a bit young, don't you think?" Mariah filled another jar.

Perhaps Felicity was being overly concerned. Anna was a good seven or eight years younger than Gabriel. She wiped off the jar's rim.

"In my estimation, Anna's more like a little sister," Mariah said. "The woman who sets her eye on my brother will have to work hard to catch him. He spends too much time thinking and not enough time noticing what's around him, if you know what I mean."

Her coy little smile told Felicity all she needed to know. To attract Gabriel, Felicity must engage his intellect on a topic that dearly interested him. She could think of just one.

The rest of that week, Felicity lived at the library, reading everything she could about orphanages and adoption. She learned about Charles Loring Brace's Children's Aid Society, which sent orphans west by train. Some praised the system, but others scorned it. Was this criticism what Gabriel's friend faced? Is that what darkened Gabriel's expression?

By the morning of the first Selection Committee meeting, Felicity was ready with questions. She bit her lip as she checked her ivory linen suit in the mirror. Navy piping accented the short jacket and fostered the illusion of crisp freshness.

Alas, the moment she stepped outside, perspiration beaded on her forehead, and the linen wilted. Not one leaf stirred in the stifling air. She fanned herself to no avail.

Smithson stood at the car holding the passenger door open, but Daddy was nowhere to be seen. "Mr. Kensington has an urgent meeting this morning and will not be able to attend."

"Are you certain?" It wasn't like Daddy to miss an obligation.

Smithson raised an eyebrow as he closed the door. "Yes, Ms. Kensington."

What could be so urgent that Daddy would miss this important meeting? She gnawed her lower lip as Smithson nudged the car down the street. Daddy and Gabriel didn't like each other, but they were civil. Besides, Daddy didn't let squabbles stand in the way of business. There must be something wrong.

The town looked normal. People hurried from shop to shop on their daily errands. Motor trucks made their usual deliveries. No one looked anxious or upset, only hot.

The car glided to a stop before the church, and Felicity went inside. The church interior felt gloriously cool. Morning sun filtered through the oaks and maples before streaming through the plate glass window to dapple the floors and walls. She'd miss those rays of sunlight dancing with dust motes. As a child, she'd believed they were God's fingers. The stained glass would cut them off.

She held her hand in the light. *Give me strength, Lord, to make the right decisions.*

Reassured, she turned to the church office. A warm light flooded from the open door. She paused outside, nerves heightened. A low murmur of masculine voices came from inside.

She took a deep breath and knocked.

"Come in," Gabriel said.

Felicity pushed open the door and saw Gabriel with a Puritanical elder sporting a closely trimmed white beard. The man's saintly face crinkled into a smile the minute he saw her.

"I'm Mr. Isaacs. You must be Ms. Kensington." His warm greeting belied the somber attire. "Your pastor has told me all about you."

Her pastor. She glanced at Gabriel. "I hope it was favorable."

"Nothing but good," Mr. Isaacs said. "You're just as lovely as he said you were."

Heat crept up her cheeks to match Gabriel's color. He pretended to examine papers, but she'd seen the expression on his face when she entered. He was glad to see her.

Gabriel cleared his throat. "Where is your father, Ms. Kensington?"

She straightened her skirt and tugged off her gloves. "He left word that he has an urgent meeting this morning and can't attend."

Gabriel scowled and rubbed his temple. "This is the most important meeting of the project. He knew that. I don't see what could be more urgent than finding good homes for orphaned children."

"It's all right, Gabriel," said Mr. Isaacs with a calm, soothing voice. "I'm sure Ms. Kensington can pass along the instructions to her father."

Though the scowl didn't leave Gabriel's face, he bowed to Mr. Isaacs's wishes. The next two hours involved going over the rules for approving and disqualifying applicants. Felicity struggled to concentrate on what Mr. Isaacs said, but it was so difficult with Gabriel sitting beside her. She marveled at his strong, steady script as he took notes. Most men scribbled. His words flowed, beautifully readable. Ink stained the tip of his index finger and the first joint of his middle finger, but his nails were clean and trimmed. Attention to the right details mattered in a man.

"A strong Christian household is most important," said Mr. Isaacs, "but we do want to take into account their family life. We prefer to place the children with families that have two parents and children around the same age. Education is important, of course. The child must attend school, Sunday school and Sunday worship."

Felicity nodded when Isaacs looked at her for confirmation, but she barely heard what he said—something about Christian education.

"The children are to share the same food as the family and work the same chores as the family's own children."

"Must a foster family already have children," Felicity asked, "or do we consider childless couples?"

"That is the committee's decision. If you feel the couple meets all other qualifications, then you may approve their application."

A child. Felicity had never thought about children, but as she sat next to Gabriel, she couldn't help wondering what that would be like. Any child of hers would not endure the long, lonely days she'd spent. She'd have many children, like Gabriel's family, bustling with activity. For the tiniest moment, she imagined being married to Gabriel with a houseful of children. Mariah would visit, of course, and they'd go on grand picnics and adventures.

Mr. Isaacs coughed, and she pulled her attention back to the business at hand.

"Though the foster family will receive a small stipend for the child's care," Isaacs said, "the bulk of the cost is borne by the family. They need to understand this upfront. Any report of neglect or abuse will bring the immediate removal of the child. You can prevent that tragedy by carefully screening the applicants. Do you have any questions?"

Felicity spilled hers all at once.

Gabriel smiled softly. "One at a time, Felic—uh, Ms. Kensington."

Mr. Isaacs chuckled. "That's quite all right, Gabriel. I appreciate an eager committee member."

After all her questions had been answered, Mr. Isaacs moved on to the itinerary. "It's best to complete the application process before the children arrive. Try to approve at least five suitable applicants, preferably more. Every child longs to be chosen. They'll be eager and nervous. Our agents will do their best to keep the children calm, but you can help by offering a warm and encouraging atmosphere and ensuring each child is matched."

"We can do that," said Gabriel.

Felicity closed her eyes and drank in his warm baritone. She wouldn't mind hearing that every day, waking up to his smile and falling asleep in his arms.

"The children will arrive on the afternoon train on Wednesday the fourteenth," Mr. Isaacs said.

"Of this month?" Gabriel was clearly surprised. "That's only a little over a week away."

"I'm confident you can have everything in place, Gabe."

Felicity started at the familiar appellation. Only Mariah used that nickname. Gabriel must know Mr. Isaacs very well.

"They will come to the church first," Mr. Isaacs said, "so the town can see them. A short hymn-sing would be perfect."

Felicity imagined arriving in a strange town and having everyone examine her like a cow on the auction block or a picnic basket on Founder's Day. The best and prettiest would get picked, but what about the rest? It would be worse than being the last one picked for a schoolyard baseball game.

"Won't they be self-conscious?" she asked.

"It is difficult," Mr. Isaacs conceded, "but you can ease their discomfort by meeting them at the train and giving them a little time alone before going to the church. After the service, the children will be brought to the boardinghouse for supper and to wash up for bed. Two agents will be with them at all times."

"Agents?" she asked.

"Representatives of the Orphaned Children's Society," Gabriel answered, lightly squeezing her hand. "They help the children through the process."

Felicity barely heard his words. She stared at her hand. He'd touched her in public. It was practically an announcement that he cared. Though she felt the dots of heat in her cheeks, Mr. Isaacs didn't seem to notice.

"Pastor Gabriel is right," said Isaacs. "You can make this the best experience in these children's lives with the proper preparation. If you allow the applicants to note preferences, do so after the children have left the room. The next day, distribution day, will go much easier for the children if the committee has already decided which families get each child. The children will arrive at the church at ten sharp for the distribution. I can't stress enough the responsibility you hold."

Felicity felt it coiled like a spring inside her, but with Gabriel's help they'd ensure the best homes for these children.

"I understand," she whispered.

Mr. Isaacs nodded. "You will need to have each applicant complete the following paperwork." He then outlined the forms to be filled out and the oath to be taken.

By the time they finished, her head spun and not only from the hundred procedures to be followed. She'd be working with Gabriel, making important decisions together.

What's more, he valued her opinion. She was glad Daddy had gone to another meeting that day.

Isaacs gathered his papers, and Gabriel rose. "Would you care to lunch at the parsonage, Mr. Isaacs? It's only roast chicken, but we have plenty."

Felicity longed to join them, but Gabriel hadn't invited her. She lingered, hoping he would.

Isaacs slid the papers into his valise. "Tempting as that is, I'm exhausted from the travel and am looking forward to Mrs. Terchie's perogies and a long nap." His eyes twinkled as he glanced at her. "You two enjoy the meal."

Felicity's cheeks burned. Was her attraction to Gabriel that obvious? She felt him stiffen beside her, but he didn't dispute Mr. Isaacs's suggestion.

"And if you change your mind, Gabriel, our door is always open." The men shook hands.

Felicity wondered what Mr. Isaacs meant. What door? Change his mind about what?

After goodbyes were said and Mr. Isaacs headed to the boardinghouse, Gabriel and Felicity strolled toward Elm Street.

"Whew, it's hot." He mopped his forehead. "No wonder Mr. Isaacs didn't want to eat roast chicken in the parsonage."

"Don't you have a fan?" Felicity thought the church supplied all modern comforts for its minister.

"It's not working."

"You should speak to Mr. Grattan. He heads the trustees. They'll get it fixed."

"Uh-huh," he mumbled, peeling off his dark jacket.

They walked in silence for a while. Gabriel seemed deep in thought, his brow furrowed.

Felicity couldn't bear to see him without a smile. Maybe asking about home would help. "How long have you and Mr. Isaacs known each other?"

"We met when I was a boy. Even though he's forty years older than I am, we became friends at once."

The young Gabriel had met the director of an orphan placement service as a boy? Was he an orphan? But Mariah looked so much like him. Unless they were orphaned siblings. It happened. Was it possible? The question bobbed on her lips until it finally burst out.

"Were you...that is, how did you meet?"

Gabriel barely glanced at her, lost in the past. "My parents believe in helping the less fortunate. From an early age, all of us went into the tenements to help. Sometimes we cleaned. Sometimes we sat with the sick. Sometimes I helped my brothers fix things."

Felicity wondered at his words. His family could not have been as poor as she'd believed if they could reach out to others.

He smiled at a memory. "I wasn't always a very good worker. Once I saw a stray tomcat along the way. He was a filthy thing, all matted and torn from battle. He probably didn't want to be saved, but I was intent on rescuing him. I got separated from my brothers, and by the time I caught up to the tom, I was lost. Luckily, Mr. Isaacs found me. He brought me to the orphanage until my parents could fetch me. I loved it there. Once upon a time, I thought that was my life's mission."

Felicity heard the passion in his voice. "Then why didn't you stay?"

A faint smile graced his lips. "Because God called me here."

His assurance stunned her. To know beyond a doubt what you're meant to do. She'd never experienced such certainty.

They reached Elm Street and stopped. The parsonage stood to the right, its broad front porch shaded by two stately elms and framed by bridal veil, which had lost its dusting of white.

"Stay for lunch," Gabriel blurted out. "We have extra, since Mr. Isaacs won't be joining us."

"I should go home," she said without a great deal of conviction. "Daddy will expect a report on the meeting."

"Of course." But his eyes caught hers and melted her to the spot.

"Mariah will be disappointed." His smile suspended time. "I will be disappointed."

"You will?" Her heart pattered.

He grinned. "Slinky will be disappointed."

"Well, if Slinky insists."

He laughed, and that warm sensation came over her again. He cared—about her of all people.

Felicity followed Gabriel up the porch steps. Somehow it felt both wrong and right to enter the parsonage through the front door.

"It's too hot to eat inside," Mariah said the moment they entered. "I fixed a picnic basket. Let's go to the park." She bustled across the parlor, blanket in hand. "Hello, Felicity. I'm glad you could join us."

Gabriel watched his older sister with a smile of bemusement. "Do you mind if Felicity checks Slinky first?"

Mariah waved her into the kitchen. "Check away. He's been pestering me all morning for some chicken."

"You didn't give him any, did you?" Gabriel held the kitchen door for Felicity. "Mariah, I thought we agreed. No more table scraps."

"It's hardly table scraps, Gabriel John."

Gabriel John. Felicity let the syllables run over her tongue. It was a good name, a strong name. She liked it.

Slinky lay on his bed watching the bustle around him.

When she knelt to check his paw, he perked up, lifting his head with its one floppy ear.

The wound was still puffy and red, though the flesh had begun to knit. "Bathe it in hydrogen peroxide morning and night, and don't take him on walks quite yet."

"Thank you, Dr. Felicity," Gabriel said.

She blushed at his teasing. "It's only common sense."

Slinky plunked his head on her lap, and she had to give him a few strokes before leaving with Mariah and Gabriel.

They ambled through the woods, which felt so cool that she longed to stay there, but Mariah selected a grassy spot under a maple at the park's edge.

They weren't the only picnickers that day. Several mothers had brought their children to the park. For a moment, Felicity wondered what they'd think of her lunching with the minister and his sister, but what did it matter? She liked Gabriel, and judging by the way he looked at her, he liked her, too.

"Too bad Mr. Isaacs couldn't join us," Mariah said as she removed the plates and napkins from the basket. "I'm not surprised though." She cast a mischievous grin at her brother.

He made a face at her. "I can't imagine what you mean."

She laughed. "So how did it go? Did your father run the show, Felicity?"

Mariah had pegged Daddy's character from the start. "He had a business meeting and wasn't there."

"Lucky you."

Felicity supposed it was lucky. If Daddy had been there, she'd never be eating lunch with Gabriel. After they'd feasted on chicken, biscuits, hard-boiled eggs and carrot salad, Gabriel leaned back with a sigh, hands folded across his stomach.

An Important Message from the Editors of *Love Inspired*® Books

Dear Reader,

Because you've chosen to read one of our fine Love Inspired Historical romance novels, we'd like to say "thank you!" And, as a **special** way to thank you, we've selected **two more** of the books you love so well, and two surprise gifts to send you— absolutely **FREE!**

Please enjoy them with our compliments...

Jean Gordon

Editor,
Love Inspired Historical

Peel off seal and place inside...

EDITOR'S
FREE GIFTS
SEAL
THANK YOU

LIH-EC-11B

HOW TO VALIDATE YOUR
EDITOR'S FREE GIFTS!
"THANK YOU"

1. Peel off the FREE GIFTS SEAL from front cover. Place it in the space provided at right. This automatically entitles you to receive two free books and two exciting surprise gifts.

2. Send back this card and you'll get 2 Love Inspired® Historical books. These books are worth $11.50 in the U.S. or $13.50 in Canada, but are yours absolutely FREE!

3. There's no catch. You're under no obligation to buy anything. We charge nothing—ZERO—for your first shipment. And you don't have to make any minimum number of purchases—not even one!

4. We call this line Love Inspired Historical because every month you'll receive books that are filled with inspirational historical romance. This series is filled with engaging stories of romance, adventure and faith set in historical periods from biblical times to World War II. You'll like the convenience of getting them delivered to your home well before they are in stores. And you'll love our discount prices, too!

5. We hope that after receiving your free books you'll want to remain a subscriber. But the choice is yours—to continue or cancel, anytime at all! So why not take us up on our invitation, with no risk of any kind. You'll be glad you did!

6. And remember...just for validating your Editor's Free Gifts Offer, we'll send you 2 books and 2 gifts, *ABSOLUTELY FREE!*

YOURS FREE!
We'll send you two fabulous surprise gifts (worth about $10) absolutely FREE, simply for accepting our no-risk offer!

The Editor's "Thank You" Free Gifts Include:

- Two inspirational historical romance books
- Two exciting surprise gifts

YES!

PLACE FREE GIFTS SEAL HERE

I have placed my Editor's "thank you" Free Gifts seal in the space provided above. Please send me the 2 FREE books and 2 FREE gifts for which I qualify. I understand that I am under no obligation to purchase anything further, as explained on the opposite page.

102/302 IDL FENX

Please Print

FIRST NAME

LAST NAME

ADDRESS

APT.#

CITY

STATE/PROV.

ZIP/POSTAL CODE

Detach card and mail today. No stamp needed. ▶

© 2011 LOVE INSPIRED BOOKS PRINTED IN THE U.S.A.

LIH-EC-11B

The Reader Service—Here's How It Works:

Accepting your 2 free books and 2 free gifts (gifts valued at approximately $10.00) places you under no obligation to buy anything. You may keep the books and gifts and return the shipping statement marked "cancel." If you do not cancel, about a month later we will send you 4 additional books and bill you just $4.49 each in the U.S. or $4.99 each in Canada. That is a savings of at least 22% off the cover price. It's quite a bargain! Shipping and handling is just 50¢ per book in the U.S. and 75¢ per book in Canada.* You may cancel at any time, but if you choose to continue, every month we'll send you 4 more books, which you may either purchase at the discount price or return to us and cancel your subscription.

*Terms and prices subject to change without notice. Prices do not include applicable taxes. Sales tax applicable in N.Y. Canadian residents will be charged applicable taxes. Offer not valid in Quebec. All orders subject to credit approval. Credit or debit balances in a customer's account(s) may be offset by any other outstanding balance owed by or to the customer. Please allow 4 to 6 weeks for delivery. Offer available while quantities last.

▲ If offer card is missing write to: The Reader Service, P.O. Box 1867, Buffalo, NY 14240-1867 or visit www.ReaderService.com ▲

BUSINESS REPLY MAIL

FIRST-CLASS MAIL   PERMIT NO. 717   BUFFALO, NY

POSTAGE WILL BE PAID BY ADDRESSEE

THE READER SERVICE

PO BOX 1867

BUFFALO NY 14240-9952

NO POSTAGE
NECESSARY
IF MAILED
IN THE
UNITED STATES

"That was wonderful, sis. I think I'll take a nap now." He pulled his straw Panama hat over his eyes.

"A nap?" Mariah swatted him with her napkin. "Is that any way to behave around guests?"

"Guests?" He peered out from under his hat. "We have guests? Oh, you mean Felicity. She's not a guest. She's practically part of the family."

Part of the family. What wonderful words, and as a newly inducted member of this family, she wanted to know more. "Is your father a minister?"

"He might as well be," Gabriel groaned.

Mariah laughed. "Dad sells motorcars."

That explained Mariah's car but not Gabriel's reaction. "Then why does your brother think he should be a minister?"

Gabriel scraped his hat to the crown of his head. "Because he's always preaching."

"Must be where you picked it up," Mariah joked.

Felicity loved their cheerful teasing. She'd lost that when she left for Highbury. By the time she returned, Blake was getting married. Sure, he'd been thoughtless at times when young, but what child wasn't? Deep down, she knew he liked her, and if they'd spent more time together, they might have developed a relationship similar to Gabriel and Mariah's.

"You're lucky," she sighed.

Gabriel looked surprised. "To have a preachy father?"

"To have a big family. Mine is so small."

"If half of us weren't adopted," Mariah said, "we'd have a small family, too."

"Adopted?" Felicity stared, openmouthed. So it was true. "You're adopted?"

"Actually, Gabe and I and our older brother Samuel are Mom and Dad's biological children, but Charlie and Rudy and Lloyd were adopted."

"That's another reason why we're so close to Mr. Isaacs,"

Gabriel explained. "Every one of us understands how important it is to grow up in a loving Christian home. When we were young, many more orphans were placed with families than today. Things are different now. The asylums have dwindled, and placements are made through government agencies closer to home. The society now works locally to put children in foster homes. I don't know how much longer it will stay open."

"I read about some of the controversy, but I can't believe there aren't as many orphans now. The war had to leave many fatherless, and then the influenza epidemic took even more. Though Pearlman doesn't have any orphans, the cities must."

Gabriel hesitated and glanced at Mariah before proceeding. "Many of the children placed out in the last century weren't orphans. They were abandoned by parents who couldn't afford to raise them."

"It was heartbreaking," said Mariah. "Our brother Charlie ran away from his drunken father after being beaten nearly to death. Rudy was left at the asylum by parents who couldn't speak English and therefore couldn't get a good enough job to support their ten children. Only Lloyd is a real orphan. His parents died in a train wreck."

Felicity saw why this placement meant so much to Gabriel. "We'll find the children good homes."

Gabriel forced a smile. "I know we will."

The responsibility could crush a person, but these children needed her. She would not let them down.

Mariah began repacking the basket. "I'd better get this leftover chicken into the icebox."

"And I'd better escort Felicity home," said Gabriel. "Her father will want a report on the committee meeting."

Felicity handed her plate to Mariah. "Are you sure you don't need help?"

Mariah waved her off. "You two go. I can handle this in one minute."

She was good to her word, packing the basket in record time. After a wave goodbye, Felicity found herself alone with Gabriel. That peculiar hum between them returned, like a taut violin string.

He held out an arm. "Shall we walk through the park?"

She could think of nothing finer. The summer air was fragrant with the smells of mown grass, peonies, sweet alyssum, roses and a thousand growing things. The sky spread out in a quilt of solid blue, unmarred by a single cloud.

"Have you thought about my idea?" Gabriel asked as they strolled in the shade along the river. "You'd be a wonderful veterinarian."

Morning glories had twined through the bushes, raising their vibrant trumpets to the afternoon sun. Their cheerful blooms seemed to suggest anything was possible, but Felicity wasn't sure that's what she wanted to do. Gabriel had heard God's call. She hadn't.

"I don't know. It's not an occupation open to women." She matched her step to his, ivory pump aligned with brown shoe.

"Not many women have chosen that path, but it is possible. I did a little checking and found a Dr. Florence Kimball graduated from Cornell in 1910 and opened a small-animal hospital in Massachusetts."

Felicity sighed. Even if his facts were correct, that wasn't the problem. Mother wanted her to go to art school and marry well. While Felicity was with Gabriel and Mariah, she forgot all that, but now, heading home, she had to face it.

"It's not possible for me," she whispered.

"What do you mean?"

She didn't quite know how to put it. "You were able to

choose your profession, even if your parents disagreed. That's not the case for me. My parents would never send me to veterinary college, and I have no money of my own." She shrugged. "It doesn't matter. I don't know what I'm supposed to do with my life anyway."

They walked in silence until the river path ended. The stream bubbled along below an overlook. Men fished there often, but today the spot was empty. They stood side by side watching the river. Then she felt his hand brush hers, politely inquiring. She reached for him, and he clasped her hand.

"You'll know," he said. "God always answers prayer."

"I hope it's soon, or Mother will send me to the National Academy."

"There are worse places to go."

She sighed. "There are better."

She felt a tremor run through him. "Are you all right?"

"Hush." He held a finger to her lips. "Do you hear it?"

She listened. "Do you mean the birds?"

He shook his head. "No, deeper."

She listened harder. The rustle of leaves, the burble of the river, the sigh of the wind. The beating of her heart.

He placed her hand over his heart, and she could feel it, too, the beating that was getting more impatient. She looked into his eyes, not up like Robert's but at her height.

"What do you see?" he whispered.

Caring and compassion. He liked her. The realization took away her breath. He liked *her,* Felicity Kensington, not her money or social status but who she really was. She saw it in the way he held her, in the way he looked at her, in her reflection in his eyes.

This time, the tremor came from deep inside her. She shivered. He wrapped his arms around her. Sunlight sparkled off the flowing river, but it could not blind her more than his affection.

"I—"

He pressed a finger to her lips then let it slide under her chin as he leaned closer. That wild sensation shot from her head clear through to her feet.

"You are so beautiful." His voice had roughened and lowered as his thumb stroked her jawline.

Don't stop. Don't stop. Every fiber of her being begged him not to stop. His breath joined hers. Sunlight crowned him with a halo of gold. She closed her eyes, and his lips found hers, gentle as a leaf falling to the ground. He touched once and waited, so close she could feel his breath. This wasn't like Robert's demanding kiss. Gabriel's was tender and considerate.

She leaned forward and placed her lips on his. Without hesitation, he truly kissed her, the way a man ought to kiss a woman, showing her she meant everything to him. She could drown in his arms and never feel a thing.

"Pastor Meeks!" Mrs. Grattan's rebuke sent Felicity flying.

A flustered Gabriel adjusted his hat. "Mrs. Grattan. I didn't realize you were here."

Judging by the redness of her face, she'd hurried to catch up to them. She glared at Felicity. "Ms. Kensington. I should have known you'd be here."

The words turned Felicity's joy to ice.

Gabriel stepped between her and Mrs. Grattan. "Whatever you have to say to me can be said in front of Felicity."

"Very well, Pastor. Have it your way, but you need to realize who's a friend and who's an enemy. I just came from an emergency meeting of the Church Council."

Gabriel visibly reeled. "Emergency meeting? Where? There wasn't a council meeting at the church."

"We met at my house," Mrs. Grattan sniffed.

"But I wasn't there," Gabriel said. "I wasn't even informed."

"They can't do that." Felicity edged forward.

"They can when it's about the pastor." Mrs. Grattan nodded firmly. "But I want you to know that Dermott Shea and I stood our ground."

"Stood your ground against what?" Gabriel said.

"Against Eugenia Kensington getting you removed, that's what."

This time Felicity reeled. Mother had tried to remove Gabriel from the church? Why?

"Then…?" Gabriel was struggling with this as much as she was.

"Oh, you're safe for now. The vote was two for removal and three against."

Felicity mentally counted the votes. Glenn Evans and Ralph Neidecker would have introduced and pressed for acceptance of Mother's resolution since their wives were her cronies. That meant Daddy had voted to keep Gabriel.

Mrs. Grattan looked straight at her. "Just remember, Pastor, who your enemies are."

Gabriel had intended to ask Kensington's permission to court Felicity, but Mrs. Grattan's news sent that plan spinning away. Eugenia Kensington wanted him fired. He'd never get approval to court her daughter.

He stewed the rest of the day. Felicity confirmed that her mother might want him removed, but she couldn't or wouldn't say why. Surely this couldn't be over that silly stained glass window.

When Mariah asked him why he was skulking about the parsonage all evening, he took a walk. The woods and the river would calm him. If he had a fishing pole, he'd toss in a line. That had always calmed his thoughts when he was growing up.

He idly picked up a fallen branch and broke off the side shoots to make a walking stick. The park was quiet at this hour when sultry dusk slipped into cool darkness. If any lovers graced the pavilion, they kept their talk to a whisper. Gabriel walked toward the river, to the place where he'd kissed Felicity.

Was that it? Had Felicity's mother noticed the feelings he had for her? Is that why she tried to remove him? He ran a hand through his hair, tugging against the unseen forces working around him.

The three-quarter moon had moved behind a thick cloud, leaving the woods dark, but Gabriel knew the way by heart now, his steps sure on the leaf-cushioned path.

When the initial threat of removal from the pastorate had evaporated, Gabriel thought he was secure. He'd expected quibbling and even criticism but not an emergency meeting to fire him. What had he done to rile Mrs. Kensington? She didn't like him. That much had been evident, but he attributed that to her designs to match Felicity with Blevins.

He stepped off the path and headed through the woods toward parsonage land. A familiar sound slowed his steps.

Clink. Clink. Rustle. Clink.

Gabriel stopped, peering into the blackness, ears pricked to catch the sound again.

Clink. There it was, to his right. *Clink. Rustle.*

And was that a murmur? If he wasn't mistaken, the sounds were coming from the direction of the old root cellar. The bootleggers had returned to remove their stash of whiskey.

Gabriel crept through the woods, moving from tree to tree one step at a time to ensure he didn't snap a twig. He held his breath as he drew near.

Yes, someone was moving around in the darkness, in fact, more than one person, but Gabriel couldn't spot a cart or pile of liquor cases in the blackness. If only that cloud would pass, the moonlight would reveal everything.

"What's the count?" said a low voice Gabriel didn't recognize.

"Twenty cases," answered a muffled voice that had to come from inside the root cellar. "But what's this? Anyone know what this is doing down here?"

At that moment, the moon finally edged from behind the cloud, and Gabriel saw the tattered satchel being lifted from the cellar.

A man straightened. "Yeah, I do."

Gabriel froze. What was Robert Blevins doing there? He was a prominent engineer from New York. Yet there he was with the bootleggers. Suppose the engineering had just been an excuse to bring him to town? Suppose he wasn't really an engineer but was a key cog in the liquor-smuggling ring? Gabriel had never liked the man. Something was false about him. Furthermore, he'd hurt Felicity. Gabriel should have wrung the man's neck when he had the chance.

A broad, shorter man stepped in front of Gabriel, blocking his view of the criminal. In the moonlight, Gabriel could see a rifle slung across the man's back, a rifle that looked all too familiar. The man inspected the satchel and then tossed it back into the cellar. "We've been found out, boys. Game's over."

Gabriel's stomach knotted tighter than a trolley screeching to a halt. He recognized that voice—Branford Kensington, Felicity's father. His suspicions had just been confirmed, but what was he going to do about it?

The cellar door closed with a thud. The men were moving off toward town, leaving the liquor behind. In moments, they'd be gone, but what could he, a single unarmed man, do to stop them? Kensington would shoot him on the spot. The man was a crack shot. He'd downed African game. He'd shoot first and call it a hunting accident afterward. No, Gabriel needed help before he acted.

He pressed his back to the tree, careful not to make a sound. Only after the woods returned to their usual quiet did he start for home.

Last time they'd moved the liquor into town during a new moon. If they followed the same pattern, the next opportunity would come in a week and a half. Between now and then, he needed to come up with a plan to trap the bootleggers and prove to the sheriff that trouble was afoot in Pearlman.

Then he'd have to figure out a way to tell Felicity her father was a criminal.

Chapter Twelve

A week later, after the distribution had been fully advertised, the committee was ready to take applications. Felicity waited in the front pew while Daddy showed Hendrick Simmons and Gabriel where to set the massive oak table. After several misplacements, Daddy settled on a spot directly before the altar. From there, the committee could oversee everyone.

Hendrick placed three chairs behind the table, looking up after each one as if searching for someone in the gathering crowd. Gabriel ushered applicants into the pews, managing to calm nerves and lighten spirits at the same time. He was everything Felicity could want in a man. The sweetness of his kiss lingered even now. She closed her eyes and imagined exchanging vows. He'd slide the wedding band on her finger and seal their bond with a kiss.

"Let's sit here," said Anna Simmons.

The voice jerked Felicity from her dream. Anna and her mother had settled directly across the aisle from her. Anna Simmons wore her Sunday best and had swept up her hair and secured it with a satin ribbon. Felicity worried the clasp of her handbag. What if Gabriel's kiss had been in haste? What if he really liked Anna?

"Let's get this show underway," Daddy bellowed and waved Felicity forward.

She dragged her attention back to business and ascended the steps to the table. Turning, she saw that half the town had gathered in the sanctuary. She had no idea so many people would want to help the children. Surely, they couldn't all be applicants.

Gabriel pulled out the center chair for her, but Daddy directed her to the right and took the middle seat for himself. Felicity silently apologized, but Gabriel didn't nod that he understood.

After the blessing, Daddy pushed a stack of forms and pencils toward her. "Hand each applicant one form and one pencil. Make sure you number the forms. The pastor and I'll handle the tough stuff."

"I can handle difficult questions," she insisted, but Daddy was talking to Gabriel and didn't hear her. She could do more than hand out forms. Gabriel believed she could accomplish anything, even veterinary college. She tapped her father's shoulder and spoke louder. "I thought each of us was supposed to give a recommendation."

"Eh, what's that?" It took a second for her words to sink in, then, with a paternal smile, he patted her hand. "Don't worry your pretty little head. We'll handle everything."

"But I intend to give my opinion. It's my responsibility."

"Yes, it is," Gabriel interjected. "No applicant will be accepted without the approval of the whole committee."

"There you have it," Daddy said, as if he hadn't just stated the exact opposite. "Straight from the horse's mouth."

With a rap of his knuckles, he called the assembly to order. "People, line up down the center aisle, husband and wife together. If you're here on your own, you can sign for your spouse, but we'll need to see both of you at the distribution."

After a period of loud shuffling and chatter, Daddy rapped on the table again. "Quiet down, people. Time's a-wasting, and we've got a lot of business to get through. Come forward one family at a time and pick up your application from my Felicity. Any questions go to Pastor Meeks or me. When you've filled out the application, give it to the pastor for verification. We'll announce our decision Thursday morning."

"When do the orphans arrive?" asked Mrs. Grattan, who'd managed to be first in line.

Mrs. Grattan wanted a child? Why? They already had four daughters and a son. Mr. Grattan's dairy might need extra labor, but the orphans weren't hired hands. They were to be loved and raised as family members.

"They arrive on the Wednesday afternoon train," Gabriel said calmly. "You may meet them here at four-thirty. After the children leave, the applicants will have an opportunity to indicate their preference."

In a few short days, five lives would change forever. Felicity assessed the applicants in line, judging who would make good parents. For each, she asked if she would like to live with the family. Many failed the most basic criteria. Why, Cora Williams wasn't even married. What could she know about children?

For the next hour, Felicity handed out application forms and explained what was needed. She didn't have time to think about Gabriel or the kiss or a future with him when faced with the more pressing business of finding good homes for the children.

Of course, Blake and Beatrice would be wonderful parents, but they didn't apply. The Sheas would be good but stern parents, and Mrs. Simmons was such a dear soul, but the Simmonses lacked income. Others had known deficiencies like a tendency toward drink or violence. Some let their own children run ragged at all hours of the night. Her hope of finding all five children a good home wore thin by the time the line ended.

When the applicants returned their completed forms, Daddy chatted with them while Gabriel verified that every item was filled in. She handed out the sheet of paper listing the terms of placement and answered questions about the foster parents' duties, but her heart ached for the poor children. She could recommend a couple homes but not five. What would happen to those not placed?

Between inquiries, she watched Gabriel with each set of parents. They'd approach nervous or fearful, and before long, they'd be smiling and confident. He had a way with people, the perfect pastor.

Someone approached her, and she blindly held out the terms of placement, unwilling to draw her attention from Gabriel.

"I don't want them rules. I wanna apply."

Felicity gasped. Before her stood Mr. Coughlin, rough and unshaven. She fought a wave of revulsion. Mr. Coughlin with a helpless child? Never. She struggled to find the right words to dismiss him. "I'm sorry," she said with her mother's stern tone, "we're no longer taking applications."

His eyes narrowed. "You saying I cain't apply?"

"That's precisely what I'm saying."

"You cain't deny me my rights as a law-abiding citizen."

Felicity didn't have a chance to answer. Daddy snagged an application from her stack and handed it to Coughlin. "Here you go, Einer."

Felicity stared at her father and then looked to Gabriel, who was too busy talking to Mrs. Simmons to notice her plea for help. "I thought the application phase was over."

"Hand him a pencil, Felicity," Daddy warned.

"But, Daddy—"

"A pencil." That tone meant her father would tolerate no arguments.

But why would Daddy support Einer Coughlin? The man was abusive. His wife had died suddenly, and his son had run away. Everyone knew he was trouble. He couldn't be given one of those poor orphans. Her stomach twisted and snapped like a flag in the wind.

She tried to catch Gabriel's attention, but he was busy verifying an application. Coughlin sat in the front pew and began filling out the form. Somehow this injustice had to be stopped.

"Daddy, it's not right."

"Everyone may apply, little one," Daddy said.

"Even horrible parents?" she snapped, cheeks ablaze with fury. Honestly, when her father acted so unconscionably, she didn't know how she could be related to him.

"Felicity," he growled, "be charitable."

Charity was all well and good, but precious lives rested in her hands. She glanced again at the stack of applications Gabriel had taken. There must be twenty-five or more—and only five children. The odds of Coughlin getting a child were slim. With her disapproval, those odds dropped to zero. Gabriel said the whole committee must approve an applicant. Well, she'd refuse, and that would be the end of Mr. Coughlin's application.

After the last application had been handed in, including Mr. Coughlin's, Daddy rapped on the table again, hushing the remaining crowd. "That's it, people. See you here Wednesday, four-thirty sharp."

Once the crowds left, Felicity, Gabriel and Daddy reviewed the applications. Seven were eliminated right away by mutual agreement. Gabriel laid the remaining twenty-one applications on the table in front of them, one of them Coughlin's. Daddy refused to reject it.

Felicity chafed to remove the Grattans and Mr. Coughlin from consideration, and she hoped Gabriel felt the same way.

"We are looking for good Christian homes," Gabriel reiterated, probably for Daddy's sake, "preferably those who have had prior experience with children or who still have children at home. Consider the way they raised their children, the education and compassion they've shown them."

"And two parents," Felicity added. "The children deserve a home with both a mother and a father."

"No one's denying that, little one," Daddy said, "but a good home with one parent is better than no home at all. I say we consider all options."

Felicity fumed. Why was he standing up for that rotten man? "I'm sure Gabriel—er, the pastor—agrees with me." She shot him a hopeful glance.

"Two parents are ideal."

She'd won. It was two against one. Mr. Coughlin was out. She removed his application from the twenty-one still under consideration. "That rules out Mr. Coughlin."

Daddy pulled the application from her hand. "Not so fast. Coughlin has had a hard go of it. He could use help on his farm."

"Help?" She choked. "We're not giving out help. This is about raising a child properly, about love and a good home. I don't think—"

He cut her off. "Don't think." He patted her hand. "Let us handle everything."

Felicity was so angry she couldn't spit out a single word. Daddy blurted out insensitive comments all the time, but she was no fool. She had a fully functioning mind.

Daddy toyed with his gold watch fob, oblivious to her fury. "In some cases, we need to be lenient. Einer Coughlin deserves our compassion after losing his wife so tragically and having his son run off." He leaned toward Gabriel. "Typhoid fever. Drove the poor woman mad. Then his son left for California." He shook his head. "The poor man's gone through a lot and deserves a second chance. Don't you agree, Pastor?"

"T-t-t—" Felicity spluttered, unable to get that single word past her rage. Typhoid? Cora Williams said Maddy Coughlin took strychnine. In Felicity's opinion, her husband drove her to it. Rumor had it the man beat her. "That's not what I heard."

But Daddy talked right over her. "Every man deserves a second chance."

"Not with a precious child," she cried, but he'd turned a deaf ear to her. What was Daddy thinking? She caught Gabriel's attention and mouthed her plea for help.

"You've been preaching on forgiveness, Pastor," Daddy continued, "on wiping the slate clean. Well, here we have a man who, thanks to us, has a second chance at a family. I say we give him that chance. Agreed?"

Felicity held her breath. If Gabriel were the man she knew him to be, he'd say no.

Gabriel shifted in his chair. Why was Kensington defending Coughlin? The two seemingly had no connection, yet Kensington was ready to break every rule to place a child with the man. It made no sense. Unless...what if the smugglers were using Coughlin's land? Suppose Coughlin knew about Kensington's role and was blackmailing him to get a child. Gabriel hated to think Kensington was so hardhearted that he'd place his own welfare above that of an orphan, but evil could worm deep into a man's soul.

"Well?" Kensington prodded.

Gabriel looked to Felicity. Denying Coughlin his due would mean the secret of Kensington's involvement with the bootlegging ring would come out. Felicity would be crushed. The moment he'd been dreading had arrived.

Kensington growled, "You have a problem deciding, son?"

Gabriel cleared his throat. "Two parents are preferred."

Felicity beamed at him, and his heart ached.

Kensington ratcheted up the pressure. "Let's not exclude a deserving man based on circumstances beyond his control. I'm sure we all know widows or widowers who did a fine job raising children. Why look at Mrs. Simmons. She raised a son and daughter after her husband died, and we haven't eliminated her from consideration."

"True." Gabriel couldn't refute that. The Simmonses were amongst the kindest people in Pearlman.

"But Mr. Coughlin is hardly Mrs. Simmons," Felicity insisted. "She is kind and respected. He is shiftless and cruel. I knew Benjamin. We can't send an innocent child to live with Mr. Coughlin. We can't." She blinked rapidly, and her voice rasped with emotion.

Gabriel had never heard such passion from her. She would fight for those children with every ounce of strength. He hadn't given her enough credit. Mariah was right. Felicity did belong on the committee, and she'd just made his decision much easier.

"I'm sorry, Mr. Kensington. I must stand for what is right for the children." He placed Coughlin's application on the rejection pile. "Mr. Coughlin simply doesn't meet the basic requirements of the program."

Kensington leaned back, his jaw tight and his gaze narrow. "That's your final decision?"

Gabriel nodded.

Kensington worked his jaw. "I'm disappointed, son. I thought you were a man who practiced what he preached. Apparently I was wrong. Unless you're willing to change your mind." His finger twitched like it was on the trigger of a gun.

Gabriel saw his career fall dead to the ground. Mrs. Grattan said Kensington voted to retain him. The next vote would come out differently, and he'd be gone, his ministry and his hope of a life with Felicity in ruins—all for doing what was right.

He could change his mind and accept Kensington's offer. He could sell his soul for the chance to spend a lifetime with the woman who dominated his thoughts and dreams. Kensington expected him to capitulate, but Gabriel Meeks was not in the soul-selling business.

He looked to heaven for assurance and saw the plate glass window, the one Mrs. Kensington planned to replace. Wrong was wrong. That first day, he'd told Kensington that he answered only to God. Well, nothing had changed.

"My decision stands." Gabriel wrote REJECTED across the front of Coughlin's application, and Felicity clapped with joy.

Little did she realize what he'd just signed away.

"What do you mean you gave up your ministry?" Mariah stopped stirring the stew and fixed her attention entirely on Gabriel.

He slumped into the nearest kitchen chair, exhausted. "It's over, sis."

"Why?" Mariah returned to the stewpot. "I don't understand how rejecting Mr. Coughlin's application warrants firing you. Any decent person can see the man's not fit to raise a child. How on earth can that lead to removal?"

Gabriel groaned and buried his head in his hands. "It's tough to explain."

"Try."

Thoughts and memories whirled through Gabriel's mind,

not the least of which was the kiss. In that moment, he knew Felicity was meant for him. She fit so perfectly, as if molded from the same bit of clay. He'd intended to ask Kensington for permission to see her. Gabriel laughed harshly at the lost opportunity.

Mariah stared. "I don't see what's humorous about this."

He rubbed his mouth, but it didn't remove the bitter taste. "I was going to ask permission to court Felicity."

"Oh, Gabe, that's wonderful."

Count on Mariah to gravitate to the positive and ignore the problem. "It's impossible."

She blinked, spoon in midair. "I don't understand. Even if you did lose the pastorate here, Felicity would go anywhere with you."

"That's not the point." He tore at his hair.

"Then what is the point, because quite honestly you're not making any sense?"

"Her father would never give permission."

"Because you rejected Mr. Coughlin's application." She laughed and returned to the stew. "Don't you think you're taking this to extremes? I'm sure Mr. Kensington is a reasonable man and in time will see that you and Felicity are right for each other. Besides, he loves his daughter. You've told me so a dozen times. Even if he is upset now, she'll eventually win him over. You'll see. Everything works for the best for those who love the Lord."

Gabriel groaned at her unshakeable faith. "We are also to expect persecution and suffering for His name's sake."

"My, aren't we gloomy tonight."

"It's not gloom. It's fact." His voice broke. The chain of events had been set in motion. Once Coughlin learned he wasn't approved, he'd expose Kensington's part in the bootlegging. Felicity was smart enough to piece together the rest. She'd hate him. "It's no use, Mariah. I've lost her."

His sister sat beside him. "What aren't you telling me?"

Gabriel took a deep breath. He couldn't hold it in any longer, and he trusted Mariah. "Something illegal is going on in this town." And then he explained it all. He detailed how he'd smelled whiskey on Blevins, the sounds in the alley and that Slinky had fallen into a root cellar full of bootlegged liquor.

Mariah grew more worried with every revelation. "You have to tell the sheriff."

"I did. He refused to act."

"But why?"

Gabriel had asked himself that question many times. That was why he hadn't told Sheriff Ilsley about Blevins and Kensington canting liquor at the root cellar. He knew only one reason why Ilsley wouldn't act. "Perhaps he's in on it."

"I can't believe that. Sheriff Ilsley is respected throughout Pearlman for his honesty and fairness."

"Even honest men can be turned by greed, especially when their superiors are." He bitterly thought of Kensington. There was no other explanation. Though the man owned half the town, it wasn't enough. Perhaps he'd lost money recently. Perhaps runs on the bank had left him strapped, and he had to turn to illegal activities for funds.

"What superiors?" Mariah asked. When he didn't answer, understanding dawned in her hazel eyes. "Do you mean, Felicity's father?"

He nodded miserably.

"Are you certain?"

He wished he wasn't. "I saw him at the root cellar with Blevins counting their stores of whiskey."

"Oh, Gabe." She hugged him, but it didn't do much to relieve the pain. "What are you going to do?"

He shook his head. "I don't know. I just don't know."

Chapter Thirteen

~❧~

Felicity arrived late at the train station Wednesday afternoon thanks to Mother, who pestered her about every little thing until Felicity finally walked out in midprotest. Judging by the crowds on the platform, everyone else in town was already there. So was the train, its black locomotive grayed by summer dust. The whistle screeched with a cloud of white steam, and the smallest children covered their ears.

The crowd hummed with the anxious excitement of bees on a hive. She slid between Mrs. Evans and Mr. Hammond, who barely gave an inch. She then skirted around the Sheas. The oppressive heat stuck to her like spun candy.

"Excuse me," she called out repeatedly. "Committee member coming through."

Most people gave her a little room, but not everyone did. Her hat got knocked askew, and more than one elbow accidentally caught her in the ribs.

At last, intact though slightly disheveled, she stood at the edge of the platform. Only a few feet separated her from the wall of the locomotive. By leaning forward over the abyss, she could see down the length of the train. To her dismay, the passengers were disembarking fifty feet away, and scores of people jammed the platform between her and there. Grown men and women jostled and craned to get a look, but Felicity didn't see the children yet.

When the conductor appeared on the metal train car steps, the crowd surged behind Felicity, nearly pushing her off the platform.

"There they are." The shout rang out, and the crowd pressed toward the passenger car, taking Felicity along with them.

She spotted the little faces in the windows, peering anxiously at the crowd below. One moment they were visible; the next they disappeared.

"They're coming," a man shouted.

Again the murmur rose, and Felicity feared the people would crush the poor children the moment they debarked.

"Step back, everyone," Gabriel urged from the train car's bottom step. He motioned the people to move, and they obediently took one step back. "Let's give the children some room." They moved back a few more inches, but not for long. As soon as he turned to the conductor, they pressed forward again.

"They're coming," someone shouted, and the pushing and shoving resumed.

"People," Daddy bellowed, "let's give the pastor here some room."

That not only stopped the pressing but for precious minutes quieted the crowd. Though Felicity was still miffed at her father for supporting Mr. Coughlin, she was glad he'd make sure the crowds didn't squash the children.

Daddy held up a hand. "Now listen up to the pastor."

Gabriel had to shout. "There will be a reception at the church at four-thirty. No one may talk to the children before then. Sheriff Ilsley and his deputies are here to ensure that, so you might as well go home."

The sheriff hopped onto the bottom step of the train car.

"Reverend Meeks is right. Not one child will get off this train until every one of you clears back."

Grumbling, the crowd backed off, all, that is, but one man. Mr. Coughlin stood alone with unfettered access to the train. He could easily reach the children by going through the unguarded end of the car.

"Stop him," Felicity cried, but no one listened. Neither could she get past the people that blocked her way. She waved at Gabriel, but he didn't see her. Daddy was chatting with the sheriff off to the side. They didn't see Coughlin.

"Let me through," she begged Mrs. Grattan, whose heavy bulk blocked her way.

Mrs. Grattan planted her hands on her hips. "Felicity Kensington, you have no more right to this spot than I do."

"But you don't understand."

"Oh, I understand all right. You think you're better than everyone else. Well, we're all equal under God and the Constitution." With a huff, she turned away.

Felicity couldn't see over or past her, nor could she get around her. She was trapped.

Mariah appeared for a moment but soon disappeared as the crowd moved forward with an "ahhh." The first of the children appeared in the doorway. Perhaps five or six, the young girl's golden curls and wide eyes ensured she'd be snapped up by someone. She hugged a rag doll and sucked her thumb.

"Isn't she darling?" cooed Mrs. Fox.

Why wasn't the sheriff waiting until everyone left? Bringing out the children now only made the crowd press close again.

Two boys around eight years of age climbed off the train. One, a sparkplug bursting with energy, waved to the crowd, eliciting laughter. The other, bronze-skinned and with a dark mop of curls, kept his gaze firmly on the ground.

The fourth child appeared, an older boy around eleven or twelve, thin and pale and terrified. Felicity's heart went out to him. The poor boy reminded her of Slinky when Coughlin was leading him to slaughter.

Abandoning all decorum, Felicity shoved past Mrs. Grattan. From there, she saw Coughlin step up to the train. The last boy had appeared on the step by then, beanpole tall and wary, his trousers several inches too short. Felicity looked around for help, but Gabriel was nowhere to be seen.

Coughlin mounted the first step. "Show me yer muscle, boy."

The lad, perhaps fourteen or fifteen, stood frozen in place until the black-suited male agent gently pushed him forward.

Coughlin squeezed the boy's biceps as Felicity watched in horror. "Mighty thin, but he'll do. I'll take this 'un."

"No," she cried. Someone had to stop this.

The boy looked ready to punch Coughlin, and though part of her wished he would, the boy was no match for the farmer. Coughlin would pummel the child into a bruised heap.

"Stop him." Felicity struggled to get to the boy, but no one let her through. If anything, the crowd was more intent than ever on the drama unfolding before them. "Please, someone."

Thankfully Gabriel leaped onto the train steps and wedged himself between Coughlin and the boy. "I'm sorry, Mr. Coughlin. The process doesn't work that way. After this afternoon's meeting at the church, you and the other applicants will have an opportunity to indicate a preference. Then the committee will meet and makes its decision. The children will be united with their foster parents ten o'clock tomorrow morning at the church."

Coughlin reluctantly backed away, and Gabriel shuttled the boy to Mariah, who was gathering all the children under the protection of the sheriff and his deputy.

The terror hammering inside Felicity eased. The children were safe now. Nothing bad could happen to them.

Yet.

Once the children were safely delivered from the turmoil of the train station into the sanctuary of Terchie's boarding-house, Gabriel could finally relax. He hadn't expected the crush of curiosity—and neither had the children. It took all Mariah's skill to calm them down. Naps were out of the question and so was eating in the dining room, where curi-ous townspeople peeked through the windows. After draw-ing the drapes, Terchie brought the paczki and milk upstairs.

The boardinghouse smelled of wax, borax and cleanser—good, honest clean. Gabriel drew in a lungful. This is why he came to Pearlman, not for the trivial sniping and prejudices. Over and over this afternoon he heard people, some mem-bers of his own congregation, weigh the merits of one child over the other—too thin, too frail, too shy, too fearful, skin too dark. He'd heard enough to make him wish he'd never agreed to this project.

"They're not behaving like Christians," he complained to Mariah when she returned. He poured her a cup of tea.

His sister blew on the piping-hot liquid to cool it. "They're behaving like people, good and bad."

Gabriel rubbed his temples. "I wish it was over. Can you believe Mr. Coughlin?"

Mariah smiled slightly. "He didn't understand the process is all."

Gabriel raised his eyes. "I never thought you'd take his side."

"Did I say I was taking his side?" She took a sip of tea. "Did you see Felicity?"

Gabriel hated to admit he'd been scanning the crowd for her the entire time. When she appeared, frantic and hat askew, he'd nearly abandoned his post to go to her. "I had responsibilities."

Mariah lifted her eyebrows. "I only asked if you saw her."

"I did." Gabriel sank into the irrational sulkiness that had dogged him since yesterday. He told himself it had to do with the disaster that would erupt when Coughlin learned he wasn't getting an orphan, but in reality, it was all about Felicity. He wanted to protect her from the pain of learning her beloved father was a criminal, and he wanted to hide his role in that revelation.

"Mmm," murmured Mariah. "Too bad there wasn't time to talk. Perhaps later."

"I doubt it," he growled.

Mariah leveled her cool gaze at him over the rim of the teacup. "Gabriel John, two people in love must talk openly and honestly. It's the foundation of any relationship. Don't make her wonder why you're avoiding her."

He squirmed in his seat. Mariah could be just like a mother sometimes. "Some things are best left unsaid."

"You have to tell her what you know about the bootlegging."

"What's this, Pastor?" Sheriff Ilsley, a tall, lean man with the sinewy muscles of a cowboy and the crooked nose of a boxer, sauntered into the room with a cup of coffee. His crisp uniform hadn't wilted in the heat, though the dust on the trousers and shadows under the arms betrayed a tough day's work. "Have you heard something more?"

Gabriel shot his sister a look that could send a grown man to his knees. It had no effect on her.

"Nothing new," he mumbled. This was neither the time nor the place to tell Ilsley that he'd seen Kensington and Blevins at the root cellar. He still wasn't certain the man wanted the bootleggers caught. "Quite a mess at the train station, wasn't it?"

"Just what I expected," the sheriff drawled. "A circus. Like I said, you shouldn't have told people when the children were coming in."

"Maybe you're right." Even a minister had to swallow his words sometimes.

"That church meeting of yours'll be even worse."

"In a house of God?" He couldn't believe that. "Surely people will behave in a church."

"Don't count on it, Pastor. These folks don't see much new around here. It's a curiosity. You can't blame 'em for wanting to take it all in."

Gabriel groaned. He did not want to go through that scene again. "Perhaps we should cancel the reception."

Mariah clucked softly. "You know you can't do that, Gabe."

"The lady's right. People are expecting a show."

"It's not a show," Gabriel protested. "This is serious."

The sheriff was unfazed. "Of course it is. I'm not saying it's not. No one here'll step out of line, not while I'm around." The sheriff tossed down the rest of his coffee. "You can count on me to make sure everything's on the up and up."

On the up and up. The words convicted Gabriel. He hadn't been forthright with the sheriff, a man who had acted with integrity today. Mariah jerked her head toward the man. *Tell him.* Gabriel didn't need to hear the words to know what she was saying and that she was right.

He swallowed, but his throat had narrowed. Coward. He had to speak up. "I might have seen something the other day."

Ilsley fixed his steel-gray eyes on him. "Seen what?"

"You said to tell you if I saw or heard anything else suspicious concerning the bootlegging."

The sheriff propped one foot on a wooden chair, which creaked under his weight. "Fire ahead, Pastor."

He gulped more tea and began slowly, "It happened near the river, behind the parsonage." And then Gabriel told the sheriff everything he'd seen that night at the root cellar—everything except who he'd seen there.

The sheriff tapped his boot idly. "Was it moonshine?"

"One of them said whiskey."

"We know alcohol's getting into town, but we don't know how. Did you recognize anyone?"

Gabriel sucked in his breath, but all he could see was Felicity's face. "It was dark and difficult to see. Clouds blanketed the moon. From what I've seen, they choose moonless nights."

"Hmm, it's a new moon tomorrow." Ilsley's tone suggested what Gabriel had already speculated.

"They might move the liquor then, and we could catch them in the act."

The sheriff stood. "We could, but you said that one of 'em said they'd been found out. Chances are they won't use the same location again."

Gabriel felt a rush of relief. "Then it's too late."

Sheriff Ilsley patted him on the shoulder. "Don't worry, Pastor. We'll stake out the spot. If they're foolish enough to come back there, we'll get them."

Gabriel hoped Kensington had the sense not to return to the root cellar, or Felicity's heart would be smashed along with the bottles of liquor.

Felicity dreaded the reception at the church, but it began better than the mob scene at the train depot. Perhaps being in a church reminded people that they should behave properly. Best of all, Mr. Coughlin wasn't there.

She sat alone in the front pew, while Daddy prowled the side aisle. Mother refused to go and even tried to talk Felicity into staying home with her.

Gabriel led a few hymns from the pulpit, and then he yielded to the male agent, who described the program in detail. Several people stifled yawns. Everyone watched the empty front pew on the opposite side, waiting for the children to arrive.

Why weren't they there yet? Felicity appreciated keeping them from the vultures, but eventually they'd have to appear. She glanced at Gabriel, but he was focused on the speaker.

"And now let's introduce the children," the agent finally said.

Felicity's nerves fluttered.

"Don't be afraid," she whispered as the door opened and the children began to enter. "I'm right here." Indeed, if Mr. Coughlin appeared and dared repeat his stunt from the train station, she'd whisk the boy away in an instant.

The crowd shuffled and murmured softly.

The beanpole boy came first, dressed in the same pair of too-short trousers. He warily scanned the crowd, for Coughlin, no doubt.

"Peter is fourteen," the agent said. "He came to us a year ago after living hand to mouth on the streets for nearly six months. His only living relative, an aunt, had died of dysentery, and he didn't know where to go, so he did the best he could. Peter is a hard worker and would like a family where he can use his hands. He's good at fixing things."

Mrs. Simmons perked up, as well she should, given the family's motor garage business. After Mr. Simmons's death and his partner's retirement last month, only her son Hendrick was left to keep it going. Another hand would doubtless be helpful, but these children weren't laborers. They needed a home.

The thin, towheaded boy came next, dressed in denim trousers and a yellowed white shirt. He looked just as terrified as earlier.

"Matthew is a bright child, though shy. He's short for his twelve years but very strong."

"Why does every child have to be measured in terms of their strength or skill?" Felicity muttered.

"He's pointing out their advantages," whispered Mariah, settling in beside her.

"It cheapens them."

"Perhaps, but the end result is a home."

"Does the end justify the means?" Felicity said. "Why not just have the families meet the children? That's what's supposed to happen."

While they were talking, the agent introduced Nathaniel, the fireplug of a boy who looked ready to box anyone who came near him. Upon cue, he demonstrated his talent on the mouth organ, and the assembly rewarded his effort with a rousing ovation.

"Luciano," the agent said as the last boy was led out.

A low murmur rippled through the sanctuary—foreigner, dirty. The insults circled like flies.

"We call him Luke," the agent continued, "just like the apostle. Yes, his parents came from Italy, but Luke was born right here in the United States."

"That boy ain't Italian," Hermann Grattan grumbled behind her. "He's half darkie."

Felicity stiffened at the racial slur. How dare he say such things? She turned and hissed, "Hush." Of all people. Mr. Grattan came from Germany. He even refused to change his name during the war. He should know better. "Keep your thoughts to yourself."

She hoped the boy didn't hear the murmured epithets, but when his little shoulders drooped, she knew he had. She wanted to hug him close and tell him it would be all right, but would it? She scanned the congregation, looking for someone who would accept Luke, and found no one. Tears burned her lids.

Please, someone help Luke.

That someone turned out to be Gabriel. He walked over to Luke and placed his hands on the boy's shoulders, confirming his worth. Luke looked hopefully at Gabriel, but a single man, even a minister, couldn't take a child. She'd enforced that rule with Coughlin. It had to hold true for Gabriel also.

Last came Grace, the golden-haired girl, now dressed in a ruffled pinafore. She still clutched the rag doll to her chest, though the thumb had come out of her mouth. Her wide blue eyes made the women sigh. At least half the applicants would name her as their first choice.

Next Mariah guided the applicants forward one at a time, so the children wouldn't be overwhelmed. Felicity watched each interaction, trying to match applicant to child. Gabriel stood behind the children like a guardian angel. Though he frequently looked out at the crowd, his gaze never fell on her.

Every couple stopped to meet the little girl, Grace. Mrs. Simmons dropped to her knees to talk. Mrs. Shea kissed the girl's head. Cordelia Butterfield, who'd lost a baby girl last November, wiped away a tear. She would make a good mother, but her husband never cracked a smile. Grace deserved happiness, not a father who couldn't even smile at her. Mrs. Grattan looked the girl over as if checking for lice. Felicity nearly intervened, but Gabriel hastened Mrs. Grattan along, noting the lateness of the hour. Felicity mouthed a relieved thank-you, but again he didn't look at her.

As the line dwindled, Felicity glanced nervously at the remainder of the crowd. Thankfully Coughlin still hadn't appeared. She shuddered to think what he would do to Peter, who stood very straight and very solemn through the entire proceeding. Though the boy put on a tough face, his lip occasionally quivered.

How horrible to stand on display, wondering who would select you or even if anyone would select you. Luke, the bronze-skinned boy, drew little notice from the applicants. Felicity looked at the remaining applicants, hoping someone would approach him. No one did. Like Slinky, he'd been deemed unfit and cast aside. If only she were married, she could take him. He would prosper in the right home, one filled with love and kindness, one like Gabriel's.

As she watched Gabriel move between the children, squatting down to talk to the shorter ones, she knew that no man would make a better father.

Gabriel, Gabriel. She'd teetered on the edge of falling in love for so long, but today cemented her feelings. Somehow she'd convince her parents that he was a good and worthy man. As the last of the applicants met the children, she went to him.

"Thank you, Pastor." The word felt strange on her lips, but not as peculiar as it once had. If their love grew, she might one day be a minister's wife. Never in all her life would she have believed she'd want that, but as she watched him with the children, she knew without a doubt that she did.

"Ms. Kensington," he said stiffly, barely glancing her way.

Ms.? Why was he using such formal language? For a moment, she faltered. What was wrong?

"How may I help?" she asked, eager to smooth over whatever was troubling him.

He avoided her gaze. "We need to get the children back to the boardinghouse."

"Let me lead the way."

"Thank you for your offer, Ms. Kensington, but we have enough help." He began ushering the children toward the door. "The committee will meet in the office in a few minutes."

Was that all? A horrible ache squeezed her chest so tight she could barely breathe.

"Gabriel?" she whispered.

His head jerked, so she knew he heard her, but he continued to herd the children to the side aisle. She followed.

"What's wrong?" Her ears began to ring, and she gulped for air.

As the last of the children walked through the door, he turned to her. Their eyes met, and she saw in his a deep sadness. For a moment, he lingered in the doorway; then, without a word, he left.

The very air seemed to go with him. She clutched the end of the pew and closed her eyes against the gathering tears.

"Felicity, thank goodness I caught you." Mother clamped on to her arm. "Mr. Blevins called on your father this morning. I believe he asked permission to see you."

Felicity's stomach lurched as she pulled herself from the brink of despair. "Who did what?"

"Robert asked permission to call on you. Your father would naturally have said yes." Mother's bloodred lips stretched into a predatory smile. "Our work has paid off."

Felicity stared at the doorway through which Gabriel had vanished. Every time they got close, something drove them apart. Dread rushed in where despair had just dwelt.

"You'll be Mrs. Robert Blevins," Mother crowed.

The words that had so enchanted her weeks before now struck a deadly nerve. She could not marry Robert, not when she loved Gabriel.

"No." The word bubbled up from the deepest recesses of her heart.

"What do you mean? Of course it will happen. If I'm any judge of character, and you know I'm the best, he'll propose by summer's end. Why wouldn't he? You have wealth and beauty. What else could he want? Come along, dearest. He's waiting for you."

"Now?" Everything was whirling out of control.

"Of course now."

"But I have a meeting. The Selection Committee." Felicity pulled her arm from Mother's grasp.

"Oh, that. Your father told me he and Reverend Meeks have already made their decisions. The meeting is just a formality."

Daddy and Gabriel had already decided without her input? Shock turned to dismay. No wonder Gabriel hadn't been able to meet her eyes. No wonder he didn't want her help. They'd gone ahead without her. Her opinion meant nothing.

"But the children," Felicity cried. "What about the children? I'm a member of the committee. My voice needs to be heard."

"Goodness, Felicity. Stop blubbering about a ridiculous little committee. Who cares about orphans when Robert Blevins is waiting?"

Robert Blevins was not her future, no matter what Mother and Daddy wanted. Felicity straightened her shoulders. Those children needed her, and she would not abdicate her responsibility. Daddy and Gabriel *would* listen to her.

Without another look at Mother, she strode to the church office.

Chapter Fourteen

Shadows cloaked the office in darkness, so Felicity pulled open the drapes. The air hung heavy with the scents of typewriter ink and Florabelle's perfume. Sharpened pencils bristled from a cup on the corner of the secretary's desk, buttressed by a Bible and a hymnal that subtly warned borrowers to return all borrowed pencils.

Felicity cracked open the window and breathed in the fresh breeze, ripe with a sunburst of summer flowers.

"Darling." The nasal tenor from behind set her on edge.

"What are you doing here?" She whirled around to see Robert sitting in Gabriel's chair. "You're not the pastor."

The chair creaked as he rose. "Neither are you." He glided to the door and shut it. The latch clicked with deadly finality. "I trust you've heard the news."

Felicity's nerves twisted into knots, and she backed against the window. Nothing bad could happen in a church, could it? Gabriel would soon be here, and Daddy must be nearby.

She crossed her arms. "What do you want?"

The tips of Robert's mustache jerked up. "Is that any way to treat your guy?"

"You're not my *guy*. We've barely seen each other in the past two weeks."

"That's my fault. Too much business, not enough pleasure. Can you forgive me, chickadee?"

"I'm not your chickadee." She looked out the window, afraid he might see the fear in her eyes. A robin hopped across the ground, cocking its head to one side listening for worms. Could she hear danger in Robert's voice? She drew her attention back to the room and jumped when she found him just inches away.

"What do you prefer to be called, darling?" He lifted a finger to her hair, and she recoiled.

"Nothing." She edged toward Florabelle's desk. "I'm not your darling or your chickadee. I'm plain old Ms. Kensington."

"Ms. Kensington? Isn't that a little formal for two people in love?"

"In love? I never told you I loved you."

"But you did. The picnic basket, the little knapsack, asking me to help on the stained glass window. A man would be a fool not to read those signs."

"Those were just kindnesses," she said to cut off the litany of mistakes. "I'm sorry if I misled you, but I never had any feelings for you."

"Now, now, chickadee." He clucked his tongue. "It's too late to play coy."

"I'm not playing coy. I didn't care for you then, and I don't now. Nothing has changed."

"On the contrary, darling. Everything has." Robert lifted her hand to his lips.

She yanked it away. "It's over."

"Yes, darling, the long wait is over." If possible, he drew even closer. "Now that your father—"

"Daddy spoke in haste. He didn't even consult me." She

slipped past him into the only open area, the little spot behind Florabelle's desk.

Robert positioned himself between the desk and the door, blocking her only escape. "Consult you about what?"

"About giving you permission to court me."

Robert laughed. "Permission to court? How quaint and old-fashioned. I suppose you go to church suppers and quilting bees, too."

Felicity flushed. "But Mother said you spoke to Daddy."

"So I did." He edged toward her.

She stepped back and ran into the bookcase. "About the airfield project?"

"Not about the airfield project and not about courtship. This is much, much better. I asked for your hand."

"M-m-my hand?" The room began to spin. "As in marriage?"

"As in engagement," he crowed, reaching an arm around her waist. "Aren't you excited, darling?" He closed his eyes and leaned forward to kiss her.

Felicity abandoned every one of Mother's rules for ladylike behavior. Like a squirrel caught in a room, she frantically looked for escape and without a thought for appearances, crawled over the desk, knocking Florabelle's precious pencils to the floor.

"Where are you going?" Robert cried, spinning about. "Felicity? Darling?"

She slipped and slid on the rolling pencils, but desperation kept her moving forward. She had to get out of the room now—before Robert caught her, before he trapped her, before her life was ruined. Arms flailing to keep her balance, she stumbled across the room and yanked open the door.

There stood Gabriel, his expression grim. "My congratulations."

He'd heard every word.

Her mouth went dry. "I-I-It's—" she stuttered, so desperate to tell him the truth that nothing would come out.

Gabriel nodded stiffly. "You also, Mr. Blevins."

That pompous fool had come up behind her. Beaming, he pumped Gabriel's hand. "I'm the lucky one."

Gabriel smiled wryly. "Yes, you are. Now, if you'll excuse me, I have work to do." He started to leave but then spotted the disarray inside the office. He looked at her with evident concern. "Is everything all right?"

"Couldn't be better," said Robert, squeezing her by the shoulders.

She couldn't stand it any longer, but neither could she explain. The words just couldn't get past the ball of anger and humiliation in her throat. Gabriel must think the worst of her.

Gabriel closed the office door. "I'll take care of this mess later." He frowned at her. "We'll meet in the sanctuary."

The meeting. How could she concentrate for the meeting? Then she remembered what Mother had said. Daddy and Gabriel had already made the decisions. This meeting was just to inform her, to lead her to believe that her opinion counted.

Tears rose as Gabriel walked into the sanctuary. The doors closed softly behind him.

"Alone at last," Robert said. "I thought he'd never leave." He ran a red-hot finger across her ear.

She jerked away. Were all men the same, thinking they could have whatever they wanted? Well she was tired of being pushed around. Her opinion did count for something. In the case of Robert, it counted for everything. Mother and Daddy and Robert could not maneuver her into a marriage she did not want.

The preposterous man tried to wrap his arms around her again, but this time she threw them off.

"Stop it. If you don't, I'll scream, and trust me, Gabriel will come running." She backed away, fists up like a boxer preparing to spar.

"Darling."

"I'm not your darling, your chickadee or any other endearment. I am Felicity Kensington, and I have no intention of marrying you."

Instead of showing distress, the man grinned.

At any other time she would have asked why, but this was too important. "I'm sorry if I led you to think otherwise, but my feelings belong to another. I could not marry you if you were the last man in Pearlman. I'm sorry, but that's the truth."

He wiped his mouth, setting one mustache tip off-kilter. "It's goodbye then."

She nodded, and he left without protest. The door slipped silently closed, and she stood for long minutes in the dim vestibule. How strangely Robert had acted, as if he'd never cared for her at all. She knit her brow, trying to figure it out, but such peculiar behavior defied explanation.

In time, her thoughts returned to duty. Behind the sanctuary doors, Gabriel and Daddy waited for her. After the pain of the last few minutes, they would understand if she excused herself from the meeting, but the children needed her—if she could stand up to Robert, she could speak her mind to Daddy and Gabriel.

She pushed one of the doors halfway open and peered inside. The two men worked closely, their heads almost touching. Daddy was speaking, too low to hear. Whatever he'd asked, Gabriel nodded agreement.

Daddy leaned back with a sigh and extended a hand. "Thank you for seeing this little matter my way."

Gabriel reluctantly shook. "I can't say I completely agree."

Felicity watched in horror. What if Daddy had convinced

Gabriel to give Coughlin a child? She couldn't think of any other part of the process that Gabriel objected to. That had to be it. No wonder they wanted to meet without her.

"I can count on you," Daddy said, "and that's all that matters. Come on up to the big house for dinner, son."

Gabriel shook his head grimly. "I have other plans."

Felicity slowly released the door so it didn't make a sound. She had to do something to stop this injustice, but what? Everyone was working behind her back—even the two men she loved most. Her legs shook as she left the church. Daddy could be hardheaded, but she'd trusted Gabriel. She thought he cared about the children. She thought he understood.

Oh, how wrong she'd been about everyone. She wiped away an angry tear. It was such a foolish plan—find a husband. What good would that do when they only wanted to control things? Marriage was no better than being subjected to Mother's scheming.

If she wanted to save those children, she'd have to do it herself. She didn't quite know how, but God always provided a way.

She'd better find it before ten o'clock tomorrow morning.

Hours of prayer didn't help. Felicity sat on her bed and searched the Bible for direction. How? *Lord, show me.* Never before had she relied so much on God, yet she was just as lost.

Her mind kept wandering back to Gabriel. Why would he agree to send an orphan to Mr. Coughlin? It went against everything she thought he stood for. He'd protected the children. He'd rejected the application. He upheld the rules. He wasn't the type of man who would then send innocent children into danger. Yet she'd heard him agree to Daddy's proposal, and Daddy had talked of nothing else but approving Mr. Coughlin's application.

How wrong she'd been about everyone, but especially Gabriel. She'd kissed him. She'd wanted to make a life with him. Tears burned her eyes. What a fool she'd been.

Now she was the only person who could save the children, and she had no idea how. Frustrated, she set the Bible on her bedside table. A breeze from the open window ruffled the pages. She started to close the book when a passage from John struck her: "In my Father's house are many mansions."

Many mansions. Many homes. Many rooms. That was it. That was the answer she needed. Invigorated, she jumped to her feet and raced down the stairs.

"Felicity? Where are you going?" Mother asked as she rushed by. "It'll be dusk soon. If you're meeting Robert, he should come to the house."

Felicity hadn't quite told her about Robert yet.

"I'll be back before dark," she said as she burst through the door. This couldn't wait. This had to be done now, even if it meant facing Gabriel.

Darkness set in late this time of year. As Felicity hurried down the hill, the sun was just dipping below the treetops, infusing the elms and maples with fiery diamonds of late-day light. Trees cast long shadows across streets and roofs, making the town look sleepy. If she had her way, Pearlman would bustle with new excitement.

She breathed in the humid summer air, ripe with scents of grass and flowers. Gnats gathered in clouds the way they always did in the evening. A month ago, she would have swatted and complained. Today, she strode right through them. What were a few gnats when God had set a purpose in her heart?

A few motorcars chugged back from the Grange Hall. There was Mr. Devlin's old Model T, its doors rusty. There went Lyle Reimer on his daily journey to Lily's, the town's only restaurant. Pearlman wasn't New York City, but it was home.

At the parsonage, she hesitated. The motorcar wasn't there. What if Mariah was gone? A light shone in the front window. She needed to broach her idea to her friend, not Gabriel. If he were the only one home, she'd lose nerve.

For the children.

She hovered on the porch, torn between fear and duty. What if Gabriel answered her knock? She chided herself. If God had sent her, He would find a way. She must simply act.

She knocked. A steady woofing announced that Slinky was home. A minute later, Mariah opened the door.

"Felicity, dear. What brings you here?" Mariah wore a dressing gown, and her hair was damp as if she'd just bathed.

"I'm sorry. I've interrupted you."

"Not at all." Mariah held open the door. "Come in. I hope you don't mind a little mess. I gave Slinky a bath and ended up taking one myself."

Felicity laughed nervously as she slipped indoors. "Slinky has a way of making everyone take part in his baths."

"I heard about that first one." Mariah led her into the kitchen, where Slinky sat with head cocked and white eyebrows lifted, as if to dispute what they'd said about him. "Gabriel loves to tell that story."

"He does?" That warm, wild sensation returned with surprising force. Despite everything that had happened, the way she felt for him didn't die.

Mariah smiled. "But you aren't here to talk about bathing Slinky. Tea?" She poured a cup from the kettle on the stove. "It's cooled a little but still delicious."

Felicity gratefully took the cup. Holding it gave her something to steady her shaking hands. "Your brother isn't here?"

"He took the children around town in the car. He wanted to point out the various landmarks, like the school and the churches and the mercantile, so they'd feel more comfortable in their new hometown. He should be back in a half hour or so. Would you like to wait?"

Felicity gathered her courage. "Actually, I wanted to speak to you."

"Me?" Mariah dropped into a chair, and Felicity took the one beside her. "You sound serious."

Felicity peered into her cup, not sure how to say this. "Something's been bothering me, but I didn't know what to do until tonight. I found the answer in John's gospel."

Mariah took a sip of her tea and set the cup on the table. "What answer is that?"

Even Felicity's fingertips tingled with excitement. The idea had come to her in a flash, but it was brilliant, the solution to everything. "The parsonage would be perfect." Hot blood pounded to her brain, muddling her thoughts.

Mariah wrinkled her brow. "For what?"

She wasn't explaining it very well. "Let me try again. I couldn't help wondering what would happen if one or more of the children aren't chosen tomorrow or if worthy applicants can't be found."

Mariah sat back, legs crossed at the ankle. "They'd return to the asylum in Detroit."

"But think of the disappointment. To be so close to getting a real home, and to have to go back, why it's worse than not coming here at all. Wouldn't it be better if every one of them gets a home?"

"Yes, but you can't force people to take on a child."

"And what if an orphan is given to the wrong family?" Felicity was treading on delicate ground now. She couldn't very well tell Mariah that her brother had agreed to give an orphan to Mr. Coughlin.

"If there are problems, heaven forbid, the child would be removed from the home. What are you trying to tell me? Is one of the children in danger? You are on the Selection Committee. If there's a problem, you need to speak to Gabriel."

That's the one thing she couldn't do. "There's not a problem yet," she admitted, "but there could be."

Mariah sighed. "I know this is difficult, but there's no sense borrowing trouble. Our Lord will see this through, as will the good people of Pearlman."

"Yes, but if there is a problem, maybe there's a better solution than sending them back to the asylum."

"I'm not following you."

"Don't you see? We could create a home for them, a sort of boarding school. All we'd need is a big enough house, a place with lots of bedrooms. Like in John's gospel, where Jesus said his Father's house has many rooms. Why not us?"

"Do you mean here?" Mariah's face dropped. "You want Gabriel and me to take in children?"

"No, no." Felicity rose and paced the room. "That's not it at all. I mean the house itself. It's so large, with lots of bedrooms. It's much too big for a parsonage, but it would make the perfect foster home and school. The children would have a place to call home. Don't you see how perfect it would be?"

Mariah hesitated. "And who would run this?"

That was the difficult part. "I would."

"By yourself? You have no experience with children or teaching."

Felicity's hands shook. "I—I hoped maybe you'd take charge at first, and I would help."

"The way you help with Slinky?" In one sentence, the masculine baritone shredded Felicity's excitement.

"Gabriel," she gasped, emotions bouncing like fireflies in a jar. "Let me explain."

"No." He set his hat on the table, and she saw the worry lines creasing his forehead. "Everything is settled, Ms. Kensington. There is no need for a boarding school."

Ms. Kensington? The last flicker of hope sputtered out. "Then they'll all be taken?" She couldn't bring herself to ask who would get Luke.

"If the applicants agree." He poured himself a cup of tea.

"W-Who?" She steeled herself for the answer.

His look accused her of abandoning her duty. "The best applicants."

He wasn't going to tell her. The only reason to hide the outcome was if he'd agreed to give a child to Coughlin. He couldn't. He just couldn't.

"But what if some still go unclaimed?" she said, frantically trying to think of some way to talk him out of this. "What if the child objects to the match? They do have that right, don't they?"

"Felicity," Mariah warned softly. "It's late."

"Yes, go home to your fiancé," Gabriel snapped.

With a gasp, Felicity realized that's why he was being so cold. He thought she was engaged to Robert.

"There is no fiancé."

For the briefest moment, his eyes met hers. She saw hope there, but then it faded. "Please excuse me. I'm tired, and there's a long day ahead of us tomorrow."

"But—"

He left the room before she could finish her sentence. He'd dismissed her. Though she looked to Mariah for support, she knew her friend could do nothing to sway Gabriel.

It was over. Just like that. Not only had she failed the children, but somehow she'd lost Gabriel, too.

The ache that had begun when Gabriel saw Felicity and Blevins together in his office accelerated with every passing minute. All parties involved had neatly planned that marriage. For a second after she refuted it, he had hope, but then he remembered Kensington's revelation.

Blevins or no Blevins, a life with Felicity would soon be impossible. He'd protested Kensington's plan to send Peter to the Grattans, but then the man told him why he wanted the match. To protect Felicity, Gabriel turned his back on what was right, telling himself that Peter would be all right with the bigoted Hermann Grattan. It would only be for two or three years, and the Grattans had no prejudice against Peter, just Luke. But Felicity wouldn't see it that way. She'd blame him—and rightfully so.

"What happened, Gabe?" Mariah's voice carried a cartload of concern.

Gabriel could not discuss what Kensington had told him about Felicity, even with his sister. "Nothing."

"Nothing? Even I can see something's wrong."

He tried to brush off the question with a wave of the hand. "I need to go to bed. Tomorrow is going to be a long day."

"Bed is not what you need, Gabriel John. Let not the sun go down upon your wrath."

"I'm not angry," Gabriel bristled, "and I don't need scripture quoted to me."

"Apparently you do. Granted Felicity's idea wasn't thought through, but it came from a loving heart. She cares deeply what happens to those children."

"I know." He did know, and that was the problem. What her father told him that evening changed everything.

"She seemed to object to a decision that was made without her. Is that true?"

"I had to," Gabriel growled. "Don't ask me to explain because I can't without betraying a confidence." As much as he wanted to tell Mariah, he couldn't. Only two people could divulge this secret, and neither had seen fit to do so in twenty-some years.

"Oh, Gabe, is something wrong? Is she ill?"

How easy it would be to agree, but he could not mislead

her. "No, she's not ill. It's nothing terrible." If a secret that shattered lives wasn't terrible.

"I see." Mariah took the teacup from his hands. "Then why do you look like death?"

Because he'd agreed to do something that grated against his conscience. Because he could see no way out. Because he'd broken a sacred trust for the sake of a woman.

He lifted weary eyes. "Please don't ask."

She looked at him long and hard. "Do you still love her?"

"Yes," he whispered. And that was the problem.

Chapter Fifteen

By nine-thirty the next morning, the church had filled to capacity. An expectant hum followed Felicity as she made her way toward the committee table, still planted in front of the altar. Everyone watched her, some hopeful and others wary.

"Ms. Kensington." Mrs. Simmons's quiet plea broke Felicity's step. "I know you can't divulge the results, but I want you to know that I've been praying for the best foster parents for each child."

"Me, too," Felicity whispered, feeling a rush of affection for the woman she'd wrongly disdained in the past.

Mrs. Simmons patted her hand. "Then I know it will go well."

Felicity wasn't quite so certain. Gabriel and her father had made other plans, terrible plans. She blinked back tears as she climbed to the table.

Daddy stopped her before she sat down. "Felicity, you don't look well. Perhaps you should go home."

"No, Daddy. I need to do my duty, all of it." She stressed the last three words, but of course he didn't understand what she meant.

"That's my little soldier." He settled her in her chair and then proceeded to direct people who didn't require directing.

A sea of faces spread out before Felicity. From eager applicants to the nervous children, seated along the wall to the left, all looked to her. The oldest boy, Peter, joked with Matthew, but whenever he looked her way, his brow creased.

Gabriel looked older and worn, as if the last ounce of energy had been drained from him. He spoke briefly with each of the children, lingering longer before Luke. The boy never raised his eyes, and Felicity couldn't tell if he understood what Gabriel was telling him.

She quickly turned away when Gabriel took his seat at the other end of the table. The three feet between Gabriel and her might have been a huge chasm. He didn't look at her, and she couldn't bear to look at him.

"People," Daddy yelled.

The crowd gradually quieted after a lot of shushing and admonitions about not talking in church.

Daddy tugged his waistcoat down. "We've reviewed all the applications. Thank you for stepping forward to help out these children. We received twenty-eight applications. That means a good many of you are going to be disappointed. That being said, let's get the suspense over with."

He motioned to the female agent, who led little Grace to stand between the altar rails. In this enormous moment of Grace's young life, she stuck her thumb back in her mouth and no amount of tugging by the agent could dislodge it.

"For this little girl—" Daddy cleared his throat and squinted at sheet of paper in his hand "—we've selected Hugh and Cordelia Butterfield."

Cordelia burst into tears. "Praise God. Oh, thank you, thank you."

Her husband helped her forward, and as Cordelia dropped to her knees before little Grace, the man's lips trembled, and he wiped away a tear. Felicity drew in her breath. She'd been wrong about him. Though solemn and stoic, he cared deeply.

The little girl wrapped her arms around Cordelia, and the woman hugged her tightly, taking into her heart the gift God had sent to replace her dead child. Many a woman, Felicity included, dabbed at her eyes. Gabriel and Daddy had chosen wisely.

Next, the tough little fireplug Nathaniel went to the Millers, who had two boys close in age. The boy instantly fell into chatter with his new brothers. Again it was a success.

The Highbottoms claimed twelve-year-old Matthew, whose shock of fair hair closely matched that of his new mother. Felicity smiled at Matthew's delighted grin. His fear was gone, wiped away by the chance to begin anew with two brothers and two sisters.

Again, Daddy and Gabriel had chosen well, but Mr. Coughlin didn't agree. He stood at the announcement, face beet-red.

"I want that 'un." Coughlin staggered to the front of the church, pointing at poor Matthew.

Daddy stepped between Coughlin and the boy, and Charles Highbottom hurried Matthew down the side aisle.

"Now, Einer." Daddy clapped Coughlin on the back. "Most people didn't get their first choice. More than twenty will go home empty-handed."

"But I'm entitled."

"Every applicant went through the same selection process," Daddy consoled, guiding Mr. Coughlin back to a pew. "Have a seat Einer, and wait it out. We still have two boys left."

Felicity's gut tightened. The only reason Daddy would tell Coughlin to wait was if he and Gabriel had approved the man's application. She looked to Luke and Peter, both terrified. They knew it, too. She tried to catch Gabriel's attention, but he wouldn't look at her. It was true. They were going to condemn one of those poor boys to a life of pain and misery.

"No," she squeaked, but it was barely audible.

"Peter, please come forward," said Daddy.

The male agent reached for Peter's hand, but the boy refused assistance. With a straightening of his shoulders, he walked to the center, directly in front of Mr. Coughlin, and faced his future with resolve.

No, it couldn't be.

"We had a hard time agreeing on the best home for young Peter." Daddy fidgeted, shifting papers around. "We had many fine applications." He glanced at Gabriel, who shook his head.

Felicity hoped that meant he would stop Daddy, but Gabriel didn't speak.

"Stop this," she mouthed, but Gabriel would not look at her.

If he would not act, she must. She rose, but her legs trembled so badly that she sat right back down again. Electricity hummed through the deathly silent room.

Daddy cleared his throat and pushed up his spectacles. The slip of paper in his hand shook. "Hermann and Sophie Grattan."

"What?" Felicity's surprise escaped in a single word. She'd expected to hear Mr. Coughlin's name, but if Peter wasn't going to Coughlin, then… She looked to Luke, who realized the fate that awaited him. He lowered his gaze and shrank against the chair, making himself as small as possible.

"You can't," Felicity gasped. "Gabriel, no."

But he no longer sat at the table. Gabriel met the Grattans before they reached Peter. "Or, if you'd prefer," he said loudly enough for everyone to hear, "you could take Luke. He's younger, and you'd have more years together."

Peter looked to Luke, who hopefully eyed the Grattans. "Luke's a good kid."

Felicity couldn't stand this anymore. How could Gabriel and Daddy put the boys through this? "Stop this. Stop it now."

That drew everyone's attention.

"Felicity," Daddy growled.

Mrs. Grattan seized the opportunity to claim her prize. "We'd love Peter."

"Come along, boy," said Hermann Grattan, taking Peter by the arm. With a final glare at Luke, he added, "We don't want no foreigners."

Felicity had heard enough. The slurs he'd cast at Luke yesterday still rang in her ears. He'd insinuated that the boy's birth somehow made him less than human.

She stood. "He's no more a foreigner than you are, Mr. Grattan. In fact, he's less. You were born in Germany. Luke was born here. He's an American."

"Felicity," Daddy warned, but she couldn't stop now.

"If my opinion had been considered, you wouldn't be allowed to take *any* child into your home. If you can't accept Luke for who he is, you don't deserve any of these precious children." She forced herself between Peter and the Grattans. "Go back to Luke, Peter."

"You have no right." Mrs. Grattan turned bright red, her jowls quivering as her mouth sought sufficient venom.

"I have every right." Felicity drew herself to her full height. "Not only am I on the Selection Committee but I'm a Kensington."

"A Kensington?" Mrs. Grattan screeched, her laughter harsh. "You're no more a Kensington than I am."

A collective gasp came from the crowd, but the loudest of all came from a voice Felicity knew well. Mother. "No-o-o." The strangled cry echoed over the crescendoing hum.

It couldn't be. Felicity looked from Mother to Mrs. Grattan, who'd gone pale as a bleached sheet. "What do you mean?"

Mrs. Grattan hitched her shoulders. "I mean exactly what I said. You can stop pretending you're high and mighty, Felicity Kensington, when you're as much a dirty foreigner as that boy there. You're no Kensington. You're just an orphan from who knows where."

The room swam, as if flooded under several feet of water. Mrs. Grattan's mouth opened and closed like a fish gasping for air. Mother's eyes bugged out, and her lips trembled. Tell Mrs. Grattan she's wrong, Felicity silently pleaded, but Mother said nothing. Neither did Daddy. He just wiped his eyes.

"No," Felicity cried. "Lies, all lies."

Gabriel reached her side. "Felicity." He tried to lead her out of the sanctuary.

She jerked away from him. This couldn't be true. "Daddy?" She reached for the man who'd been an anchor in her life, but he was busy berating Mrs. Grattan.

"Sophie, you broke your promise."

No. Her head split. The room spun.

It couldn't be true, but it was. She wasn't a Kensington.

At that moment, Coughlin figured out how he fit into the puzzle. "I don't want no foreigner." He stabbed a finger at the man Felicity thought was her father. "Whatcha tryin' to pass off on me? Them foreigners ain't good fer nothin' but thievin' and lying."

Gabriel led the unhappy Mr. Coughlin aside while the agents whisked Luke from the sanctuary. Luke. What would happen to Luke? Would he be sent back on the train? Felicity stumbled after him, but Daddy stopped her.

"Let's not make a scene, little one."

She whirled around to see everyone watching her, waiting

to see her collapse, but she wouldn't. She was a Kensington. No she wasn't, but if she wasn't Daddy's daughter, who was she? A foreigner? A street urchin? Is that why Mother ordered her around? It all made sense now—the fine schools and fancy clothes and desperate need to marry her well. Her parents had to make her more than she was and marry her off before the truth came out. And Sally's snide remark. She knew. Eloise must have told her.

"I'm sorry," Mrs. Grattan mumbled, shuffling Peter toward the center aisle. "I thought she knew. Everyone knew." She faced the congregation. "After all these years, I thought they would have told her."

She began to march Peter from the room, but Gabriel stopped her.

"I'm sorry, Mrs. Grattan, but Peter will need to come with me. Peter, rejoin the agents in front of the church. I'll be there shortly."

Mrs. Grattan protested. "You can't do that."

"Let it go, Sophie," Daddy growled as Peter escaped from the sanctuary.

She visibly shook. "You haven't heard the last of me, Gabriel Meeks." With a harrumph, she marched out, head held high.

Felicity wobbled, the last of her strength gone, and her father rushed to support her. "D-Daddy?" Tears strangled the word.

"Come along with the pastor and me."

Gabriel gently steered her toward the side aisle with Daddy plowing ahead of them. As she passed the five empty chairs where the children had sat, she remembered Luke.

"Gabriel?" She gripped his arm with all her strength. "Don't let Mr. Coughlin get Luke. Promise me." This was more important than anything else. She could not let the poor boy endure scorn a hundred times worse than had been directed at her by Mrs. Grattan.

"Don't worry, Felicity," Gabriel assured her. "Mr. Coughlin was never going to be given a child."

"But then why? Why all that with Peter and Luke?"

He sighed. "It's a long story and one that can wait. You have more important matters to address now." He squeezed her arm. "Talk to your parents, and listen."

Her parents? She stared at Daddy's broad back.

She had no parents.

The church office afforded privacy for this most painful of conversations. Felicity stood in the center of the room, numb. Daddy pulled Gabriel's chair from behind the desk while Mother sobbed into her handkerchief at Florabelle's desk.

"Mother?" The word suddenly sounded peculiar.

Eugenia Kensington didn't lift her eyes.

Daddy pointed to the empty chair, and Felicity tentatively sat. Whatever he had to say would hurt, but she had to know the truth.

"Who am I?"

He took her thin hands in his meaty ones. "You are our daughter."

"But not by blood." Her fingers, her legs, even her cheeks had gone cold.

"What's blood?" Daddy said.

Mother lifted her face from the handkerchief to wail, "I knew this would happen one day. I knew it. You should never have done it, Branford."

Felicity stared at her mother. "You shouldn't have adopted me? Is that what you're saying? Or am I not even adopted?"

"Of course you are." Daddy turned red. "I'll show you the papers if you want, but all that legal stuff doesn't matter.

You're ours. We're yours. We raised you as our own and gave you everything you could ever want."

As their own but not their own.

Again Mother wailed, this time from within the handkerchief.

"Eugenia, stop it. This is our daughter, the joy of our lives. Show a little backbone."

"B-but now Mr. Blevins will never have her."

"Maybe he doesn't deserve her." Daddy glowered at Mother, who was too busy sobbing to notice.

"And the National Academy," she cried.

Daddy snorted. "If they won't take my Felicity, then they won't get one penny."

"But how will she ever marry well now?" Mother cried. "Now that everyone knows the truth."

Felicity's parents argued the ramifications of the announcement. Why couldn't one of them hug her and tell her it was all right? Why did it always come back to money and social status?

"Stop it," she said softly. "Just stop."

Her words went unheard as the discussion descended into bickering. Mother blamed Daddy for not taking enough precautions. Daddy claimed Mother had pushed for too much. On and on it went until Felicity couldn't stand it anymore.

She stood. "Excuse me. I need to go to the washroom."

They barely noticed her departure.

She walked through the now-vacant church. The sanctuary was dark and quiet, bearing no witness to the turmoil that had occurred moments before. In front stood the empty cross.

"Where were You when I needed You?" she said aloud.

Only the whistling of the wind answered.

Empty and lost, she walked out of the church onto the shaded walk. The noon sun blazed, but she didn't feel its heat. Kensington Drugstore stood across the street, flanked by Kensington Mortuary and Pearlman Actuarial Services. She no longer recognized any of them. The town she'd known her whole life had become foreign.

She wasn't Felicity Kensington, only daughter of the richest man in Pearlman. All the fancy clothes in the world couldn't hide the fact that she was a castoff, unwanted and unloved.

She was no one.

Where could she go? Though she instinctively walked home, the moment she saw the stately Federal, she halted. The same trees still lined the sweeping drive. The gardens still smelled as fragrant. The roses still bloomed in a profusion of scarlet and pink, but somehow it had changed. She no longer belonged.

She wiped her eyes for the hundredth time, trying unsuccessfully to stem the tears.

In front of the carriage house, Smithson washed the old Stanley Steamer. Daddy never drove it anymore. Daddy. He wasn't her father, not really. Whenever he tired of her, he could set her aside like an old motorcar, for they didn't share one drop of blood.

She bit her lip against the tears.

As blustering as Daddy could be at times, she loved him. He had bounced her on his lap and let her make entries in the ledgers that he later had to erase. He hugged her when she cried. In all her memory, Mother had never held her. When she was little, there'd been nannies and nurses. Later, Mother instructed, but she never just held her. It was all about how to behave, about clothes and being the best, about the rules for ladylike behavior. But what did that matter now? The truth was out.

Felicity turned away from the house, unable to bear the pain of looking at it any longer. Ms. Priss strolled past without stopping, as if even she knew Felicity wasn't worth the attention.

She stumbled down the hill. She couldn't go home, and she had nowhere else to go. Mariah was her closest friend, but Felicity couldn't go to the parsonage, not when Gabriel was there. Oh, what a mix-up that was. For so long she'd disparaged his lower social standing, but now the tables were reversed, and he outranked her.

Her cheeks burned with mortification. No doubt, Robert would laugh over his narrow escape, and the tale would spread throughout Newport until every soul had heard what happened to Felicity Kensington.

She could never show her face again, not even in Pearlman. She'd have to go elsewhere, but where and how? She had no money of her own and no belongings, not even clothes.

Kensington Estates, that beautiful section of Pearlman with its stately homes, meant nothing to her now. She walked away from it into the unknown. At the bottom of the hill, the park bustled with activity. The Renauds celebrated a birthday, and the children laughed and squealed. She longed for just one day filled with such delight, but watching it today proved too painful.

She wandered along the river, hoping to find solitude. At the rapids, a fisherman cast his line, seemingly unaware that the world had tilted on its axis. Through the trees, she could see glimpses of the parsonage's white fence, lost to her now. How reluctant she'd been to enter the yard the day that Gabriel took in Slinky. Now she would give anything to live within its warm embrace.

Where to go?

Many years ago, when she needed to think things through, she would hide in a little cave upriver. There she would talk to God, and there He always answered. It had been a long time, but maybe He would still listen to her.

She hurried along the path, looking for the spot where she used to climb down the riverbank to the cave. The trees and bushes had grown over the years, obscuring the markers she'd used as a child.

Finally, she found the cave, hiding behind drooping grasses and a tangle of undergrowth. It looked small and inhospitable. A grassy knoll by the river's edge was better. There she sat and thought until the warmth of the sun made her drowsy, and she nodded off.

When she awoke, she saw the sun had dipped low. Hours must have passed. She rubbed her eyes. Then she heard a rumble of thunder. Dark clouds threatened from the west, obscuring the setting sun. The air smelled of rain. A crack of lightning brought her to her feet. She needed shelter, and the only one in sight was the cave.

She pushed through the undergrowth, though it tore out the hem of her skirt. She stopped to brush off the seeds and bits of dried leaves. Thunder rumbled, long and loud, then, with a crack, lightning struck nearby. She dove through the grasses into the cave just as the first raindrops fell.

The cave was shorter and darker than she remembered. She couldn't stand up nor could she see. After her eyes adjusted, she could make out a stump, or rather a foot-thick segment of tree trunk that would serve as a chair.

She brushed it off and shrieked when a bug darted away. She'd forgotten about the centipedes and earwigs and other creeping insects that lurked in caves. Still, the thunder had grown louder, and there was no place else to get out of the weather.

If only she could have gone to the parsonage. She squeezed her eyes shut. Gabriel could never love her now. It was all well and good to help orphans, but marrying one was another matter altogether. The Sophie Grattans in the congregation would murmur about the inferior wife. Oh, they wouldn't say it that way. They'd hide their barbs behind complaints over little mistakes or say that he didn't present the proper figure for a man in his position. But the real cause would be her.

She sucked in her lower lip. Every bit of the life she'd known was gone, shattered into pieces too small to repair. Why hadn't Daddy told her? If she'd known who she really was, she would have lived differently. She would have treated others better. She would have cultivated friendships. She wouldn't have looked down on her neighbors. Instead, she'd ruined everything.

She'd have to begin anew, somehow. She'd have to forget Gabriel. For his sake, she'd have to pretend she didn't love him. She'd have to forget the way his lips pursed when he was deep in thought, forget the little indentation of worry between his eyebrows, forget the way he'd lain prone after trying to catch Slinky and then snorted with laughter when she thought he'd hurt himself, forget the unruly curls and even the rolled-up shirtsleeves.

She missed him. Each memory hurt almost more than she could bear, yet she heaped on more: how he'd caught her when she fainted, the awkwardness when she'd given him Slinky's leash, how he'd encouraged her to go to veterinary college, how he'd respected her treatment of Slinky, how he'd wanted her on the Selection Committee.

Dear God, help me.

She rocked as the thunder boomed and the lightning flashed, knees hugged to her chest. Where could she go? What could she do?

"Who am I?" she whispered, lifting her face only to have water drip on it.

She buried her head in her knees again and wept, letting

the despair flow out until finally she felt nothing. The storm had quieted, and in the stillness, a verse from the hymn "Amazing Grace" came to mind: "I once was lost but now am found."

"But I'm not found, God," she muttered into her knees.

She let the emptiness take hold, yet one small corner of her soul refused to give up. Surely others had lost much. The apostles had left their families to follow Jesus, yet they never complained of loneliness. Gabriel had left his family to minister in a strange town. Peter and Luke and the other children had lost families. All survived.

"I am with you always; even unto the end." The verse came vividly into her mind. Felicity didn't realize she still remembered the scripture she'd memorized as a child. During the years at Highbury, she'd stopped reading the Bible. She figured the verses had slipped away as well.

Yet now this verse returned, a calm reassurance that in this bleakest of hours, God saw her, felt her pain and was with her.

"I'm so sorry, Lord," she prayed. With throat clotted and tears flowing, she confessed her pride and selfishness, and as the rain calmed to a steady nourishing shower, she felt the most amazing renewal. If she opened her eyes, she could almost believe she'd see Jesus beside her, holding out a hand. She reached out and somehow felt His touch, reassuring her deep inside that she was loved.

God was and had always been her Father. He had never left her, even when she turned away. His love was constant. He would see her through this and every moment of her life.

"But what do I do?" she whispered.

She waited, listening to the silence for the answer.

It came in the oddest of sounds, like oars splashing in the river followed by an odd clink of metal on metal. It was very close, perhaps just below the cave. If a boat had been out in the storm, they might need help. She scurried toward the entrance, then heard a thud and a low masculine voice.

"Bring 'em up, boys."

She froze. The muffled voice sounded vaguely familiar, yet she couldn't quite place it.

"We'll stash them in the cave," the man said.

Then the undergrowth in front of the cave parted, revealing a man, outlined by the light of a half-shuttered lantern. The only things visible were his legs, his hands and a pistol.

"What on earth did you think you were doing?" Mariah demanded after putting Luke to bed for the night.

Gabriel knew he'd asked a lot of his sister. She'd come to help him keep house for a few months until he found a suitable wife or hired a housekeeper, and now he'd saddled her with a child. She'd had to open up a room and clean and feed and bathe the boy.

Meanwhile, he'd hid in the library, frantically reading scripture and praying for guidance. The whole fabric of Pearlman was splitting apart, and he had no idea how to stop the rupture. When the sheriff arrested Kensington for bootlegging, it would shatter the last shards of Felicity's life.

Felicity. The look on her face would haunt him forever.

The truth wasn't supposed to come out. That's why he'd reluctantly agreed to send Peter to the Grattans. That's why he'd tried to get the Grattans to back off by revealing their prejudices. That's why Kensington had confided in him, but all that effort had come to naught. He'd been able to rescue Peter but not Felicity.

"A child," Mariah scolded, "is not a dog."

Slinky whined and raised his white eyebrows.

She ignored the protest. "Gabriel John, you simply cannot take in every stray you find. Mom and Dad might have let you, but not me. There are consequences to your actions. That boy deserves a real family, with a mother and father."

"I know."

"Then why did you take him on?"

He couldn't answer.

She threw up her hands. "Don't tell me. I know. Felicity."

"She was right about the Grattans," he said quietly.

"Granted, but that doesn't mean you had to take in Luke. Another family could have taken him. There were twenty-eight applicants. Mrs. Simmons took Peter. Surely you could have found someone else."

Gabriel wrapped his cold fingers around the cup of tea. Though the evening was warm and sticky, he'd been chilled since the distribution. "I don't have any answers, Mariah. I just know it's the right thing to do."

She studied him for a long time. Then, sighing, she rose and retrieved the teakettle. "It's not just that, is it? It's about Felicity's boarding school idea," she said as she refilled their cups.

He shook his head. "I can't explain it, Mariah. I just know I couldn't send him back on the train, not after…"

"What happened to Felicity had nothing to do with the distribution," she said in a gentler tone. "You know that, Gabe. Her parents should have told her long ago. In fact, it's amazing no one spilled it before now, considering how small the town is. Secrets don't stay secret in small towns."

Gabriel groaned and buried his head in his hands. "That's the problem."

"What's the problem? Tell me, Gabe, because honestly I don't see why you're acting this way."

He didn't know if he could put words to it himself. That he loved Felicity? That he'd tried desperately to protect her and failed? That the worst blow was yet to fall?

"What's going to happen when the bootleggers are caught?" he asked miserably.

Mariah drew in her breath sharply. "Her father."

He nodded and dug his fingers into his hair, tearing at it like the penitents of the Old Testament. Why had he gone to the sheriff? Why had he come up with the idea of catching the criminals at the root cellar? Tonight's new moon meant the bootleggers would likely act and the sheriff would trap them. On top of all Felicity had endured today, she'd lose her father.

A rumble of thunder rolled in the distance.

Mariah put an arm around his shoulders. "Good will prevail, Gabe. You have to believe it."

"I don't see how," he mumbled.

A flash of lightning lit the kitchen windowpane, and a loud knock sounded on the kitchen door.

Mariah lifted her head. "Who could that be?"

His heart raced. He knew who he wanted it to be. Felicity. He leaped to his feet, hoping God had answered his prayers, and yanked open the door.

"Pastor." Branford Kensington pushed past him into the kitchen. "Ms. Meeks." He nodded stiffly and shoved a flashlight into a pocket of his canvas hunting jacket.

Gabriel stuffed down his disappointment. "Mr. Kensington." Aside from being angry with himself, he was furious with Kensington for not dealing straight with his daughter.

Kensington scanned the kitchen. "I'd hoped my Felicity was here."

If Kensington didn't know where Felicity was, who did? "I thought she was with you."

The man looked worried. "Haven't seen her since she left the church, about noon."

"Dear Lord," Mariah gasped, covering her mouth with her hand.

The fear in the room escalated, driven by the accelerating storm. Blinding lightning was followed by a crack of thunder. It had struck close. Seconds later, wind and rain lashed the house. Kensington buttoned his jacket and set his jaw. "I'll find her."

Gabriel grabbed the raincoat hanging by the door. "I'm going with you." Whether Felicity was lost, had run off or was hurt, she was out in this storm. Gabriel's heart pounded slow and hard, like a fist thudding into a punching bag. "We'll find her."

Kensington nodded grimly. "Let's hope we're not too late."

Chapter Sixteen

Gabriel followed Branford Kensington into a steady, light rain that beaded off his coat. The man might be a criminal, but he loved his daughter. On that they agreed.

The storm had cleared the mugginess from the air, bringing a chill. If Felicity were caught outdoors, she would be cold and soaked through, ingredients for a fever. They needed to find her quickly.

"After me." Kensington strode toward the side of the house where Mariah parked her car.

Gabriel reached back to close the door, but Slinky slipped out. He grabbed the dog by the collar and tried to shuttle him into the kitchen, but Slinky refused to budge.

"Come on, boy. I don't have time for this."

Mariah poked her head out the screen door. "You'd better take him. Here's his leash."

Kensington called from the side gate. "What's keeping you, son?"

Gabriel struggled to attach the leash. The rain made the metal cold and slippery. "Slinky thinks I'm taking him for a walk."

To his surprise Kensington said, "Bring him along then. The mutt might have a good nose."

Count on Branford Kensington to treat this like a hunting expedition. Finally Gabriel clipped the leash in place, and Slinky took off.

"Where should we start?" Gabriel asked, struggling to hold the dog back.

"I was hoping you'd know. Already checked the cinema and the drugstore."

Gabriel cringed at the mention of the drugstore, but clearly Kensington wasn't referring to the blind pig in the back. Honestly, Gabriel couldn't see Felicity at any of the places Kensington mentioned. She was more likely to stroll in the park. Other than the mercantile, he'd never seen her in any Pearlman business.

Kensington closed the gate behind them and headed toward the street. Gabriel racked his brain. Where would she go?

The constant dripping of the rain dampened his hopes they'd find her unharmed. Think...he had to think.

"Let's work from what we know," Gabriel suggested, coming up on Kensington's heels. "You said you last saw her at the church?"

"She excused herself to go to the washroom but never returned. At first I thought she went home, but none of the servants saw her come or go."

A knot twisted in Gabriel's stomach. What would Felicity do? She'd gotten a terrible shock, one that had unhinged her entire world. In the past, when faced with adversity she took shelter behind her family name. Remove that, and she had nowhere to hide. Kensington owned nearly every business in town. She wouldn't go into any them, except... His mouth went dry.

"I hate to mention it," he said slowly, "but have you checked the train station?"

"Allington says he didn't see her. She definitely didn't buy a ticket."

"Thank God. Would she have gone to her brother's house?"

Kensington shook his head. "He's checking with everyone she knows."

"Did you talk with the sheriff?"

"He's not in," Kensington growled.

They'd reached the junction of Elm and Main. From there, Gabriel could see the church steeple, backlit by the receding lightning. Felicity had stood up to her mother about that stained glass window. She'd refused Blevins. She'd come to him with the idea of the boarding school for orphans. She was strong, and she was also tied to this community. She wouldn't leave, even after getting the shock of her life. That meant she was still here, but where?

Unfortunately, he was out of ideas. "What do you suggest?"

"Comb the town. Knock on doors. You take one street, I'll take the next."

It seemed an inefficient way of searching, but Gabriel didn't have a better idea. "What are her favorite places? Who are her friends?"

"I'm not sure." Kensington frowned. "I should have spent more time with my children, but one business or another always needed my attention."

Gabriel had heard his father lament the same tugging between family and the need to provide, but Dad had chosen family more often than not.

"She liked to walk in the park," Gabriel suggested.

Kensington shook his head. "In the dark? We're wasting time here, son. I say you take Main and I'll take Oak."

Lacking a better plan, Gabriel started to cross the street,

but Slinky had other ideas. He dug in, tugging Gabriel the opposite direction with insistent barking.

"What's with that dog?" Kensington said.

"I don't know. He won't cross the street." Gabriel tried again with the same result. "He probably needs to do his business."

"Make it quick, then. Without the sheriff's help, we're undermanned."

The sheriff. If Ilsley wasn't in the office, he must be staking out the root cellar. Felicity said she'd played around the homestead when she was a child. What if she'd gone there to get out of the rain? If so, the sheriff might have found her by now. She'd be rescued or... His pulse quickened as he thought of another scenario. Both the smugglers and the sheriff carried guns. In the dark, either side might mistake her for the other. She could be a hostage or worse.

Gabriel clutched Slinky's leash so tightly that his hand ached. Rain drummed against his raincoat. "I have an idea, Mr. Kensington, and could use your help." He had to hold his hand to his brim to shield his eyes from the rain. "There's a root cellar out behind parsonage land. Felicity said it was part of the old Warren homestead. Do you know the place?"

Kensington's expression glimmered with hope. "You think she might've taken shelter there?"

"It's a possibility."

Even in the dim light of Kensington's flashlight, Gabriel saw his mouth tense. The man knew what that meant, especially if a delivery was scheduled that night.

"Think you can find it in the dark?" Kensington asked.

Odd. The man clearly knew its location. He'd been there before. Yet he asked Gabriel to lead the way. A delivery must be underway, and Kensington didn't want to blow his cover, even with his daughter missing. Gabriel couldn't get the nasty taste from his mouth. Apparently for Kensington, business came before everything, even his daughter's life.

"Well?" Kensington snapped. "Do you or don't you know how to find it?"

Gabriel shook off a warning shiver. "I think so. Actually, Slinky's the one who found it. Maybe he'll lead the way. Come on, boy. Find Felicity."

Slinky strained on his leash as he ran into the park. Gabriel could swear the dog understood the urgency of the situation and was leading them directly to Felicity.

They proceeded through the park at a quick pace, keeping to the paths. Eventually they'd have to set off through the woods, but Gabriel wanted Kensington to reveal his hand. When they reached the point where they'd have to trudge into the forest, he'd ask Kensington if he knew the way. Until then, they walked in silence, led by Slinky's panting and rustling.

Kensington apparently didn't want to talk, even about Felicity. By the time they reached the pavilion, Gabriel couldn't stand the quiet any longer. "She had no idea she was adopted?"

Most people would balk at such a personal question, but not Kensington. "We thought it best she never know. It's a small town."

"And people would talk?"

Kensington nodded.

Once again, they walked in silence, with only the patter of rain to accompany them.

At the river, Gabriel headed toward parsonage property, but Slinky tugged to go in the opposite direction. "That's odd. We never walk that way."

"Probably got a whiff of a rabbit," Kensington grunted.

Gabriel tugged, trying to point Slinky toward the root cellar, but the dog whined and cowered, the way he had the day Coughlin had hold of him. The moment came back in vivid detail. Felicity running after Coughlin in her stockings, insisting he not kill the dog. Gabriel had to intercede, and then somehow he'd ended up with the stray. Though he'd made Felicity promise to find Slinky another home by the end of summer, the dog had stamped a permanent place in Gabriel's heart.

"Come on, boy," Gabriel urged. "This way."

"That's no way to make a dog heel." Kensington grabbed the leash and gave it a yank.

Slinky whined, as fearful as he'd been with Coughlin. Gabriel instinctively took the leash from Kensington, but as he did, a thought crept into his mind. What if Kensington—and perhaps Coughlin—had run into Slinky while delivering bootlegged liquor? Maybe that's why the dog had gone to the root cellar during the picnic. He knew where to hide things, and he knew where things were hidden. His reaction to Kensington told Gabriel the two weren't strangers. If Gabriel had needed any confirmation of the man's guilt, he just had it. All he had to do was trap the man in his lies.

He tossed out a little test. "I'm not sure I can find the cellar from this direction. Do you happen to know the way?"

Kensington glared a moment, then handed him the leash. "Follow me. If the dog won't come, leave him."

Gabriel's suspicions were confirmed. Kensington knew how to find the root cellar. He was the shorter man with the rifle that Gabriel had seen that night. If the sheriff had staked out the site tonight, Kensington was walking right into the trap. Within moments, the truth would be out.

Gabriel knelt to stroke Slinky's head. He could use a friend on his side. Kensington might not be carrying a rifle, but the bootleggers would have guns. "Come with me, Slinky," he said loudly and then whispered, "and keep quiet. This is important."

The dog's upright ear pricked as if he understood. With any luck, they'd find Felicity before the sheriff ambushed the bootleggers. And if they didn't? People could get killed— and that included Felicity.

Felicity backed into the farthest reaches of the cave. Spiders, bats and insects. Every one made her skin crawl, but a man with a gun trumped them all. Lord, this wasn't the type of help she wanted.

She crouched low in the inky blackness, hoping the man wouldn't shine the lantern into the back of the cave. She reached behind her, and her hand met a wall of cool, damp earth. She couldn't go any farther.

"Quick now," the man commanded.

He held up the lantern, revealing his face—or at least the part she could see. He wore a tattered old hat pulled low and a cloth tied around his face like a bank robber in a moving picture show. He swung the lantern into the cave, and she pressed against the dirt wall. A knobby root dug into her back.

God, help me.

She didn't dare breathe lest the man hear her.

Someone grunted and set a small crate or box near the front of the cave.

"Hurry, before we're spotted," the leader said.

Though Felicity couldn't make out what was in the crates, she knew it had to be illegal. A spidery cold sweat crept over her limbs.

Painful seconds later, another man brought a second crate and stacked it atop the first. As he adjusted it, something clinked. She'd thought that sound was metal on metal before, but it wasn't. It was glass.

Alcohol. It had to be alcohol. Vanesia Lawrence's blind pig got liquor from somewhere. It had come in during state

Prohibition, and it continued to arrive during federal Prohibition.

The leader waved his pistol. Alcohol and guns were a bad combination.

She made herself small as crate after crate was stacked across the opening of the cave to form a low wall. At first she was relieved, because the crates partially hid her, but then she realized that soon they would box her in. If the wall was only one crate thick, she could push through, but if the men made several rows, she'd be trapped, unable to get out. She had to leave now, before all hope of escape was gone.

Several deep breaths calmed her racing mind, and soon she saw the way. Crates arrived every fifteen to twenty seconds. Between deliveries, the leader faced toward the river to watch his men. He didn't realize someone was behind him in the cave. He wouldn't see her if she slipped past while he was watching his men, but she had to be quick—and quiet.

She waited until the deliveryman headed down to the river and the leader turned to watch him. After taking a deep breath, she crawled forward on her hands and knees. Stones bit into her flesh, and the dampness drove a chill deep into her bones.

She paused at the narrow opening, ready to dart out, when the leader turned and coughed. In a flash, she scurried behind the wall of crates and waited to see if she'd been discovered.

"Hurry," the leader growled to one of his men.

She could breathe again. He hadn't spotted her.

Soon she heard the thrashing of the deliveryman. There was only room for a couple more crates, and then the cave would be sealed shut. She waited until she heard the crate drop and then stifled her alarm when the man pushed it into the empty space. She'd have to climb over it and hope she was quick enough and quiet enough to avoid detection.

Her palms were clammy and her breath shallow. She had no choice. She had to attempt it.

She crouched, poised to jump, and the moment she heard footsteps moving away, she scrambled over the crate. Then she froze. The leader stood too close to the front of the cave. She had barely a foot of space to slip behind him. How could she get past without drawing notice? But she had no choice. If she went back into the cave, she'd be trapped.

Heart pounding, she slid sideways behind the man, praying he didn't sense her.

"Your turn," one of the men at the boat grumbled. "I done more'n half already."

"Quiet," the leader hissed, stepping forward.

The exchange gave Felicity the diversion she needed. She sprinted toward the path, but on the third step the ground gave way and she crashed downward, making enough noise to alert the entire town.

The leader whipped around and shined the lantern at her. "Who's there?"

Felicity flattened herself against the ground. *Lord, please make me invisible.*

"What are you doing?" the leader said much more clearly. He'd removed the handkerchief from his face.

Shock prickled her skin with a thousand sharp needles. She knew that voice, only now it didn't reflect the simpering idiocy of the dandy. This Robert Blevins was strong and sure and most decidedly not the man he'd claimed to be.

She heard him step closer, and then he cocked the gun.

Dear God. She was going to die.

Gabriel followed at Kensington's heels. The woods were quiet that night, too quiet for a smuggling operation. Perhaps Gabriel had been wrong and the bootleggers had moved to another location. That would explain Kensington's lack of concern that they were headed to the site of his illicit activities.

The man crashed through the woods, guided only by the weak glow of the flashlight. Of course he knew the way. He'd spent his entire life here. Unlike Gabriel, who had to use a bent tree as a marker, Kensington could head right to the spot.

Within minutes, they reached the root cellar. No one was there, not even the sheriff. Kensington shined his flashlight at the cellar doors, not bothering to disguise the fact that he knew its location.

"All right," Kensington grunted as he lifted the first door. "Let's see what we have." He directed the light inside. "Felicity?"

The woods came alive with a flurry of crackling and shouts.

"Freeze and put your hands in the air."

Gabriel jumped and raised his hands, even though he knew it had to be Sheriff Ilsley.

Kensington didn't bother. "What on earth are you doing, Sheriff? I went to your office looking for help finding my Felicity, and now I see you're sitting out here in the woods."

Ilsley lowered his gun. "Felicity's missing?"

"Didn't I just say that?" Kensington growled. "Now put that thing away and help me find her."

Ilsley looked at Gabriel. "But if you're here, then where...?" He didn't finish, but Gabriel knew the question. Where are the bootleggers?

Gabriel shrugged. "We don't know." The answer fit equally well with a missing person or a missing group of bootleggers.

Ilsley still looked confused. He directed his gaze at Kensington. "But I thought..."

"There's no time for talk," Kensington said gruffly. "My

Felicity's missing, and it's getting cold. Are you going to help me comb these woods?"

The sheriff holstered his pistol. "Of course, but let's not go about this like chickens with their heads cut off. We need a plan of attack." The sheriff pulled off his hat, ran a hand through his hair, and then replaced the hat. "Is she alone?"

"As far as I know," Kensington growled.

"Any ideas where she might have gone?"

Gabriel hated covering the same ground while Felicity waited somewhere for rescue. "We've discussed this already, Sheriff, and we've checked everywhere we thought she might be. Her brother, Blake, is calling her friends and acquaintances. I thought she might have taken a walk in the park and got lost."

"Lost?" said Kensington. "She's lived here her whole life."

"Except for school," Gabriel pointed out. Highbury School for Girls. If Mariah's friends were correct, the society girls there would have eaten Felicity alive. "She did go to school in New York City, right?"

Kensington dismissed his idea. "A person doesn't forget their hometown in a few years."

"Gentlemen," Ilsley interrupted, "this is getting us nowhere. I say we split up to cover as much ground as possible." He quickly assigned sections of town to two of his four deputies. "The rest of you come with me."

Still, Gabriel felt they weren't looking in the right place. Rain streamed off his hat and down his neck. Felicity couldn't stand a night exposed to these conditions.

"Pastor, you take Main Street," Kensington said. "I'll take Oak. All right, boys, let's spread out."

Ilsley looked at Gabriel. "Perhaps we should pray first."

The suggestion shot through Gabriel with clear precision. He should have been the one to suggest it. He was the minister.

Ashamed, Gabriel bowed his head. Slinky still pulled at the leash, and worry riddled his thoughts. He couldn't hear God's still voice when the woman he loved was in danger. He said a rudimentary prayer and hoped God would understand.

As soon as he finished, the sheriff split them into teams of two. Gabriel found himself paired with Kensington again.

"You take the area from the parsonage through Kensington Estates, and I'll head toward the Grange Hall," the sheriff said. "We'll find her, Branford."

"Follow me," Kensington said, heading toward the parsonage.

At that moment, Slinky chose to tug at the leash, pulling Gabriel in the opposite direction, toward the river. In a flash, he remembered how Slinky had wanted to go upriver rather than toward the root cellar. Did the dog sense or smell something?

"Wait a minute, Sheriff, Mr. Kensington," he called out, bringing the men to a halt. "I have an idea. Follow me."

"Where?"

Gabriel gave Slinky free rein and took off toward the river. "Just follow me." It would take too long to explain and argue out the merits of following a dog. It was better to go on faith.

They crashed through the woods and were soon back on the path, headed upriver. They passed the pavilion, dark and silent, and reentered the forest.

"Where are you going?" Kensington huffed as he struggled to keep up the pace. "My Felicity would never walk this way. She's too delicate."

Gabriel just kept plowing forward, more and more certain with every step. Slinky pulled hard on the leash, leading him closer to the river. Now he could hear the water rushing past, tumbling over the rocks that made up the little rapids.

Aside from their bumbling and panting, the forest was quiet. Even the rain had stopped, and Gabriel unbuttoned his coat. The cool night air felt good but not as good as knowing they'd soon find Felicity.

"Come on, boy," he urged. Gabriel was almost running now, his feet as sure as a boy's. Roots, branches and stones meant nothing in the pursuit of Felicity.

Then, off to his right, he heard a man yell in surprise. A second later, a gunshot rang out and a woman screamed.

Gabriel dropped Slinky's leash and ran.

Chapter Seventeen

～

Felicity stared at the barrel of the gun. The puff of smoke had drifted off, but Robert kept the pistol pointed at her head. Her heartbeat swooshed in her ears, and she couldn't have stood even if she could get her legs to move.

"R-Robert," she stammered, unable to think coherently. He'd just shot at her. Robert, the man she'd once wanted to make her husband.

"Shh," he hissed. "Not a word. Do you understand? Not one word."

She heard the menace behind the words as well as their implicit threat: *or else the next bullet will be in your head.*

She couldn't swallow, could barely breathe. Her arms ached from the awkward position, but she dared not move. If she flinched, he'd kill her. His hand stayed steady, the pistol level. Next time he wouldn't miss.

Is this how the buffalo had felt before Daddy shot him? And the gazelles and antelope? Had they cringed and prayed for salvation? Had they recounted every mistake they'd made?

How wrong she'd been about Robert. He was no engineer. It had all been a pretense to cover his criminal activities. She should have known. A real engineer wouldn't constantly forget his instruments or carelessly leave them lying about. A real engineer would have assessed the weight problem of the stained glass window in minutes.

If only Gabriel was here. She'd known he was the man for her that first day but hadn't wanted to accept she could love a poor man with no social standing. What a fool she'd been to throw away the best man she'd ever known. Now she faced death never having told him how she really felt.

The rest of the smugglers readied the boat in haste, no longer caring how much noise they made. "Ready, boss."

Robert cocked the gun again, and she tensed, steeling herself for the pain of the bullet. Would he aim for her head or her heart? Would the shot be true? She feared the pain, not death, for God had promised her a heavenly home if she placed all her trust in Him.

She closed her eyes and prayed. *Dear Lord, please forgive my countless offenses. I'm not worthy, but I pray You will remember me and let me enter Your kingdom. Above all, please look after Luke and give him a loving home where he will be cherished and grow strong. Let him know that You will always be his Father.*

Somehow, praying for Luke brought peace. She waited for the sound of gunfire, waited for the searing pain of the bullet tearing through her flesh. Instead, a dog barked. A dog? Even in the dim light of Robert's shuttered lantern, she recognized the black-and-white bundle of fur.

"Slinky."

And by his side stood Gabriel, her Gabriel. Hope surged, but fear came quick on its heels.

"Robert has a gun," she warned.

"I see that." Gabriel knelt by her side and wrapped his raincoat around her shoulders.

Didn't he understand? "He'll hurt you. H-he'll kill you." Her teeth started chattering uncontrollably.

"Maybe you'd better listen to her, Reverend," Robert snapped.

Gabriel paid him no attention. "Shh," he whispered, holding her close. "I'll never leave you."

"Gabriel." She buried her face in his wonderful cotton shirt. "I'm so sorry. Don't risk your life for me."

He lifted her face and looked deep into her eyes. "I will risk everything for you. I love you, Felicity Kensington. Never doubt that. I love you."

The last of her strength disintegrated. "You do?" The tears returned. "B-but why? I was so prideful. I treated you terribly."

He smothered her confession with a kiss, and at last his words sank in. He loved her. He truly loved her, no matter who she was.

He cupped her face in both hands, and in the light of the lantern, she saw such love that the tears flowed again.

"Don't ever leave me again," he said. "Promise?"

She nodded, eyes brimming.

Robert sneered, "Very touching, Reverend. I could almost fall for that little show of concern myself. What you didn't tell her is why you're really here tonight."

Felicity glared at Robert. "What are you talking about?"

"I'm talking about the reverend's real agenda, if he even is a minister. That's right, Ms. Kensington. Everything is not what it seems. Tell me, Reverend, how you knew where to find us. Care to tell me why first Ms. Kensington appeared and then you showed up tonight."

Gabriel tensed, and she wanted to comfort him, but he stepped away from her to face Robert.

"Considering *you're* the one leveling a gun at *us*," Gabriel said, "you have some gall to claim I'm the one with the false agenda. Shoot me, if you must, but let Felicity go. She has nothing to do with this charade you've concocted."

"No," she cried. Gabriel couldn't die, not when she finally realized how much she loved him. She stood beside him. "If you shoot Gabriel, you'll have to shoot me."

Gabriel pulled her behind him. "Don't be a martyr."

Her heart pummeled her rib cage. Her knees wobbled. She hardly felt like a martyr.

Robert's head suddenly jerked toward her left, and he lowered the pistol. "Sheriff. It's about time." He tucked the gun under his jacket.

"What?" Felicity blinked, utterly confused. Robert acted like he expected to see the sheriff, who scampered down the riverbank with a deputy on his heels.

Gabriel pointed at Robert. "Arrest this man."

Robert just smirked.

Felicity looked from Robert to the sheriff, searching for answers. Had the entire world gone off-kilter? She reached for Gabriel, trying to find something solid.

"I waited for you at the root cellar," the sheriff said to Robert. "That was the plan."

Felicity's hope sank with a heavy thud. If Sheriff Ilsley was waiting for Robert and Robert was waiting for the sheriff, that meant they were in on this together. Why hadn't she seen it before? Mrs. Lawrence's blind pig never got raided, even though everyone knew she sold liquor. The only reason Mrs. Lawrence stayed in business must be because the sheriff looked the other way. For a cut of the profits, he let men like Robert smuggle liquor into town unchallenged.

She sucked in her breath. That meant she and Gabriel were far from safe. The sheriff would not want anyone to know about his part in the bootlegging operation. He'd kill them and ensure their bodies were never found.

"Lord, help us," she whispered as Robert consulted with the sheriff.

Gabriel drew her close. "He will."

At least they'd die together and walk hand in hand into the Lord's kingdom. She pressed to his side, waiting for the inevitable report of a gun firing and the subsequent blow of the bullet piercing her body.

Gabriel cleared his throat. "Excuse me, Sheriff, but your bootleggers are getting away down the river."

How could Gabriel think the sheriff would care about the bootleggers when he was clearly one of them?

To her astonishment, Ilsley directed his deputy to head toward the river. "DeWalt, you'd better join us."

"DeWalt?" Who was DeWalt? She didn't know anyone by that name in Pearlman.

"DeWalt?" Gabriel echoed, but the men, including Robert, were already crashing down the slope, Slinky close behind.

They'd left Gabriel and her alone, free to escape.

"What's happening?" she whispered.

"I don't know, but I'm not waiting around to find out. Follow me."

Felicity held tight to Gabriel. "But I can't see."

"Wait for your eyes to adjust," he whispered back. "I can already see the trees."

She panicked. "I can't."

He held her close. "Just put your arms around my waist and follow me. I'll get you home safely."

Home? The thought sent another flood of tears to the surface. "I have no home."

He hugged her close. "You always have a home, just as you always have a Heavenly Father."

The calm assurance she'd felt in the cave returned. Yes, she did have a Father who would never abandon her.

"Be brave," he said.

Brave. The word brought a surge of strength. With God's help, she could be brave. She could survive.

"I'm ready," she said. "Lead on."

He positioned her arms at his waist, and then slowly, bit by bit, they inched upward. Her foot slipped, and he caught her. Branches whipped her face. She endured. Her sleeve tore. She ignored it. Soon she'd be home with the man she loved.

Before long, the ground leveled out, and Gabriel stopped.

"Why—?" she began, but he hushed her.

In the still, moonless night, she heard it, low at first but then louder—a crackling, rustling sound punctuated by the heavy fall of footsteps. Someone was coming. They hadn't made it to safety. She pressed close to Gabriel. It must be DeWalt. Maybe their pursuer wouldn't be able to see them in the dark. Then she spotted a wildly bouncing beam of light headed straight toward them.

"Dear God," she breathed.

"This way," Gabriel whispered.

He led her away from the oncoming person, but she couldn't keep up his pace. One hand slipped off his waist and then the other. Meanwhile, the bobbing light was drawing closer. They were going to get caught.

She yelped when the top of her foot caught a log and sent her tumbling. The impact shivered up her arms to her elbows, but worse than the jolt was losing Gabriel.

She cried out for him, and his strong hands lifted her to her feet. "Are you hurt?"

"N-no," she admitted.

But it was too late.

The bobbing light rounded a corner and shone directly in her eyes. They were caught.

"Felicity. Thank heavens," said a familiar voice, gasping and panting.

"Daddy?"

The flashlight dropped to the ground, and she could see his haggard face. "Little one. I...your mother...I'm just so glad to see you." He blew his nose and wiped his fogged spectacles. "We were so worried." His strong shoulders sagged, all vigor gone.

"Daddy," she whispered, her heart aching for the man who'd raised her. He'd worked a little too much perhaps, but he loved her. She knew it as surely as the sun would rise in the morning.

"I love you, too, Daddy."

As soon as Felicity went to her father, Gabriel missed her touch, but they had a bigger problem to address. Felicity was shivering.

"Let's get out of here," he barked, breaking up the father-daughter reunion. Felicity needed time with her father, but not now and not under these circumstances.

Kensington looked at him sharply. The man clearly wasn't used to taking orders.

"She needs to get warmed up," Gabriel said.

That kind of reasoning Kensington understood. He picked up the flashlight and headed Felicity back toward the park. That left Gabriel to bring up the rear. Neither Felicity nor her father had much fortitude left, and with every step the pace slowed. At this rate, Blevins would catch up to them before they reached town.

"Let's go to the parsonage," Gabriel suggested. "It's closer."

Felicity shivered, and Kensington altered direction. Gabriel took the lead. He'd get Felicity into the warmth of the kitchen, where Mariah would revive her with hot tea and a thick blanket.

"Where's your dog, son?" Kensington huffed as Gabriel forced the pace.

"With the criminals," Gabriel said tersely.

"What criminals?"

Gabriel tensed. How could the man pretend he didn't know what was going on tonight? "The bootleggers."

Felicity sighed. "Robert turned out bad, Daddy."

Kensington chuckled. "I could have told you he wasn't the man for you."

"That's not what she meant," Gabriel said stiffly. "Mr. Blevins is part of a gang smuggling liquor into town."

"He tried to shoot me, Daddy."

Kensington waved off Felicity's comment. "Nonsense. He wouldn't shoot you. He's in on everything."

"So we found out." Gabriel boiled. Of course, Blevins was in on everything, the same as Kensington was in on everything. What father would jeopardize his daughter's life for money? Gabriel could not keep down the bile. "Blevins and his gang were storing the liquor in the old Warren root cellar until they were discovered. Apparently they've shifted to a spot upriver, but then you know that, don't you?"

"What?" Kensington halted just outside the parsonage fence.

Gabriel had made a mistake, a bad mistake. This was not the time or the place to confront Kensington, not in front of Felicity.

"What do you mean, Gabriel?" Her plaintive voice tore through him.

For weeks, he'd dreaded how Felicity would feel when she learned the truth, but he'd never imagined he'd be the one to reveal it. "I, uh." Nothing could explain away his words.

The dim, yellow glow of the flashlight made her look pale and weary. "Tell me what you mean. How would Daddy know anything about Robert's bootlegging?"

Gabriel stood mute.

She did not. "Are you accusing my father of being involved with Robert and those criminals?"

Gabriel could think of no way out. If he told the truth,

he'd lose her. If he lied, he'd lose his soul. He swallowed hard, searching for help.

That help came from a most unlikely source. Kensington shook his head. "Robert's not a criminal. He's a Prohibition agent working with the sheriff to stop the bootleg liquor coming into town. Unfortunately, the pastor and I broke up the sheriff's stakeout at the root cellar. Hopefully he caught the bootleggers at the river."

Gabriel's heart sank. He'd been wrong? Had everything he'd believed been wrong? As he put together the pieces, his shame grew. Not only had he insulted an agent of the law, he'd also accused Felicity's father in front of her.

He tried to apologize, but her dismay stopped the words in his throat.

Tears clotted her voice as she rebuked him. "How could you?" She sagged against her father.

"Let's get you home, little one," said Kensington. "It can all be sorted out in the morning."

Morning alone could not cure the pain Gabriel had wrought. He watched Kensington lead his daughter along the outside of the parsonage fence to his car. Moments later, they drove away, the car's headlights finally disappearing up the hill.

At that moment, Slinky trotted up, leash dragging behind him. He wove around Gabriel's feet, whining.

"I know." Gabriel picked up the leash. "You don't have to rub it in."

He'd lost her. This time for good.

Chapter Eighteen

Though a bath and clean clothes helped Felicity feel almost like her old self, she couldn't sleep. Her parents had promised to answer her questions. In fact, she could hear Daddy prowling the hallway, his steps uncharacteristically nervous. She towel-dried her hair but didn't bother to comb it out.

Daddy stopped pacing the moment she opened her bedroom door. With expectant concern, he asked, "Are you ready?"

She nodded and took his arm, like a bride being escorted up the aisle. There'd be no wedding this summer—maybe not ever. Robert wasn't what he pretended to be, and Gabriel... How could he accuse her father of being a criminal? She thought he was a man who cared for people and thought the best of them. How cruelly wrong she'd been.

Daddy squeezed her hand. "I love you, little one."

Felicity shoved the sting of Gabriel's betrayal to the back of her mind. Now was not the time to lament lost romance. Tonight she needed to know who she was.

The hall and parlor lights blazed even as the clock struck midnight. Mother paced below, her pallid face untouched by rouge and her hair mussed. Felicity had never before seen her at less than her best, even when sick.

"Felicity." Mother's lips quivered, and her eyes were puffy. "You worried me sick." She wrung a handkerchief, made an aborted attempt at an embrace and retreated to the parlor.

Oh, why couldn't Felicity have a normal mother, one who kissed away bruises and shared tears? How she longed to really talk with her, to share fears and hopes. Instead, there'd always been a distance between them. When she was little, she didn't understand why. Now she knew. She wasn't her child.

They walked into the parlor, where the heavy velvet drapes had been drawn shut. Pearlman would not see what transpired in the Kensington house that night.

"Sis." Her brother unfolded his long legs and stood up from the sofa.

"Blake? What are you doing here?"

"Dad asked me to come over," he explained, offering her the seat beside him.

Instead, she chose the love seat and left enough room for Mother to join her. Her mother poured two cups of steaming liquid from the silver coffee service while Daddy took his position at the folding whist table where he'd assembled a stack of very official-looking papers.

He cleared his throat. "I wanted everyone to hear this at the same time."

Mother handed her one of the cups. "Hot chocolate. It'll make you feel better." But instead of sitting beside Felicity, she hung nervously at arm's length.

Felicity dutifully took a sip, though her stomach couldn't handle food until she knew the truth. "Tell me everything."

Mother handed the other cup to Daddy. "Where do we begin, Branford?" Her voice quavered, and at that moment Felicity caught a glimpse into her soul. She was terrified, so afraid of rejection that she couldn't even reach out to her children.

Daddy leaned back and tugged on the sash of his smoking jacket. "You were a baby, Felicity, when I first saw you. What was she, Eugenia, six weeks old?"

Felicity shook her head. That wasn't what she wanted to know. "Start at the beginning. When did you decide to adopt? Was I sent here on a train? What happened to my parents? Where did they live?" She choked out the hardest question of all. "In the tenements?"

"No," Mother exclaimed, glancing at Blake, "certainly not. We'd never take in a filthy street urchin."

Felicity cringed.

As usual, Mother failed to notice Felicity's discomfort and the prejudice in her words.

"You were to be Blake's sister, after all." She smiled at her son.

Blake's sister. Even now she couldn't be valued for herself.

"Then where was I born?" Felicity asked before she lost nerve.

Daddy exchanged a glance with Mother.

"I need to know who my real parents are," she insisted. "I need to know who I am."

"We are your parents," Mother insisted, but she wouldn't look at Felicity.

Daddy rose. "Let me handle this, Eugenia." He pulled a paper from the stack and gave it to Felicity. "Here's your adoption certificate."

Felicity took it gingerly and scanned the document for any indication of her origin. "It gives my name as Felicity Anne Kensington and lists you but no birth parents."

"We named you at once. You didn't have a name."

Not even a name. What couple doesn't name their baby? A couple that doesn't want a child. "Then I was abandoned?"

Daddy shook his head. "You were orphaned. Your parents died from typhoid soon after your birth."

Typhoid fever. A horrible sadness swept through her for the parents she'd never known—to hold a newborn baby, dreaming of the wonderful life you'd have together and then to have it snatched away. The little fingers, the tiny toes... how they must have hoped for their future, but then disease took it all away.

Daddy stroked his mustache. "Let me back up. You wanted to know when we decided to adopt. It was after your mother lost a baby girl—stillborn."

Felicity had never heard this before. She looked to her mother, who'd gone ashen, eyes downcast. Twenty-one years later, the loss still hurt. No wonder she was afraid to become too attached.

"Doc Stevens said your mother couldn't have another child, so I decided we'd adopt, quickly and without fuss. I went to an orphanage in Detroit and saw you. You looked so much like Blake that I knew you were the one."

Felicity let every word and action sink in. Mother's hands knotted around that handkerchief. Daddy was in control as always. "Then I'm from Detroit?" she whispered.

Mother and Daddy glanced at each other before he answered. "The agents said your parents died aboard ship."

"Aboard ship." Felicity knew what that meant. "Then I'm an immigrant, a foreigner." Just like Luke. Just like Mrs. Grattan said.

"You're an American," Mother said sharply.

"But I wasn't born here. Where did my parents come from?"

Again Mother and Daddy exchanged glances. Again

Daddy spoke. "The agency wasn't certain. Either Hungary or Romania, they think."

"Hungarian?" Felicity's ears hummed. How the Highbury girls had ridiculed Eastern Europeans, calling them Gypsies. She waited for Blake to make a joke, but he stayed mercifully quiet.

"You might be royalty," Mother suggested.

Blake snorted.

"It's possible," Mother insisted.

"No, it isn't," Felicity said. "Royalty doesn't emigrate to America anonymously and pennilessly. Admit it, Mother. I'm common stock." Somehow saying the words felt good, even liberating.

"Don't say such a thing," Mother said. "A lady is always confident and secure, no matter her circumstances. Grace and manners cover a multitude of sins."

Felicity felt her cheeks heat. "Being born common and foreign isn't a sin."

Mother gasped. "I didn't mean it that way. I meant the circumstances of your birth don't matter."

"Exactly," Daddy stated emphatically. "You're our daughter, and that's all that's important. Birth is nothing. It's what you do in life that matters."

Perhaps to Daddy, but Mother talked of nothing but status. "Then bloodlines—"

"Mean nothing," Daddy finished for her. "We loved you the moment we saw you. You're my little girl and always will be."

"Oh, Daddy." Felicity thought she could never cry again, but back came the tears. No matter what, she could count on her father.

He took her hand. "Besides, despite what your mother would have you believe, neither one of us has the purest blood."

"Branford," Mother hissed.

"It's true, Eugenia, and our children deserve to know it. Your mother's family made its money in meatpacking, and I'm a self-made man. My parents sharecropped. There's not one drop of blue blood."

Mother wailed into her handkerchief, but Blake burst out laughing. "You don't say. That's a relief."

Felicity stared, openmouthed. That's why she had never met her grandparents, only heard stories that were apparently complete fabrications. All of Mother's pretensions had been based on nothing. "Why didn't you just tell me? I would have understood."

Daddy glanced at Mother. He didn't need to say a thing for Felicity to understand. The facade all centered on Mother.

"I understand," Felicity said quietly, "but you could have at least told me I was adopted."

Daddy shook his head. "We wanted everyone in Pearlman to treat you as our biological child."

"But Dr. Stevens knew," Felicity pointed out. "And so did Mrs. Grattan. How did she find out? Or am I the only one in Pearlman who didn't know?" Eloise and Sally surely knew, and Gabriel didn't look the least bit surprised when Mrs. Grattan announced the truth. Stricken, yes, but not surprised.

Daddy looked at Mother. "Sophie Grattan was the attending nurse at the stillbirth."

Felicity had forgotten that Mrs. Grattan was once a nurse.

"We swore her to secrecy." Daddy's face grew dark. "Apparently her word meant nothing."

"She always held that over me," Mother wailed. "Every society meeting. Everything I tried to do, she'd always bring it up. I lived in terror."

"Then you should have told me." Felicity didn't want her parents to descend into bickering again when they'd finally opened up their hearts. "If you'd told me the truth, none of this would have happened."

Mother stiffened. "We didn't want you to suffer any stigma for being..."

"A foreigner?" Felicity recalled the epithets hurled against Luke.

"Don't ever say that again," snapped Mother. "You're a Kensington."

But no amount of pretending would rub away the truth. "You're ashamed of me."

"No, dearest," Mother cried, "I only wanted what was best for you—the best schools, the best husband, the best marriage."

"It was the same for me," Blake chimed in. "You know how Mother has to orchestrate everything."

"B-but all I ever really wanted was to be loved for who I am," Felicity whispered. The words sank like a balloon filled with cold air.

Mother's face twisted up again. "I did my best. I thought you knew how I felt."

As Felicity watched her mother weep, she realized that she would have to initiate any change in their relationship. Mother was too afraid to reach out, even when told that love would be reciprocated. Hesitant, she looked to Daddy for encouragement. He nodded, his walrus mustache shaking, and wiped his face with his handkerchief.

Mother had collapsed into a sobbing heap, head on her knees, shoulders heaving. Everything Eugenia Kensington valued had been stripped away: wealth, status and control. For the first time in Felicity's life, she wasn't afraid of her mother. She pitied her.

"It's all right, Mother." Though it took every ounce of will, she went to the woman who'd tried so hard in all the wrong ways. Kneeling, Felicity embraced her. Mother's bony shoulders shook, but she didn't pull away. Then came the most difficult words of all, those of forgiveness.

"I love you," Felicity whispered.

Mother lifted her head, face mottled. "You do? I—I never knew for certain." She bit her lip, looking for once vulnerable. "I love you so." She battled a sob. "Daughter."

Felicity threw her arms around her mother and wept as Mother stroked her damp and tangled hair for the very first time.

No matter how close Gabriel sat to the kitchen stove, he couldn't get warm. The events of the night tumbled through his mind over and over, always coming out badly. Every time he made the fatal accusation, every time she asked what he meant, every time she walked away.

Moments before he'd held her close, professing his love, then one careless moment cost him everything. No wonder so many scriptures decried the tongue.

He clutched the cup of coffee.

"She'll need time to heal," Mariah said, taking a seat at the kitchen table, "and work things out with her parents."

"I know." He blew on the coffee, sending a cloud of steam against his face.

"Then why so glum?"

How could he begin to tell her? Yet even clergy needed someone who would listen to the deepest anguish of the soul. Mariah had always been that for him.

"I lost her." Every word bled.

"How?"

He gulped the strong brew. It scalded his throat. "Have you ever withheld knowledge to spare someone?"

"Do you mean the bootlegging ring?"

"It slipped out at the worst possible time. Why couldn't I

leave it alone? Why didn't I listen to you and leave it in the sheriff's hands?"

"Because you can't bear injustice."

"I thought I could expose the crime without hurting Felicity. I thought I knew best."

"In other words," Mariah scolded, "you played God."

The best confessor could dredge the most carefully buried sins from a man's soul. The truth hurt. The truth tore his pride to tiny pieces. He licked his lips, eyes burning. "The worse sin of all—pride. I deserve her rebuke."

"Yes, you do."

He buried his face in his hands, scourged by the blazing whip of self-realization. All this time he'd cried out against Felicity's pride, when the most prideful actions of all came from him.

"I was so concerned with the splinter in other people's eyes that I didn't see the plank in my own," he said miserably. "What a fool I am."

"Without God, we all are."

His eyes burned. "But how can I mend the damage? H-how do I…?"

"Get her back?" Mariah looked him square in the eyes. "You apologize."

But he'd seen her face, the hurt, the betrayal. "It's too late."

"Perhaps, but you still must ask." Mariah scraped back her chair. "But not tonight. Pray, get some sleep and you'll think more clearly in the morning." She paused, staring at something outside the kitchen window. "Are you expecting someone?"

Gabriel rose as she opened the door.

"Would you care for coffee, Sheriff?" She offered to take the man's hat and raincoat.

"No, thank you, ma'am." Though Gabriel pulled out a

chair, the sheriff declined that, too. "I need to get back to the jail. Thought you'd want to know that we caught them."

Gabriel should have rejoiced. This was what he'd wanted all along, what he'd preached against and strived to correct. It's why he'd been called to Pearlman. At least that's what he used to think.

"Who was involved?" He held his breath.

"Mostly out-of-towners."

Gabriel recalled Coughlin's assertion that city folk had torn down his fence. "From where?"

"Detroit. Rumrunners bring the liquor across the St. Clair River from Canada by boat and then transport it across the state by motorcar, truck, train, plane and small boat. This gang used the Kalamazoo River to move shipments across the southwestern part of the state and even out to Lake Michigan. They sell whiskey along the way in towns like Pearlman. What's left makes its way to Grand Rapids or Chicago. That's why we brought DeWalt into the operation."

That name. "Is DeWalt Robert Blevins?"

The sheriff nodded. "He's a federal Prohibition agent out of Detroit. I'll tell you, Pastor, for a while, he suspected you."

"Me?"

Mariah burst out laughing. "Oh, what a tangled web."

Ilsley didn't crack a smile. "Perhaps, ma'am. Truth was, Pastor, you happened to arrive at the right time. DeWalt had gotten a tip that the ringleader was going to be in town during the Founder's Day celebrations. Since you were new, he had his eye on you."

Gabriel recalled the night he'd seen Blevins, or rather DeWalt, and Kensington at the root cellar. He swallowed the lump in his throat. "I saw him with Branford Kensington at the root cellar."

"Mr. Kensington has been a key part of our attempts to break up the bootlegging ring. They were checking to see if any of the liquor had been moved. The broken bottles and tipped-over case threw them for a bit."

"Slinky," Gabriel muttered. "The cellar door must have been left open, and he fell in."

The sheriff chuckled. "That's what Mr. Kensington told us later. Apparently, his daughter played some part in that."

"She is skilled with animals," Gabriel said, but all he could think about was his horrible error. He'd lost Felicity for nothing. All his clues could be explained. The smell of whiskey on Blevins might have been done on purpose, trying to trip him up. So, too, with Kensington's offer of a drink that turned out to be sarsaparilla. The root cellar, the noises behind the drugstore, Kensington's visit to the blind pig... everything could be explained.

"The ringleader? Did you catch anyone?" Gabriel held his breath.

The sheriff cleared his throat. "We've brought in Hermann Grattan. Apparently, he was using the dairy trucks to smuggle liquor all over the area."

Mr. Grattan? Gabriel reeled. The man was a bigot, but he'd never suspected Grattan was running liquor.

Mariah shook Ilsley's hand. "Thank you, Sheriff. I'm glad to learn the bootlegging has stopped."

"For now, but they'll be back, Ms. Meeks. Until people lose the taste for whiskey, there'll always be someone willing to risk arrest to supply it."

"Then it's not over," Gabriel said. Justice had only won a battle, not the war.

"It's never over, Pastor, not 'til Judgment Day." The sheriff tipped his hat. "As far as I'm concerned, your job's the better one. I can only punish 'em after they commit the crime. You can stop 'em from going astray in the first place. You change what's inside a man. If crime is ever going to be wiped out, that's where it has to start." He opened the door. "G'morning, folks."

"Morning?" Gabriel looked out the window. So it was. The sky shimmered dove gray while a rim of orange licked up from the eastern horizon. A new day.

God had given him a second chance. This time he'd follow where God led, not his own stubborn path. *Thy will not my will.*

Lord willing, he could reclaim people's hearts and turn them to good. He could truly minister to the congregation. Felicity was right about creating a home for orphaned children. Two boys needed such a home right now. They'd need to find the right house and fix it up, but he could involve the community, starting with Einer Coughlin. Maybe if the man had something positive to work toward, his anger would melt away. It would take time, but it could be done.

He grabbed his hat.

"Where do you think you're going?" Mariah asked.

"I need to see Felicity."

Mariah pressed her back against the door and wagged her finger at him. "Not at this hour, you aren't. Whatever you have to say to Felicity can wait." A bold knock startled Mariah from her perch. "Who now?"

She opened the door, and Gabriel saw a weary Branford Kensington on the stoop.

He handed Mariah an envelope. "Tell your brother a special meeting of the church council has been called for two o'clock this afternoon." He tipped his hat and left.

"Gabe?" Mariah turned to him with wide eyes.

Gabriel didn't need to open the envelope to know why he'd been called before the council. With Sophie Grattan and Eugenia Kensington leading the way, he had no doubt.

He was going to be fired.

Chapter Nineteen

Luke.

Felicity awoke with a start. What had happened to Luke? Though Gabriel had assured her Coughlin wouldn't get the boy, Luke could still be sent back to the orphanage.

She couldn't let that happen.

Sunlight streamed through her bedroom window. The clock read nearly one-thirty…in the afternoon. She flew out of bed and donned the first dress she found, a dull old cotton frock. She added work shoes, a quick swipe of the hairbrush, and she was ready. She clattered down the staircase and ran to Mother's sitting room.

She wasn't there.

She tried Daddy's study. Maybe she could convince him to adopt Luke or at least give the boy a temporary place to stay. Why not? They had plenty of room. She pushed open the door and peered inside—empty.

Where was everyone? The house was deathly still. Even the cook seemed to be away. At last she found Smithson watering the lilies in front of the house.

"They left for a meeting," he informed her with a sniff, "at the church."

What horrible timing. Probably a Ladies' Aid Society meeting. Felicity had stopped paying attention to those the moment they'd postponed the stained glass window project.

She ducked back inside to grab a hat. The afternoon train left at three-thirty. That gave her less than two hours to find Luke a home and even less time to find Daddy. He probably went to the bank or the mercantile after dropping off Mother. Without checking her hair, she plopped the hat on her head and flew outside.

"If Daddy returns, tell him I'm looking for him," she told Smithson. Then she added, "Please."

The butler raised his eyebrows but didn't comment on her uncharacteristic politeness.

"I'll be in town," she added.

Ms. Priss strolled up and stroked against her legs. She instinctively bent to give her neck a scratch and noticed the little darling looked far more plump than normal.

"Ms. Priss, are you going to have kittens?"

The cat meowed and arched her back for more petting.

"You'd make a good mother."

Of course. Luke needed a home with children and a loving mother, someone like Beatrice. She'd ask Blake. At this time of day, he'd be at the airfield. Blake would listen. He might balk at first, but she could convince him.

She raced down the hill and reached town by the time the clock at city hall struck two. Pearlman bustled with activity. Mrs. Evans drove by and honked her horn. Felicity waved. Cordelia Butterfield passed on the other side of the street with little Grace at her side.

"Thank you so much, Felicity," Cordelia called out. "You've made me the happiest woman on earth. May God bless you."

"And you, too." Felicity couldn't help but be cheered by

everyone's warmth. She fairly skipped past the park, which was filled with families and children. A group of boys played baseball, and their ball rolled in front of her feet.

"Sorry, Ms. Kensington," young Freddie Highbottom said as he tracked it down.

Ms. Kensington. To the children, nothing had changed. She tossed the ball to the boy. "That's quite all right, Freddie."

At the corner of Elm and Main, Mrs. Simmons hailed her. Though Felicity was anxious to reach Blake before the train left, she couldn't refuse Mrs. Simmons.

The widow clutched a threadbare cloth handbag, and Felicity recalled her shelf full of unused bags. She'd make a point of sending a couple to Mrs. Simmons.

"What can I do for you?" Felicity asked politely.

"Do tell your mother I'll be late to the society meeting tomorrow."

"Tomorrow? But if the society is meeting tomorrow, then what's the meeting today?"

Mrs. Simmons shook her head. "I don't know, but Felicity, I must tell you." She looked ready to burst with excitement. "Pastor Gabriel said I could take Peter for now."

"He did?" Felicity regretted her harsh words about the Simmonses. No one would love Peter more. "What wonderful news. Peter will be very happy at your home."

"Oh, thank you, Felicity. He and my Hendrick are getting on famously. He already wants to be a motor mechanic." She chuckled. "And Anna, well, if she wasn't older than young Peter, they'd be quite a pair." She leaned close to whisper. "I think he's taken a bit of a liking to her."

Felicity couldn't help smiling at the thought of fourteen-year-old Peter pining after seventeen-year-old Anna, who would have nothing to do with him. Anna wouldn't settle for a boy when she loved a man. "She's a wonderful girl, but I think she has someone else in mind."

Mrs. Simmons clucked her tongue. "Aye, but there's no spark between those two." Her eyes twinkled. "I think the pastor's set his cap elsewhere."

Despite last night's betrayal, Felicity's pulse raced at Mrs. Simmons's words. She shook her head. "I'm afraid that's beyond hope."

Mrs. Simmons touched Felicity's arm. "There's always hope. When two are meant to be together, nothing can keep them apart." She blinked back tears, and Felicity realized she must have been thinking of her husband.

"I'm sorry," she whispered. As Mrs. Simmons wiped her eyes, Felicity understood the power of those two words. They could bridge vast chasms and heal years of pain. Perhaps they could even mend the break between Gabriel and her. All he had to do was apologize.

"Enjoy every moment you have," Mrs. Simmons urged. "You never know how long you'll have together."

The knot of pain in Felicity's chest tightened. What if Gabriel never reconciled with her? What if she never saw him again? What if he got ill or died in an accident? Felicity's birth parents hadn't lived to see her grow up. Ecclesiastes said that everything has its season. What if their season together was over? Gabriel had a lot of pride. He'd never apologize first. That left her. Like with Mother, she alone could heal the breach.

After she saved Luke. "I'm sorry, Mrs. Simmons. I need to go." She looked toward Baker's Field. With luck, she could reach Blake with plenty of time to spare.

"I'm so sorry, dear, keeping you here when you have important business." Mrs. Simmons gave her arm a squeeze. "And when you find him, don't let him go."

"I—I don't know what you mean." But she did know. Gabriel. Find Gabriel. But it wasn't that simple. Too many questions lay unanswered between them. She couldn't let him into her heart until she knew he regretted accusing her father.

It was much easier to concentrate on Luke. First, she had to find Blake. Baker's Field was a good half mile away, but she could save precious minutes by cutting behind the parsonage and then through Coughlin's land. *Coughlin*. His name brought dull, metallic fear. Coughlin had threatened her last time, and after being denied an orphan, he'd be even more irate, but Luke's well-being outweighed that fear. She headed into the park.

The sky was that creamy blue of midsummer, when the light filtered through the trees and buzzed off the grass. Crickets hummed and couples strolled lazily in the shade. The white of the parsonage fence peeked between the rustling trees, making her wish for happier times like the day she rescued Slinky and Gabriel in turn rescued her. She'd saddled him with a dog that day, and he'd accepted the stray into his home.

Would he accept Luke? She halted, shocked by the thought. Gabriel would be the perfect father, but he wasn't married. The Orphaned Children's Society would never allow an unmarried man to adopt. What if he married? Heat flushed her face. She was mad to even think such a thing. She squeezed her eyes shut, and when she opened them, she saw Mariah in the yard hanging the wash.

"Felicity?" Mariah called out. "How are you faring?"

She didn't have time for pleasantries when Luke would soon be put on the train. On the other hand, Mariah might know what had happened to the boy. She hurried into the yard. "Where is Luke?"

Mariah didn't note the urgency in Felicity's question. "After I finish hanging the wash, I'll show you."

"Then he's not at the train station?" Felicity took the end of the sheet that Mariah handed her and attempted to pin it to the clothesline. It slid free, and she caught it just before it touched the ground.

"Double-over the fabric," Mariah instructed.

This time the pin held. "You didn't answer me. Is Luke going back on the train? He's not with Mr. Coughlin, is he? Gabriel promised he wouldn't send him there."

"That was never a possibility," Mariah said calmly, affixing the last clothespin.

At that instant, the back door of the parsonage swung open, and Slinky burst out with a loud bark, followed by none other than Luke.

"He's here?" Felicity watched the boy in amazement.

Mariah nodded and then called out to Luke, "Play quietly, or you'll rile up Slinky."

Luke laughed as he threw a stick as far as he could, and Slinky took off after it.

Mariah heaved a sigh. "I'm afraid playing quietly is impossible for eight-year-old boys."

"Then he's not going to be sent back on the train."

Mariah smiled as she watched the boy. "He's not. Gabriel took him in, just until a proper home is found, but he couldn't bear to send Luke back to the asylum." She shook her head. "How I lectured him on that one, but Luke is already a blessing. He's going to be a challenge, too." She sighed. "He clings to Gabriel as if he's afraid he'll disappear. That's probably why he hasn't spoken yet."

"He doesn't speak?" Felicity had no idea.

"Only to Slinky."

Felicity's heart ached for the boy. She knew what it felt like to be unwanted. "Gabriel will love him."

Mariah nodded. "He has a tough road ahead, though. Luke's father abandoned him at the asylum last December. I understand he promised Luke he'd return once he made his fortune. Poor Luke waited every day at the front window for his father to return. Of course he never did. I don't know if Luke will ever trust again."

Felicity blinked back tears. How could anyone leave that beautiful dark-haired little boy? By the grace of God, he'd found Gabriel, whose heart was wider than the ocean and deep enough to take in so many hurts—even hers. The way he'd avoided her gaze and refused to speak to her hadn't been because he was giving a child to Coughlin. He was trying to protect her, and there was only one possible reason why.

"He knew, didn't he," Felicity said. "Gabriel knew I was adopted."

Mariah sucked in her breath, confirming everything. "Your father told him in an attempt to prevent Mrs. Grattan from spilling the news. That's why Peter went to her at first, though it destroyed Gabriel to do so."

It all made sense now, and the weight of anger lifted from Felicity's shoulders. How Gabriel must have tormented himself over a decision that would hurt someone no matter what he did. She would talk to him later, but Luke's giggle reminded her of what was most important now.

The boy was wrestling Slinky over a strip of leather. The dog gave unconditional love. That's what Luke needed, and she could show him he'd always have it. For once in her life she could truly help another soul. She knelt and petted Slinky.

"Too bad he can't talk," she said to Luke, "because he'd say that he's your friend."

Luke watched her with wide eyes and tightly clamped mouth.

"See his eyebrows?" She pointed out Slinky's white markings above the eyes. "Those tell you what he's thinking. See how he lifts them when he looks at you?"

Luke nodded.

"That means he likes you a lot. In fact, I'll bet you're one of his best friends."

Luke threw his arms around Slinky, who patiently bore the smothering embrace. A sob struggled out of the little boy.

"He won't leave you," she whispered, rubbing the thin, heaving back. "And neither will Pastor Gabriel. He loves you." She choked back tears. "I know he does. He's a good man with love enough for everyone. He'll be a real father to you."

Luke buried his face in Slinky's fur and covered his ears with his arms. He wanted her to leave, but this was too important. Somehow she had to make him see that an adopted father was every bit as good as a birth father.

"I'm adopted, too." The words sounded strange, and she realized that was the first time she'd admitted it aloud.

He unblocked his ears.

She said, "And my new parents love me very much."

He unburied one eye and gave her a look filled with questions.

"Even if I had no father on earth, I'll always have a Father in heaven." She kissed the top of his head, full of dark curls so much like Gabriel's. "He loves you and will never leave you. I promise. And I'll be here for you. Pastor Gabriel will, too."

Mariah cleared her throat and motioned for Felicity to come with her.

"What is it?" Felicity sensed trouble but followed her

friend a few paces away. "I meant my promise, and I know your brother would never give up on anyone."

Mariah's eyes had darkened. "It's not that simple. Gabriel is standing before the Church Council as we speak. He's been asked to resign."

"Resign? Gabriel would never resign."

"He may have no choice."

Felicity could barely comprehend Mariah's words. Was that where Mother and Daddy were? Of course. Daddy sat on the council and Mother had tried to remove Gabriel before. Smithson said the meeting was at the church.

"But why? What possible cause could they have?"

"There's been a complaint of improper behavior," Mariah said softly.

"Improper behavior? Impossible. I don't know anyone more proper and caring in the world. This is another unfounded attack. He'll fight them."

Mariah shook her head. "Not this time."

"But he has to fight, for Luke's sake, for you, for the community."

"Maybe by resigning he is."

Felicity stared at her friend, struggling to understand. "Are you saying he's resigning for a reason? Why?"

"Only Gabriel can tell you that."

But if Felicity waited until after the meeting for an explanation, it would be too late. "Whatever the reason, we have to stop him."

"Only one person can do that."

"Who?" Felicity's pulse thrummed a little harder.

Mariah did not answer. She did not have to.

"Do you mean me?" Felicity asked. "How can I? I don't have any say on the council. Daddy might listen to me, but the others won't." Yet even as she said the words, she knew that Mariah was right. No one else had the slightest chance. No one else could convince Daddy that even though Gabriel had wrongly accused him, he had done everything for her sake. "When does the meeting start?"

"It began at two."

At least fifteen minutes ago. She might be too late. "I need to hurry. Please tell Luke I'll see him later."

"Godspeed," Mariah called out after her.

Felicity ran like never before. Nothing had ever mattered so much. Her lungs burned by the time she reached the pavilion. She was gasping for breath when she skirted the ball diamond.

"Where are you going, Ms. Kensington?" young Freddie Highbottom asked, ball in hand.

"To the church."

"I never heard of someone running to church before." Nonetheless he, Matthew and a half dozen other children raced along beside her.

She reached Elm, and after glancing in each direction to ensure a motorcar wasn't coming, she crossed the street. There was only a block to go.

"Felicity?" asked Mrs. Simmons, exiting from the secondhand store. "What's wrong?"

"The church," she gasped, unable to get more than one or two words out at a time.

"Slow down, dear, there can't be anything so important that you need to make yourself ill."

Felicity waved off her instructions. "C-council." Deep breath. "Gabriel." Deep breath. "Resign."

Somehow Mrs. Simmons put it all together. "Gabriel's resigning?"

"Forced."

Mrs. Simmons nodded. "Then we have work to do."

By the time they reached the church, Felicity and Mrs. Simmons had rallied a dozen residents to their cause.

"You tell them, Felicity," Mrs. Hammond said. "I've never had a better customer. All his trouser legs need to be shortened."

"And he bring many customer to boardinghouse," added Mrs. Terchie. "Good-paying ones, too."

They'd reached the church, and Felicity paused at the door to catch her breath and her nerve. The big oak door stood for authority. Her father headed the council. He'd sided with Gabriel before, but would he now? Not if both he and Mother attended. And Mrs. Grattan would now speak against Gabriel. She'd been furious that he took Peter from her. When added to Mr. Evans and Mr. Neidecker's votes, Gabriel didn't stand a chance.

She turned to the small crowd that had joined her and saw Mariah and Luke standing on the periphery. Luke needed Gabriel. This town needed Gabriel.

She summoned her courage. "Thank you all for joining me. Your support means a lot, but I want to address the council first." She glanced at the door, darkened around the brass handle by the touch of hundreds of hands. "Give me a few minutes."

Mrs. Simmons squeezed her hand. "Don't let him go." The twinkle in her eye told Felicity she meant something entirely more personal than saving the pastor's job.

Felicity pulled open the door and stepped into the dark interior. She squared her shoulders. With God's help, she could do this.

The council would be meeting downstairs. She walked carefully down the dark staircase. The door at the bottom was drawn closed, meaning the meeting was still in session. She pressed a hand and then an ear to the cool door. Silence.

Finally one lone voice spoke. "Then you don't deny the allegations." Daddy.

The hammering in her ears threatened to blot out the response.

"No." That was Gabriel, calm and strong. "I accept the council's recommendation."

Why? Why would Gabriel capitulate? Why would he resign? If he refused to save himself, she'd have to do it.

"If God be for me, who can be against me?" Felicity whispered and threw open the door. Gabriel stood in the center of the room, facing the five-member council.

"Felicity." Daddy rose from his place at the council table. "This is a closed meeting."

Mother appeared from somewhere to her side and tried to tug her out the door, but Felicity would not be deterred.

"Why? This is my minister. I have every right to speak."

Mrs. Grattan whispered something to Mr. Neidecker.

Felicity refused to let the woman distract her. "If it hadn't been for Pastor Gabriel, I would never have been able to weather the shock of learning I was adopted." She looked to Gabriel, and those deep brown eyes gave her even more strength.

"That has nothing to do with this meeting," said Mrs. Grattan.

"Yes, it does," Felicity insisted. "Since Pastor Gabriel came, my faith has grown stronger. He has touched many hearts, including those of five children who now have loving homes." She gulped. Was that why Gabriel had been brought before the council? Mrs. Grattan must have initiated the action, but why would the others agree?

"Felicity, this is not the place," Daddy cautioned.

"Why not? Why can't I witness to the good Gabriel has done?"

"Did you hear that?" Mrs. Grattan sniffed. "She calls him by his Christian name. Have you ever heard anything more disrespectful? Do you need more proof of impropriety?"

Gabriel said, "Thank you, Felicity, but you should leave this to me. Please?"

"Listen to the pastor, little one," Daddy echoed.

She didn't understand. Gabriel should be grateful for her help, not try to lead her away. Daddy and Gabriel were acting exactly the same as always—trying to protect her, but from what?

Mrs. Grattan smirked and nodded to Mr. Neidecker and Mr. Evans. Judging by their expressions, she had her majority. What had Mariah said they were accusing Gabriel of? Improper behavior?

Gabriel gently led her toward the door. When he reached for the handle, she saw Slinky's leash hanging from a hat peg. Of course. One other person saw her give the leash to Gabriel. One other person saw their first kiss: Mrs. Grattan. The improper behavior was Gabriel's relationship with her.

"I'm not leaving." She turned around and strode toward the council. "This is about Gabriel and me, isn't it?"

The council sat silent.

"We didn't do anything improper." Felicity scanned the five grim faces and knew Gabriel was doomed. If true, she had nothing to lose and everything to gain. "In fact, I love Gabriel Meeks."

Mother gasped, but Daddy leaned back in his chair grinning.

"If the reason you've called Gabriel before the council is his relationship with me," she said boldly, "then I confirm everything."

Mother buried her face in her hands.

"I knew it," Mrs. Grattan gloated. "Branford, I believe we are ready to vote."

"Not so fast, Sophie. Let's hear my daughter out."

Felicity gratefully acknowledged her father. This had to be said, no matter what rumors it stirred up. "Yes, we washed a dog in the parsonage's backyard. Yes, I spent time alone with him. Yes, I kissed him. I'm not ashamed of that because I love him." She stared right at Mrs. Grattan. "No woman could do better than a man of God."

Mrs. Grattan's jaw dropped, but Felicity didn't care. Let her think whatever she wanted, for the only person who mattered was Gabriel, and he was giving her the most wonderful look.

"You love me?" he breathed as if he didn't believe her words.

She could understand his reluctance after the way she'd treated him last night, never giving him a chance to explain. "Can you ever forgive me for being angry with you yesterday?"

"I deserved it." He brushed a lock of hair from her forehead. "I'm the one who behaved like a cad. I jumped to conclusions, the wrong conclusions. Will you forgive me?" His eyes darkened like one of those deep pools in the river.

She sank willingly into them. "Always."

Then he kissed her in full view of the Church Council. Daddy laughed, and Mother wailed, but Felicity could have danced with joy. Gabriel loved her so much that he'd been willing to suffer scandal in order to protect her reputation. Every action he'd taken had been for her sake. Sometimes he was a little too protective and sometimes he was wrong, but she couldn't fault him when he did it from love.

"And there are a lot of other people who love him, too," said Mrs. Simmons, ushering in the crowd who'd followed

Felicity down the street. "Don't you have something to say to Ms. Felicity, Pastor?"

Gabriel nodded solemnly, knelt and took Felicity's hands. "I made a lot of mistakes, and I'm bound to make even more, but I love you. If you're willing to accept an imperfect man, I would be honored if, in due time, you would be my wife."

She gazed deep into his eyes. "There is nothing I'd rather do."

"Even if it means eventually taking on a small boy?"

"Especially if it means being a mother to Luke."

He rose, but his gaze never left her. "I'll wait for you to finish veterinary college."

She shook her head. "Maybe later, but now I most want to be a wife and mother."

Gabriel still hesitated. "This has to be done properly, with your father's blessing."

"Daddy?" Felicity raised hopeful eyes to her father.

"And a proper period of courtship," Gabriel added.

Her father chuckled. "You have it, son. You always had it."

Felicity threw herself into Gabriel's arms, and he kissed her again to seal the vow. Mrs. Simmons and nearly everyone else clapped. Daddy quickly called for a vote, which came out four to one in Gabriel's favor.

"Well, I never." Mrs. Grattan gathered her bag and stomped from the room, but no one paid her much attention amidst the congratulations and Mother's racking sobs.

Felicity tried to console her. "It's all right, Mother. In fact, everything's perfect."

"I—I j-just wanted the best for you." She blotted her eyes with a lace-edged handkerchief. "New York. The Academy."

"Don't you understand? I have everything I could ever

want right here in Pearlman." Felicity held out her hand, and Gabriel joined her.

His eyes twinkled, and he grinned mischievously. "If it makes you too uncomfortable, Mrs. Kensington, I'll have Mom and Dad leave the Astors off the guest list."

Mother miraculously stopped weeping. "*The* Astors?"

"They've been friends for years, but I wouldn't want their presence to make you uncomfortable."

"But—" She looked from Gabriel to Daddy in disbelief.

Daddy roared. "That's right, Eugenia. Mr. Blevins never summered in Newport, but Pastor Gabriel did."

Mother's jaw dropped, just for an instant, and then she did the only thing a woman of her breeding could in such circumstances. She fainted.

Epilogue

"Throw the bouquet now," Mother instructed.

She hovered near Felicity on the church steps as the bells pealed. The clear blue October sky glowed with the first scarlet maple leaves. The town's unmarried girls had gathered beyond the bottom step. Sally Neidecker jostled Anna Simmons aside, but Eloise Grattan, by virtue of her superior size, claimed the front spot.

"Really, that's such a ridiculous tradition," Mariah said under her breath.

Felicity laughed at her best friend and new sister. She'd had to plead with her to don the taffeta maid of honor dress. Gabriel squeezed Felicity's hand and inspired cries from the gathered guests to give her another kiss.

"Show us how it's done, Pastor," one man called out.

Gabriel blushed slightly, warming her heart so completely that she thought she would burst. Then he cast aside any embarrassment and obliged, kissing her until she tingled clear to her toes. When they broke, she had to blink to clear away the tears. Everything was perfect.

Gabriel then bent to pick up Luke, who had been waiting quietly by his side after finishing his solemn duties as best man. The boy wrapped his arms around his new father, and Felicity gave him a kiss.

"You did a wonderful job."

He gave her a broad, semitoothless smile, for he'd lost two baby teeth in the past week.

"Throw it to me," the gathered girls cried, jostling for position.

"All right," Mariah groused, "if you must throw the bouquet, you'd better get it over with."

Felicity did hate to give up her bouquet. It wasn't a fashionable Bernhardt bouquet or even a hothouse posy. No, she carried a rather ragged bunch of chrysanthemums that Luke had gathered from every garden in Pearlman. The patchwork whites and yellows and rusts didn't match the elegance of her gown, but no bouquet could have been dearer.

Yet she had to let it go. Quicker was better. She whirled around and tossed it over her head, eyes closed.

"Ouch!"

That was Gabriel.

She opened her eyes in time to see it bounce off her new husband's head and land square in Mariah's hands. Everyone stared a moment in shock, and then Beatrice started giggling. Felicity followed, and before long everyone was chuckling. Mariah, who preferred to be single and had no use for marriage, had caught the bouquet.

"Embarrassed, sis?" Gabriel teased.

"It's the cold," Mariah said, patting her red cheeks. She held the bouquet out to Felicity. "Throw it again."

"No, no, dear sister," Felicity laughed. "The bouquet has been thrown. You'll need to get married now."

"That's right," said Gabriel. "You can't live at the parsonage any more now that I'm bringing a bride home."

Mariah crossed her arms. "Tease all you want, Gabriel

John. I promise I won't be in the way. When Mr. Simmons has my car ready, I'll be off."

Felicity shook her head at Mariah's plan to drive home alone, but she didn't have time to dwell on it because the whole family enveloped Gabriel and her in a big embrace. Even Slinky barked his approval.

"Welcome to the family, son." Daddy clapped Gabriel on the back, making him cough. "I always knew you were the one for my girl. No one else would put up with all the strays she's going to bring home."

Gabriel laughed, though she knew he was still uneasy around her father. Daddy had a way of intimidating people, and Gabriel didn't quite understand how much her father adored him. Why, he'd told her in all confidence that he hired Gabriel because he knew he was perfect for her. And when she hesitated, Daddy asked Robert to play the suitor. Felicity didn't appreciate her father's interference but seeing as he'd been right and did it from love, she forgave him.

"Mrs. Meeks?" Mrs. Grattan stood quietly before her, hands gripping her bag tightly. "My congratulations."

Felicity wasn't quite used to her new name, but as soon as she realized Mrs. Grattan meant her, she extended a hand. "Thank you so much."

Two months ago, Felicity might have had difficulty forgiving, but Mrs. Grattan had suffered a great deal thanks to her husband's involvement with the bootlegging ring. The prosecuting attorney wanted him sentenced to prison, but Gabriel's plea for a reduced sentence and community service won out.

Mrs. Grattan tentatively accepted her handshake. "I'm sorry…for what happened."

Felicity warmly grasped her hand. "I'm glad you spoke up that day. If you hadn't, I wouldn't be here now."

The color returned to the woman's face.

"And I look forward to your ideas and suggestions in the society meetings," Felicity added.

Tears welled in Mrs. Grattan's eyes, and Felicity was glad to let go of past hurts. On this day, all of Pearlman was family, even Einer Coughlin, who'd worked with Gabriel to repair the broken fence and even stood outside the church during the wedding ceremony. Maybe one day he'd set foot inside.

Gabriel's father surveyed the town from the church steps. "I think you might have been right, son. It's a fine town. You'll do well here."

Gabriel gazed at her with such love. "I already have, Dad."

Then he took her hand and, with Luke, they got in Daddy's old Stanley Steamer, gleaming bright in the sunshine. With a puff of steam and a tug on the whistle, they started the procession through Pearlman to the cheers and clapping of the people they'd grown to love.

As they passed by the park with its little wooden pavilion, Felicity couldn't help recalling her goal to marry by the end of summer. She hadn't quite made that deadline, but she'd married well, and that, in the end, was the better plan.

* * * * *

Dear Reader,

I hope you enjoyed Gabriel and Felicity's journey. They're bound to have a full house in coming years, the perfect way for them to share the love they've found in each other.

What we now call orphan trains began in the mid-nineteenth century with the Children's Aid Society train from New York to Dowagiac, Michigan. Other organizations joined the movement, sending children by train from what people believed to be the "squalor" of the cities to "healthy" small towns. The orphan trains ran into the late 1920s and early 1930s. Several books have been written on the topic, and many articles can be found on the internet. I've noted a few on my website.

I dearly love hearing from readers. If Gabriel and Felicity's story touched your heart, please send me a note in care of Love Inspired Historical or through my website at http://www.christineelizabethjohnson.com.

Thank you for joining me, and may God bless you richly.

Christine Johnson

Questions for Discussion

1. At first, Gabriel considers Felicity proud. Why? What does she do to give that impression?

2. Sometimes fear and self-doubt make a person raise defenses against getting hurt. What defenses does Felicity use? Have you ever shielded yourself from emotional pain? Looking back, how might you have done things differently?

3. Why is Felicity so attached to animals? What does she see in them that she doesn't see in people?

4. What in Gabriel makes him less threatening than the other people Felicity knows? What in him touches her heart?

5. How is Mr. Coughlin the embodiment of Felicity's deepest fears? Have you ever faced someone who frightened you? If you did, what happened?

6. Felicity drifted from her faith while she was away at school, yet the Lord never forgot her and the Bible verses she learned as a child stayed with her. Have you ever drifted away? How did the Lord call you back?

7. Gabriel is torn between protecting Felicity and saving the town from bootlegging. How could he have handled this problem better?

8. Instead of telling Felicity the truth about her background, her father and mother hide it. Why? What did they hope to gain?

9. Why does Felicity's mother treat her so coldly?

10. Felicity decides she must forgive her mother first. Why? How do you think this will lead to a closer relationship in time?

11. During World War I, German Americans faced prejudice and many changed their names. Mr. Grattan did not. How might that experience have led to his actions in this story?

12. Gabriel lets his anger with Mr. Kensington overcome his better sense when he accuses Felicity's father of leading the bootlegging ring. Have you ever let anger take hold of you? In retrospect, would things have worked out better if you had reacted differently?

13. Mrs. Grattan judges Gabriel and Felicity based on what she saw. Which other character(s) rush to judgment? How does that affect their relationships? How would events have unfolded differently if they'd given others the benefit of the doubt?

14. Felicity finally stands up for Gabriel in front of her parents and the church elders. Would the old Felicity have had the nerve to do this? What changed to give her this courage?

INSPIRATIONAL

Inspirational romances to warm your heart & soul.

TITLES AVAILABLE NEXT MONTH

Available September 13, 2011

COURTING THE ENEMY
Renee Ryan

ROCKY MOUNTAIN HOMECOMING
Pamela Nissen

THE RELUCTANT OUTLAW
Smoky Mountain Matches
Karen Kirst

THE ARISTOCRAT'S LADY
Mary Moore

LIHCNM0811

REQUEST YOUR FREE BOOKS!

2 FREE INSPIRATIONAL NOVELS
PLUS 2
FREE
MYSTERY GIFTS

Love Inspired.
HISTORICAL
INSPIRATIONAL HISTORICAL ROMANCE

YES! Please send me 2 FREE Love Inspired® Historical novels and my 2 FREE mystery gifts (gifts are worth about $10). After receiving them, if I don't wish to receive any more books, I can return the shipping statement marked "cancel." If I don't cancel, I will receive 4 brand-new novels every month and be billed just $4.49 per book in the U.S. or $4.99 per book in Canada. That's a saving of at least 22% off the cover price. It's quite a bargain! Shipping and handling is just 50¢ per book in the U.S. and 75¢ per book in Canada.* I understand that accepting the 2 free books and gifts places me under no obligation to buy anything. I can always return a shipment and cancel at any time. Even if I never buy another book, the two free books and gifts are mine to keep forever.

102/302 IDN FEHF

Name	(PLEASE PRINT)	
Address		Apt. #
City	State/Prov.	Zip/Postal Code

Signature (if under 18, a parent or guardian must sign)

Mail to the Reader Service:
IN U.S.A.: P.O. Box 1867, Buffalo, NY 14240-1867
IN CANADA: P.O. Box 609, Fort Erie, Ontario L2A 5X3

Not valid for current subscribers to Love Inspired Historical books.

**Want to try two free books from another series?
Call 1-800-873-8635 or visit www.ReaderService.com.**

* Terms and prices subject to change without notice. Prices do not include applicable taxes. Sales tax applicable in N.Y. Canadian residents will be charged applicable taxes. Offer not valid in Quebec. This offer is limited to one order per household. All orders subject to credit approval. Credit or debit balances in a customer's account(s) may be offset by any other outstanding balance owed by or to the customer. Please allow 4 to 6 weeks for delivery. Offer available while quantities last.

Your Privacy—The Reader Service is committed to protecting your privacy. Our Privacy Policy is available online at www.ReaderService.com or upon request from the Reader Service.

We make a portion of our mailing list available to reputable third parties that offer products we believe may interest you. If you prefer that we not exchange your name with third parties, or if you wish to clarify or modify your communication preferences, please visit us at www.ReaderService.com/consumerschoice or write to us at Reader Service Preference Service, P.O. Box 9062, Buffalo, NY 14269. Include your complete name and address.

LIH11B

*When private eye Skylar Grady is kidnapped and
abandoned in the Arizona desert, she knows her
investigation has someone scared enough to kill.
Tracker Jonas Sampson finds her—but can he keep her
safe? Read on for a sneak preview of LONE DEFENDER
by Shirlee McCoy, from her HEROES FOR HIRE series.*

"The storm isn't the only thing I'm worried about." He
didn't slow, and she had no choice but to try to keep up.

"What do you mean?"

"I've seen camp fires the past couple of nights. You said
someone drove you out here and left you—"

"I'm not just saying it. It happened."

"A person who goes to that kind of effort probably isn't
going to sit around hoping that you're dead."

"You think a killer is on our trail?"

"I think there's a possibility. Conserve your energy. You
may need it before the night is over."

"I still think—"

"Shh." He slid his palm up her arm, the warning in his
touch doing more than words to keep her silent. She waited,
ears straining for some sign that they weren't alone.

Nothing but dead quiet, and a stillness that filled Skylar
with dread.

A soft click broke the silence.

She was on the ground before she could think, Jonas
right beside her.

She turned her head, met his eyes.

"That was a gun safety."

He pressed a finger to her lips, pulled something from
beneath his jacket.

A Glock.

They weren't completely helpless, then.

He wasn't, at least.

She felt a second of relief, and then Jonas was gone, and she was alone again.

Alone, cowering on the desert floor, waiting to be picked off by an assassin's bullet.

No way. There was absolutely no way she was going to die without a fight.

A soft shuffle came from her left, and she stilled as a shadow crept toward her. She launched herself toward him, realizing her weakness as she barreled into the man's chest, bounced backward, landed hard. She barely managed to dive to the left as the man aimed a pistol, pulled the trigger. The bullet slammed into the ground a foot from where she'd been, and she was up again.

Fight or die.

It was as simple as that.

Don't miss LONE DEFENDER by Shirlee McCoy, available September 2011 from Love Inspired Suspense.

Love Inspired HISTORICAL

Gaining the confidence of widow Savannah Elliott could help undercover agent Trent Mueller derail a plot to sabotage the U.S. war machine. With so many lives at stake, he can't afford to feel guilt at his deception…nor should he find himself captivated by Savannah. Can love withstand the ultimate test of loyalty?

Courting the Enemy

RENEE RYAN

Available September wherever books are sold.

www.LoveInspiredBooks.com

LIH82883